PRAISE FOR
THE LEGEND OF THE GREAT HORSE *TRILOGY*

BOOK I: *ECLIPSED BY SHADOW*
Winner of the
Eric Hoffer Book Award for Young Adult Fiction
Mom's Choice Award Gold for Young Adult Fantasy

"Veteran horseman Royce combines history and myth with action and adventure to create a fast-paced, well-informed tale..." ~ *Library Journal*

"One of those works you will remember forever..."
~ *Reader Views Literary Awards*

"Page-turning ... a vivid historical tale through the ages!"
~ *Historical Novel Society*

"Thrilling and intelligent fantasy..." ~ *US Review of Books*

BOOK II: *THE GOLDEN SPARK*
Winner of the
2012 Written Arts Award for Science Fiction/Fantasy
Independent Publisher Highlighted Title - Summer 2011

"A rip-snorting tale and an overall fun read ... I'm greatly looking forward to the conclusion of this series, and expect that the trilogy will become at least a minor classic, if not a more respected work over time." ~ *Amazon Vine Voice*

"Lots of Horsepower Here!" ~ *Free Lance-Star*

"Don't listen to anyone who tries to label this trilogy as a work of juvenile fiction. It is much more than that."
~ *Amazon "Hall of Fame" Review*

"With a good focus on history and horses, THE GOLDEN SPARK is a fun and enjoyable read, highly recommended."
~ *MBR Bookwatch Featured Review*

The Legend of the

Great Horse

- Book III of III -

Into the Dark

by John Royce

MICRON PRESS
BOSTON

For information, please contact:

Micron Press
inquiries@micronpress.com

Although the author and publisher have made every effort to ensure the accuracy and completeness of information contained in this book, we assume no responsibility for errors, inaccuracies, omissions, or any inconsistency herein.

First Printing 2012

Royce, John Allen.
     Into the dark : the legend of the great horse (book III of III) / by John Royce.
       p. cm.
       ISBN 978-0-9724121-7-9 (Hardcover)
       ISBN 978-0-9724121-0-0 (pbk.)
       Includes bibliographical references and glossary.
       Series : The legend of the great horse.
       Summary : Meagan is transported through time by her horse, Promise, to the American West in 1861, a horse race during Prohibition, a cavalry charge during World War II, the 1968 Mexico City Olympics, and finally, to the future.
[1. Horses --Fiction. 2. Horses --History --Fiction. 3. Cattle drives --History --Fiction. 4. West (U.S.) --History --Fiction. 5. Prohibition --Fiction. 6. World War, 1939-1945 --Cavalry operations --Fiction. 7. Olympic Games (19th : 1968 : Mexico City, Mexico) --Fiction. 8. Time travel --Fiction. 9. Historical fiction.] I. Title. II. Into the dark : the legend of the great horse (book three of three). III. Series.

PZ7.R81597 In 2012
[Fic] –dc23   2012940521

Edited by JENNIFER AHLBORN
Special editing by ASHLEY WELCH
Illustrations by MARTI ADRIAN
Cover design by CAROLYNNE SMITH

PRINTED AND BOUND IN THE UNITED STATES OF AMERICA.

To our silent partner in civilization

- THE LEGEND -

MRS. BRIDGESTONE LOOKED toward the window for so long, it seemed the elderly woman had forgotten her two visitors. She turned back with bright eyes and pointed to a small lamp beside the couch. Under the lamp's light was a letter creased with folds, lying flat in an envelope of plastic. "Would you read the letter out loud, dear? I'd like your mother to hear."

Meagan went to the table. The document was written in a strong flowing script, the ink blurred but still legible:

Captain Beardon,

I have new dreams. A path into light is fading. I have heard a poem of whispers foretelling a birth. I give the words I remember.

A hundred years hence on this westmost shore,
The Great Horse comes to men once more.

History lights the future's course,
A journey taken with the horse;

Now born of loss and mother's grief,
The Great Horse takes a mighty leap,

Eclipsed by shadow, the golden spark
Shall wing her rider into the dark.

If this is a warning the intent is clouded to me. In my dreams every night the Great Horse is mounted and darkness falls.

Hear with your own ears for the Spirit speaks to your people in ways not heard by my own. You are to have this message. So I believe. At least this duty has been met.

Captain Beardon, sparing my horse and companion was an act of a people that can know righteousness. I am proud to call you friend.

Joseph
June the 21st, 1901

Jennifer took a deep breath. "That *is* interesting—isn't it interesting, Meagan? *My*."

The elderly woman spoke softly. "I had an investigator search the state's veterinarian records. Seven female foals were born in California at exactly dawn on June 21ˢᵗ, 2001. I have acquired all of the foals ... all, that is, except yours."

"Of course, Mrs. Bridgestone," Jennifer said breezily, "you don't take this seriously?"

"Oh, but I do, dear. Most seriously."

"Mrs. Bridgestone?" Meagan asked, hesitating under her mother's cautioning expression. "Do you really think my horse, Promise, could be the *Great* Horse?"

"Yes, dear, I do." The woman's tone was solemn. "My sources call her the Traveler, with power to bring darkness to the world. Of course, we wouldn't be sure unless the Great Horse was actually ridden, but that must never happen." Meagan's eyes were wide. "I admit it is strange. In all my readings, Great Horses have never done evil. Perhaps this event has something to do with the millennium change. I can't explain it."

"Maybe it's a *good* kind of darkness," Meagan suggested hopefully.

"Unfortunately, there is more. Chief Joseph was not certain of the meaning of his dreams, but I have found other references that are less reassuring."

Jennifer interrupted. "*Less* reassuring?"

Welcome to the conclusion of
THE LEGEND OF THE GREAT HORSE *trilogy*

Those who have not read the first two books of the trilogy may have missed the warning of an elderly eccentric named Mrs. Bridgestone, who informed young Meagan that her beloved filly, *Promise*, was a legendary Great Horse come to "wing its rider into the dark."

Perhaps if the warning had been a *bit* more clear, 17-year-old Meagan Roberts would not now be sleeping in a 19th century horse-drawn carriage.

Since accidentally departing from her backyard aboard Promise and being taken back into history, Meagan has traveled in 'jumps' coming steadily closer to her own time. Our intrepid equestrienne has met all challenges—prehistoric horse-hunts, Roman chariot racing, Mongolian hordes, knights, conquistadors, and courts of the European Renaissance—with only her knowledge of horsemanship (and a year of High School Latin) to help her survive.

Let's revisit the last chapter of Book Two, *The Golden Spark*, to make sure everyone is mounted up.* We join the story in an English tavern of 1816, as Meagan and her former employer, Danvers Chadwick, celebrate a semi-successful fox hunt...

* *Please refer to the* GLOSSARY *for unfamiliar terms.*

"There you are, Meagan! I *told* Molly you were here, but she wouldn't believe me. Couldn't convince her that Banjo wasn't for the Parson Jolly to ride. He's been missing, you know. The congregation is in arms."

Meagan squinted, trying to keep the image of Danvers from splitting into two as she sat down at the wide table. A full mug was set before her, again. She pushed it away.

"I tried to have her wait." Danvers pulled a neighbor's sleeve and slurred in his ear. "You did see my lovely wife, Molly Chadwick?" The man shrugged him off. Danvers grinned vacantly. "Wasn't Molly angry! She always knows where to find me at the end of a hunt day. Clairvoyant is what she is."

"Molly?" Meagan was filled with sudden longing to see her. "Did you really mean Molly is here?"

"*Was* here, yes, I did say that, love. She took the horses home. Tied them to the carriage and said I could walk it off. She didn't mean it, she's a love. But the horses are gone just the same, and we're walking."

"Molly is gone?" Meagan said sadly. It seemed hard to accept. "Is she coming back?"

Danvers swung to his feet and grasped the back of his chair to steady himself. "Let's hope not. She's never in as good a temper the second trip. Come on, love, *up!* We've got to be getting home."

Meagan resisted. "All day, Danvers Chadwick, *all* day, with "come on, love" and "hurry up, love," or "get out of the ditch, love." Well I'm tired, love."

"It *was* a grand run, wasn't it!"

Meagan looked over the top of the mug. The people around her seemed to be speaking very loudly, but she could not understand a word. Yes, the day *had* been grand. One of her best rides ever, maybe the best. Now all she wanted was sleep. She lowered her head to the table, just for a moment.

Danvers put a hand underneath her arm. "All right, lass. We've had enough and it's me, Danvers Chadwick, saying it. Home is just an hour's walk but it's not coming closer." He propelled Meagan out the tavern door and into the late dusk. Together they stumbled past tethered horses.

"How far to Mr. Percy's?" she asked. "An hour you said?"

"What I *said*, love, is we're having no more of that cheat! You're coming back home with me. We've money again. In fact..." Danvers halted before a carriage. "We could bloody well use a ride. You there, is this carriage for hire?"

Meagan had not noticed the driver sitting hunched over, buried beneath his patched brown blanket. "Tuppence," the man mumbled.

"Very good." Danvers bowed low to Meagan. "Your carriage awaits, m'lady." Meagan raised her chin and stepped up, settling into the spare cushions.

"Wait a moment." Danvers walked to the front of the carriage. "I *do* know him ... it's Dover Beach! Driver, how long have you had this horse?"

"Nowt but a few 'ours, sir. Came to me through an acquaintance. Not much of a 'orse, truth be told."

"He used to be—oh, he used to be! In his day this horse could hunt from sunrise to set and pull all the way. Meagan, come down and meet a horse!"

Meagan struggled back out of the carriage.

"Here is the ruination of a wonderful animal. I recognized him by his roman nose and that big star on his forehead, though you can hardly see it in his gray hair. It's Martin Percy's old stud horse! Used to win all the stakes races with him, back when I was starting out. Made his fortune with this horse. Many's the time I cursed Dover Beach, I tell you."

Meagan looked at the horse more closely. A dusting of white covered his muzzle and circled dark, patient eyes that held a faraway expression so familiar... "Danvers, I know this horse too! He was at the Percy's farm this morning. His wife made him call a veterinarian. He didn't want to."

"Percy doesn't like sick horses. He probably told Candella the poor beast died and sent him out. He *will* die too, out here like this. Bloody shame. Beecher was a great horse in his day."

The aged animal was almost in desperation. Head sagging on a thin neck, his eyes were lidded and his ears set low. A regular wheeze accompanied his panting.

"Ungrateful, this is. There was a winter night when this horse saved Percy's own wife and child. Candella was in trouble and Percy had to ride for the doctor. It was snowing a near blizzard that evening—a soul should never have been out. When Percy reached the doctor's, he handed the reins over, and Beecher brought the doctor to his wife over eight miles of dark snow. It's a disgrace what he's come to! A great horse, he was."

"Come on, get into the coach," the driver growled, stirring. "The nag will get you where you're going. We'll be there in a few lashes."

"Yes," Danvers said distastefully.

Meagan reached to stroke the horse's soft nose; he sniffed her hand with tickling whiskers. "Danvers, I don't think I can."

"Oh, no worries. Watch closely, love. This is why Molly will leave me someday and she'll be right for doing it. Driver, I am buying this horse from you—three pounds, and I'll sell you one of my geldings when we get to my farm. Now let the poor animal walk as slowly as he likes and don't let him know you have a whip."

"I can't let the 'orse go, sir," the man protested. "It's my bread and butter."

"Bother! You can buy two better horses for the price. I have just the one in mind too, a good bay. Don't bargain with me. I know horses, and I know where this one came from. Now get on toward the miller's and have him rest as he wishes."

Meagan watched as the carriage gently crunched forward. "That was nice of you, Danvers."

"Nonsense. I always wanted Beecher and now I have him. He'll be good company for the General. I'll tuck him in a warm stall with a few armloads of hay. Hot apple mash will put him right."

Danvers walked briskly to another parked carriage and spoke to the driver. He boarded and the new carriage moved toward Meagan. Danvers helped her climb into the carriage's seat. "Now, love, we're both about done for, why don't I stretch out on the front bench while you cozy in back? We'll follow Beecher home."

Meagan nodded. She was still thinking about the stricken old horse. Something was bothering her, and tired as she was she could not stop the feeling.

The horse's eyes haunted her. She thought about the way his whiskers tickled her as he sniffed her hand. Meagan sat up straight, remembering where she had first seen the horse. It was not this morning in the Percy's paddock, but the very first day she had come here: Beecher had been the aged horse standing behind the fence nuzzling her. "Danvers..."

"Yes, love?"

"This horse, Beecher—you said he was a 'great' horse?"

"Most horse I ever saw—does anything you ask. Watched him build up Percy's farm as a sire and a champion. He's one of those horses..." His voice trailed off. "Well, he and me both are getting long in the tooth, any road. It's time to settle down. Past time, some would say."

"So you know he's a Great Horse?"

"I do," he said wistfully. "The eyes tell it. Great horses all have a faraway look. The look of kings ... or better, I guess."

"Maybe Moses *wasn't* the Great Horse," Meagan said to herself, confused. Her head was cloudy from the day. *Why would this matter?* "I'm sorry, Danvers. I'm not making sense."

"No, no, you are," the man said softly. "I've always known Beecher was special. Horse does anything you ask. Now rest up, love. You're almost home."

She pulled the second-hand hunt coat around her shoulders more tightly. "Beecher," Meagan called drowsily. "Would you please tell Promise to come back?" She fell asleep listening to the horse's rhythmic footfalls and looking up at the friendly stars gently rocking in the sky.

---

*The travels in this story are fiction,
but the intention is to present historical accuracy.
Where license is taken, it is to portray the
spirit of the times.*

---

*Disclaimer: According to observation
and science, horses cannot fly.*

Into the Dark

THE LEGEND OF THE GREAT HORSE

~ BOOK III OF III ~

Timeline of Meagan's journey so far ...

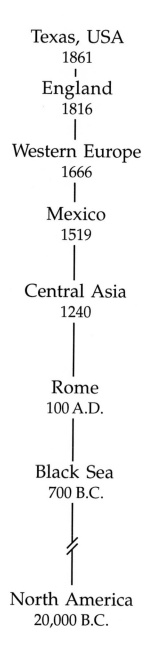

Texas, USA
1861

England
1816

Western Europe
1666

Mexico
1519

Central Asia
1240

Rome
100 A.D.

Black Sea
700 B.C.

North America
20,000 B.C.

Something About a Horse

"WHAT'D YOU FIND, Red?"

Meagan felt a blast of horse breath in her ear. She raised herself on her elbows, squinting at shaded figures in the bright sun. Dry dust coated the inside of her mouth and her head throbbed with pain. *Promise, I don't think is home.*

"You okay?" a mocking voice asked with more curiosity than concern.

"I'm doing great." *I know the secret now—ask Beecher.* Meagan leaned over and spit out alkali dust.

"So you're just laying out here in the sun?"

"Just laying." As her eyes adjusted to the light, Meagan could see a man sitting back on his haunches studying her. He wore a hat so floppy and ancient it seemed to have no spine at all, mashed down to squelch a mat of unruly hair. His jaw was set, jutting, and she could just see dark eyes through his squint.

"Thinking to steal my horse?" he asked.

"Excuse me?"

"Because it's strange, you alone out here with him. Been hunting that horse all night and here he be. A bit peculiar, wouldn't you say?"

"No, not as things have been going."

"So you *was* thinking to steal him."

"If I were trying to steal him, wouldn't I be *riding* him?"

The man shrugged. "Never ask, never know. Maybe you got off to sit."

"Got off to sit?" Meagan looked at the empty, dry landscape around her. *Promise, you are a very bad girl.*

"I said it was peculiar. But facts is facts."

Meagan groaned as she sat up. She was stiff everywhere, but her backside and head complained the loudest. At least the temperature was not so cold here.

"He threw you, didn't he?"

"*I wasn't trying to steal your horse!*" Meagan put her hand to her head, sorry for raising her voice.

In all directions were empty hills and grassland, wide sky and high clouds. Two horses stood close: a dark sorrel under a western saddle, reins trailing the ground, and a stout buckskin wearing only a halter. All three stared at her. "Are you an actress, maybe?" The man whistled, looking at her red riding coat and grinning. "Or something else?"

"Definitely something else. Pardon me, but *where* are we?"

"About nowhere. Where you wanting to be?"

"You wouldn't believe me if I told you. What year is it?"

"Funny question. 1861 ... does that suit?"

Ugh. Meagan lay back down in disgust. She had not traveled long enough. A shadow crossed over her. A large horse head blocked the sun.

"That's just Red coming to say goodbye," he said cheerfully. "We don't much like horse thieves, do we Red?"

Meagan raised herself painfully onto her elbow and sat up again. The horse nuzzled her, sniffing. His name is Red?"

"Yep. His last owner called him Blue, but he don't look blue to me at all. More like *Red*, least his lower-downs get red from prairie dust. Then I got that cussed sorrel who didn't have a name at all, but ol' Blue *did* sort of fit. So there they are, my horses."

"Red and Blue?" She smiled. "I'm sorry to bother you, but is there a town anywhere nearby?"

"There is, in a manner of speaking. Needing a ride?"

"That would be very nice, thank you. Sorry, you surprised me and I don't feel that well just now. My name is Meagan Roberts."

"Nice to meet you, Meagan Roberts. Name's Dan Beardon. Why you out here, really?"

"Would you believe I'm lost?"

Dan shrugged. "Harder to believe you weren't. Just let me check Red and make sure nothing's missing." He took up the lead rope, walking to each side of the buckskin. "I guess you ain't hurt him. Nothing looks broke or fallen off. What're you giving me in return for the ride?"

"I'm sorry, I haven't any money. None I can use, anyway, unless you take shillings."

He grinned. "Maybe we could think of something, you and that fancy get up."

Meagan looked at her rumpled hunt coat. It probably *would* fit the man. "Well, sure. If you'd like." She started taking off the coat to hand over.

Dan held up his hand. "Naw, naw. Not here, *sheesh*. Wait until we get into town." He picked up the buckskin's lead rope. "Here, get on up. Red'll take you."

"Aren't you going to put on his bridle?"

"Nope, I aim to put you in tow. I'm not handing over my Red to a suspected horse thief. No offense."

"Of course not." Meagan walked stiffly to the buckskin and looked in his eyes, and saw the faraway gaze she had come to know. "Hello, Great Horse." She looked again at the sorrel named Blue—at least she *thought* she knew. She had been mistaken before. The buckskin bumped her for a treat, and when none was forthcoming, lazily cocked a hind leg and sighed.

"Look sharp now, Red." Dan helped Meagan mount and threw the lead rope casually over his shoulder as he led them to his sorrel horse. He mounted and moved out, ponying the buckskin—and Meagan—behind him.

———

The town, such as it was, did nothing to announce itself. The rutted track simply squeezed between two rows of plank buildings and terminated in choppy mud. They stopped before a structure whose sides were warping under chipped paint. Meagan would have thought it abandoned except for the loud voices inside.

Dan led the horses around the back of the building, to a short row of horse heads sticking out over slat-front stalls. Handing the horses to a sullen stableboy, Dan turned to tramp back to the main building. He stepped onto a side porch and, unsticking the door, turned back to Meagan. "After you, m'lady," he said, bowing low.

"Thank you," she said, ignoring his wink. She walked into a room lit by smoking lanterns and shafts of sunlight shining through cracks in the wooden plank wall. Men at square tables talked and played cards.

The bartender greeted them. "Afternoon, Beardon. You're back awful quick. Changed your mind on Dodge City?"

"Hello, Geez. No, not yet. I found a lady lost in the wilderness on my way out and thought I'd escort her home. She found my horse too, convenient style."

The heavyset barman looked at Meagan; his eyes arrested on her red hunting coat. "She be wanting a room?"

"No, thank you," Meagan said, turning to Dan. "I haven't any money, remember," she whispered.

"I'll pay, honey. Set us up, Geez. Just a cupboard up top." Dan gave Meagan a grin that made her feel uncomfortable, as he took her by the elbow and propelled her toward the stairs. A few customers looked over. One whistled.

The bartender went ahead of them up the stairs and along a balcony overlooking the saloon floor. Fumbling with his keys, Geez swung open the door to a tiny room. Its only furniture was a bed made of rough cut planks and a spittoon. What the bed's single, ragged blanket left uncovered was stained brown and yellow.

"Well, go on," Dan said, still grinning.

Meagan walked carefully, watching where she stepped. "I don't know how to thank you. Really, I don't."

"You can lay your clothes over mine," he said politely.

"Pardon me?"

"To keep them clean. You can lay your clothes over mine."

"*What* did you say?"

"All right, don't, but I'd chance the floor before the bed." He reached for her and she gave him a mighty kick, well aimed. Dan gasped and fell against the wall—she opened the door and shoved him out, bent double, against the balcony railing. He slid to the ground. From the floor below came spiritless laughing. Meagan slammed the door. It had a lock, and she used it.

Meagan leaned against the closed door, catching her breath. Impossibly, the bare room seemed even seedier than before. She had to think. The appalling person outside—no, *he* didn't bear thinking about. Though, unfortunately he was the owner of the Great Horse.

"All right, lady, what's it to be?" the harsh voice of Geez came from outside.

Meagan spoke through the door. "What do you mean?"

"Pay or get out. You don't treat customers like that."

"Oh? What about how he treated *me?*"

"That's between you and him."

"Very well, I'll just be going. Thank you for your hospitality." Meagan opened the door and started out indignantly, but Geez's hulking form blocked her way.

"You owe me for an hour. House minimum, two bits."

"*I* owe? How do—*fine*." Meagan dug angrily into her vest pocket and pulled out an English shilling.

The bartender squinted. "Is that a joke?"

"No, I haven't anything else."

"Then you'll be in back helping Ethel." Geez grabbed Meagan's arm and pulled her downstairs and through a hall so dark and narrow she preferred to walk sideways. It ended with a grimy, windowless room in which a bent old woman was tossing the contents of a basin out the back door, letting it slosh over the steps. When she shut the door the room darkened, but not before Meagan had a glimpse of a lined face and gray hair.

"Ethel! Here's another who can't pay and her caller won't. Put her to work."

Ethel peered at Meagan with watery eyes that glittered in the light of a smoking oil lantern. She tilted her head toward a side of the room, and Meagan's stomach tightened. Haphazardly stacked at either side of a waterlogged wooden tub were piles and piles of dirty dishes.

"Can't we at least open the door?" Meagan asked again, but Ethel's expression was obstinately blank. Meagan was trying to be nice. Ethel's birthday had been yesterday: the ancient creature was thirty-one.

Left alone with her thoughts, Meagan passed the time remembering home and her own time, and her travels since leaving. Setting aside the frustrating question of the purpose for the journey—which she *still* didn't know—she wondered instead what Danvers Chadwick had done since she had gone missing after their grand ride together. She hoped he and Molly survived being "horse-poor" and rebuilt their rambling property back to prosperity. Standing within dimly-lit walls that seemed to amplify the barroom noises, memories of the Chadwick farm seemed as distant as ancient Rome.

As for her current circumstance, the saloon operated as a restaurant before dark, and the job paid a healthy twenty cents an hour. It included a room whose features were a broom inside a bucket she stayed away from, and a bed so foul she slept on the shabby plank floor. However, the pay was reasonable: a large plate of fried something and a fair helping of vegetables could be had for fifteen cents, and her new gingham print dress *and* leather shoes had cost only a day's wages. She converted her saved shillings into ten paper dollars, losing more to miserly currency exchange than to a half-century's inflation.

Though she liked the smells of horses, whiskey and leather, Meagan hated the saloon's other features of smoke, spit and the more woeful products of alcohol consumption. Her one consolation was being near the most probable candidate for the current Great Horse: the stock horse named Red—even if he was owned by an obnoxious, mean-spirited cowboy. She had no idea what to do next, except to bide her time quietly and stay out of trouble.

"Fetch spittoons," Ethel suggested with her usual economy of words. Meagan groaned quietly. Cleaning spittoons was one of the foulest tasks imaginable, except that nothing had to be imagined: it was spread all over the outside and dripped on the floor. Meagan grabbed a towel.

The main room was filled with its usual human menagerie with various smells and degrees of filth. Smoke hung like toxic fog. The bar carried a dust layer, and clean swipes made by drinks and elbows on the countertops were quickly recoated. Meagan had steeled herself to retrieve the first spittoon when she heard a voice she recognized.

"Can't take less'n thirty-five dollars. He's a real work horse and I'll take what he's worth." It was Dan Beardon, who had first rescued and then accosted her. He was talking quickly to two men as they exited together out the front door.

Concerned, Meagan decided to begin with cleaning the spittoon by the front window. She walked to it and casually rubbed a spot in the foggy saloon glass to see out. The dark sorrel horse, Blue, and the buckskin, Red, were standing tethered to the establishment's hitching post. Dan and his two prospects were walking around Red, patting his backside. *He was selling the Great Horse!*

Dan seemed to recognize Meagan as she walked outside to join them, but he deliberately looked away and kept talking. She crossed her arms and listened.

"Now, you two look like upstanding gentlemen of the community," Dan was saying. "This buckskin is too, he's pure genuine Presbyterian, he takes things that calm and easy."

"What about that one?" asked one of the prospective buyers, pointing to the dark sorrel standing tied. "He for sale?"

"Blue? Naw, there's no reasoning with that horse—he's Baptist plumb through—but my *Red* here, *he* can outrun the devil! Make top speed from a standstill to that post. I hate to sell him, but I've got to make Dodge City before summer sets in and I need the cash. Got a job waiting."

"Thirty-five dollars, you say?" asked one of the buyers.

"Yup. And I'll throw in the halter."

Meagan made herself think quickly: she *had* to stay near Red ... an idea was forming: "Excuse me, sir, is this the horse you ponied me into town on?"

The buyers glanced at her as Dan scowled. "Yes, I think I'd remember *that* tale of woe."

"It can't be ... how did you get rid of his spavins?"

"Ignore her," Dan advised. "The poor girl is touched." He made a tapping gesture on his temple for illustration.

"Why, it *is* the same horse," Meagan peered closer, sounding impressed. "Tell me, is he over that wheeze? Oh, that's right, you said it was just heaves."

The two buyers looked at each other.

"This horse never had spavins nor heaves," Dan hissed. "Now *get*."

Meagan stepped up to the buckskin's head, patting him gently. "Nice teeth," she said innocently, opening the buckskin's lips, "for a parrot." Smiling, she sidled up to a potential buyer and pointed at the horse's rear portion. "You look like a horseman, so tell me ... would you say the horse is sickle-hocked, or just cat-hammed? It's hard to tell, isn't it, on account of the goose rump?"

Dan simmered, turning crimson. "Lady, I'll tell you this just once—if you don't get back inside, I'm contacting the establishment. This is pure harassment of the clientele."

"If you come back here," Meagan led the two prospects to stand a distance behind the horse, "you can see a rare thing. A horse pigeon-toed in front and cow-hocked behind!"

"That's it! I'm getting Geez!"

"What's the matter, Beardon?" asked one of the buyers. "Can't answer the young lady's questions?"

"That's no lady, if you catch my meaning."

"Oh?" Now Meagan reddened too. "At least I'm not trying to pawn off a slab-sided, ewe-necked wasp-belly with no wind and asking thirty-five good dollars for it." Meagan smiled at Dan's murderous expression as the two ex-buyers mumbled something and went back inside.

Dan went to Red and tossed his lead rope over the buckskin's neck. "All right, that one's going to cost you. See I felt sorry and didn't press charges before, but I had witnesses. I think I'm going to poke into the sheriff's station and see what's what."

"I'll buy the horse," Meagan said quickly.

"The hell you will—you *can't!*"

"No, I'm serious. I'll pay you forty."

Dan stopped and narrowed his eyes at her. "You didn't have a damn cent three weeks ago, and now you've got forty dollars? Business been that good?"

"I'll pretend I didn't hear that. Here's ten dollars. I'll have the rest for you soon, I promise."

"Oh, you *promise*. Couldn't steal him, so you have to resort to actually paying? My, hard times. Sorry, can't wait. I'm getting out, like I was about to when I had the misfortune of saving your life."

"Look, I'll have the rest in a few weeks. Take the money. Please? I need this horse."

"This horse? In particular, *this* horse? Well, if it comes to that, I don't see why getting the animal of your choice should come so cheap."

"Because he really is sickle-hocked, and if his teeth were any more bucked you could open a bottle with them."

Dan grimaced. "Okay, put him in the shed. But I'm telling the boy to let me know if that horse steps one pigeon-toe out of town." He snatched the money from her hand, wadding it and shoving it into his pocket. "I was only hoping for thirty anyhow." He handed Meagan the reins and went to the buckskin's side, flipping up the stiff leather and un-cinching the saddle's girth.

"Wait, what are you doing?"

"Taking my saddle. What's it look like from over there?"

"But I *need* the saddle," she said hotly, angry with herself for not thinking of it.

"Yep, you sure do."

"How much do you want for it?"

"Don't know. Good stock saddle's sixty, seventy dollars."

"The *horse* was only forty dollars!"

"Actually, that's a lot for a cow horse. You got taken pretty bad. Red here's worth about twenty-five, *maybe* thirty if I stuck some oats in him."

"What? A saddle costs more than a horse?"

"A saddle will outlast a bunch of horses, plus saddles aren't busy making little saddles neither."

"Ok, fine. I'll pay you as soon as I can."

"No, I think I'll need cash payment for this item." Dan pulled the heavy saddle from the buckskin and perched it on his hip. "You know, you had any decency you'd work some-place else, knowing this is my stamping ground."

"How could I know that?"

"Well now you do."

There is something about the outside of a horse
that is good for the inside of a man.
- Winston Churchill (1874-1965)

MEAGAN BEGAN WORKING all possible hours for extra money, scrubbing the main room after the last customer had passed or stumbled out. Early each morning, under the stable boy's watchful eye, she brushed Red and took him for a short ride, jogging bareback down the single, short street to the edge of town and back, hinting. She wanted to give the Great Horse every opportunity to take her home ... but all were untaken.

On the brighter side, Meagan truly liked Red. Fifteen hands high, the gelding was built like a bulldog but moved with the grace of a cat. He had classic American Quarter Horse conformation: high muscular hindquarters, low withers, wide chest and thick neck. His breed were specialized sprinters, named for the short, quarter-mile raceways hacked through woods by early American settlers.

Red stood quietly while she brushed him, sighing and swishing his thick tail. She wore her riding breeches under a skirt, a look meant for pre-dawn hours. When her weight came down on his back, Red lifted his head; when she clucked lightly, he moved forward in a ground-eating stride. Another cluck and he slipped into a slow, easy jog. The street was too short to ask for more.

One morning Dan stepped from the saloon's stoop as she returned from her brief ride. "They all said you just rode up and back, but I thought they was funnin' me."

"I'm getting used to him. Good morning, by the way."

"Yes, it is. A good morning for heading out. Seems that job in Dodge City pays extra for second mounts, so I've come to get my horse."

"What do you mean, 'get *your* horse?' He's *my* horse now."

"Was." Dan held out ten straight, crisp dollars. "As I've recently come into some cash money, I'll be taking him back."

"Well, you can't have him back. We made a deal."

"Yeah, *well*, I'm changing my mind. Hurry and get down from that horse, or I'll take you off myself."

Meagan set her jaw. "I'd like to see you try."

"Lady, you woke up the wrong passenger." In an instant Dan had Red by the bridle. He reached quickly under Meagan's leg, grasped her calf and flipped her off the other side. She lay dazed a moment as ten dollars fluttered over her. "Mighty obliged." Dan tossed the reins across Red's neck and lifted a foot to mount. The buckskin stepped aside, avoiding Dan. "Whoa now, what's got into you, Red?"

Meagan sat up. "I told you, he's my horse now."

"The hell he is. This horse saved my life a hundred times—damn it Red, stand *still!*"

"Then you shouldn't have sold him. Please take your money and leave my horse."

"I suggest you mind your business, lady. I've had about enough. I've been nice, but just keep away." Growing more angry, he positioned Red against the hitching post so the horse couldn't move away. Dan tightened the reins and jumped up, throwing a leg over. Settling over Red's back, Dan gave Meagan a triumphant gesture and found himself floating weightless a split second before he hit the ground. Stretched on his back, it took him a moment to open his eyes, and when he did he saw the back of Red's hindquarters being led to his stall. Ten crumpled dollars lay on his chest.

———

Meagan had her proof now: the legend said no one could ride the Great Horse without permission and it had held true.

Of course, like the others, *this* Great Horse seemed in no hurry to take her home.

She hated nights in the barroom: dreary, sodden evenings of scraping chairs and loud remarks. Meagan could hardly dignify the perpetual leering and comments with anger, let alone friendly retorts. She had been nicknamed the "cold fish." It didn't bother her at all.

"Set some down, barkeep!"

It was a common enough request, but Meagan looked up when she heard the unfortunately familiar voice. Dan Beardon stood inside the front door, arms spread wide. His clothes still had dirt on them from the morning. He had clearly been drinking his ten dollars, and when his fogged eyes settled upon Meagan he winced and staggered to the bar.

"Yep—*that'd* be the fancy ma'am who's ruin't my life. I was finally outta this stinking dust hole—no offense, Geez—when behold the vision of a woman appeared, laying flat out cold in the open prairie. *With* my horse, mind you. Should of left her there, I'd be happy in Dodge City by now. Let my misfortunes be your instruction. Never do a good turn."

Hearing this, Meagan almost felt sorry for the horrible person's situation. In a way, it *was* her fault. "Dan, don't you think you should sit down?"

"*No, I don't think I should sit down,*" Dan mocked in falsetto before turning to Geez. "She did something to my horse, Geez. Spooked him something awful. Red won't even let me on him. It ain't the same animal."

Geezer poured a drink of brownish liquid and placed it before Dan.

Meagan intercepted it. "Haven't you had enough?"

"What the—see what I mean? She's a terror. A public scourge."

"*Really,* Dan. Can't I get you coffee or something to eat?"

"She's ferocious. She'll be the death of some poor fool. Or many."

"Meagan," the bartender suggested, "perhaps you'd better get on to the back."

"Yes, perhaps you should," Dan slurred.

Meagan set the glass down and looked coolly at the proprietor. "You're not helping him, John."

"His name's Geez and he's helping just fine." Dan looked around the dark interior. "Where is everybody? Heck, in Dodge City they're just getting started."

"You're not *in* Dodge City, Dan."

"Don't I know it," he said absently, pushing away from the bar and grabbing his drink. He took half of it in a swallow and peered narrowly at Meagan. "How're you at cards?"

"Terrible. Don't you need some sleep?"

"Terrible's just the quality I'm looking for. Come, sit right here and let's deal a set."

"No, thank you. I'm still working."

"Aw, Geez'll let you sit a hand, won't you Geez? Just until I win my horse back."

The front doors to the main room opened and two short, wiry men walked in cautiously, as if confused about the purpose of such a place.

Dan raised his voice. "You gentlemen care for a round of poker?"

Meagan felt a quick pang of guilt; they looked sober, and likely to take the rest of Dan's money. "Fine. I'll do it," she said quickly. "Sit down and we'll play a hand, just you and me."

"Move aside, little lady. You should know poker's a man's game. Say, Geez ... if you don't mind, your hired help is disturbing your patrons."

The two new players circled Dan and took chairs. The owner gave Meagan a nod. She threw her towel in disgust and went into the back to help Ethel.

"*Men,*" Meagan said to the silent woman, who gave her a look of perfect understanding. They worked together silently, Meagan struggling to get to the end of the dishes, futilely, while Ethel puttered and cleaned in the eternal way she had, a perpetual motion machine turned maid, burning her life away in the dark back room of a grimy bar in a tiny, dirtball town in the center of nothing...

Meagan sighed. *I'm depressing myself,* she thought, and put down the tray she was scraping. She went to stand by the back door. Ethel hated to have the door open, but the night was warm and clear, and Meagan made her suffer. The air was tinged with tar and manure, honest scents that vanished in the lightest breeze. The stars were a span of points brushed over with thin clouds. It seemed strange that in the midst of such beauty men could make something as ugly as this town, and choose it.

Shouting came from the street. Another fight. Meagan was about to pull the door closed when she recognized Dan's voice.

"Come on, listen to me. I can get you cash." Dan walked behind the two cardplayers from the bar, heading toward the stalls. He tried to take one of the men's arms and was brushed back.

Meagan stepped down from the porch and let Ethel close the door behind her. When she saw a cardplayer walk into Red's stall carrying a rope, she was off the stoop and shouting. "Wait—that horse is mine! Tell them, Dan! "

The men paused long enough to see she was a woman alone and thus ignorable. They opened the stall door and led the buckskin out.

Dan caught her arm. "It's no good, Meagan. I lost him in a hand, fair and square."

"You lost Red—in a *card game?*" She struggled, but Dan's grip was iron. "If you don't let me go right now, Mr. Beardon, I will remind you why we're not friends."

"Would you pull in your horns and *listen* a second," he said softly.

"They're taking my horse!"

"We'll get him back. *Listen!*"

She looked him in the eye, waiting.

"All right," he said, loosening his grip slightly. "Now, we have to get Blue too."

Meagan snatched her arm away. "What about Blue?"

"I lost him first." Dan waved at the pair of cardplayers leading the buckskin out to the street. "Bye, boys. Good game." Meagan started after them, but Dan caught her again. "Don't do it, girl. They're real armed. I have a plan. Go upstairs and get your stuff and meet me in front of the schoolhouse where I've been keeping Blue."

"There's a *school* here?"

"Quiet. Go to the right, to the edge of town. Don't forget Red's bridle—I know it's in your room—and you're fancy riding clothes won't hurt neither. Now get a wiggle on, *go.*"

Meagan suppressed a sincere urge to slap him and ran back into the saloon. She bounded upstairs, hurriedly pulled her riding breeches on under her dress and slipped back downstairs. Geez was in the front bar, so she ducked down the narrow hall, past Ethel and around the building to the street.

Dark forms were gathered a short distance away. She stopped when she saw that one of the cardplayers held a large pistol, cocked and pointing at a shadowed figure standing, hands against the building. Dan.

Meagan recognized the second player coming toward the street, leading another shadow Meagan recognized as Blue. "The saddles were inside," he called to his partner. "Put this one on the buckskin."

"*Mira!*" One of the players pointed to Meagan. "It's the woman again, Ráfe." Though she could not see either man's face, their low voices were clear enough. "You came to get your horse, eh, *chica?*"

"Actually," Meagan said, swallowing, "I ... came to give you advice: the horse likes carrots but not apples. And he loves sugar but it's bad for his teeth."

The two cardplayers chuckled. The one leading Blue threw the reins over the dark sorrel's neck. The other began cinching Red's saddle.

"And he can't stand dirty water pails," she added.

"No dirty pails, we promise, *chica.*"

"Or old hay. It has to be leafy. Second cutting is the best."

One of the players mounted Blue and reined him viciously, making the horse throw his head and skitter backwards. "Is that a bridle you're holding, *chica*? Ráfe, look, she has a bridle, *péro* she has no horse!"

"*Verdad* ... and I have a horse and no bridle! We make it better, no?" He withdrew a pistol from his side and walked toward Meagan. She avoided his gaze as she held the bridle out to him.

"Anything else you want to tell us, *chica?*" he asked, taking the bridle and pulling it on Red.

"Yes, there is one other thing..."

The horse thief swung himself up, barely settling before Red lowered himself as if to bow—and thrust himself into the air. All four feet left the ground as Red twisted and threw the rider sideways into the dirt.

Blue's rider let out a short cry and fell, squirming as he lay on the ground. The sorrel swung his hindquarters around, and Meagan saw Dan holding his reins. She didn't wait but ran to Red, reaching him just as Dan alighted on Blue. She leaped on Red's back and grabbed his mane, clapping her heels to his sides as she heard a gunshot.

The first seconds of a quarter horse's sprint are an explosion of muscle and wind. The G-force of moving from a standstill to forty-five miles per hour in four strides seems to suck the air from one's lungs. Meagan was unready for such acceleration, and her tight hold on Red's mane was her only security. The ground streaked past under pumping, violent power, and she was almost more afraid of what she had summoned beneath her than of the gunfire. There was no road, no town—only sound and wind. Red's hooves did not touch but slammed the earth.

Before reaching the edge of town, they caught up to Dan and Blue. For a long time the two horses ran together, not with the charging sprint of the first few hundred yards but in a steady gallop that ate up the distance. It was Dan who pulled up. He studied her a moment in the dark, panting.

"That was a great plan," she said.

"I'm heading to Dodge," Dan grumbled. "Do you know where that is? Any idea at all?"

"No."

"Well I *do*, so you listen to *me*, girl. Because I don't need all this, I really don't." Dan clucked and jogged on.

Meagan followed. It was all they said throughout the warm night.

———•———

A line of dawn showed at the horizon. Dim shades of gray changed to color like a developing photograph, as the sun rose into the sky with eager rays already warm. "Shouldn't we stop to let the horses graze?" Meagan asked finally.

"Once we get to some water. I want to make sure we got enough of a start. We stole these horses, you know. They had witnesses. Some places are mighty particular about horse thieves."

"Correction. *You* lost the horses in a card game—you're the horse thief, not me."

"A fine moral distinction. See if your rope don't feel about the same."

Meagan changed the subject. She would not admit it, but her bunched-up long skirt was chafing her legs on the steady ride. "How far is Dodge?"

"What difference does that make? Any place else you got to be?"

"Do you intend to be like this the whole way, Mr. Beardon?"

"No, just the talky parts."

"Fine." Meagan pulled up and dismounted.

"Now what are you doing?"

"Changing clothes and letting my horse rest."

"I told you we were waiting to get to some water."

"Go on, then. Get some water."

"Damn fool woman," Dan spat, clucking to Blue and walking on.

Meagan watched them go, then wriggled out of her skirt to just her breeches. She rolled the dress up and tied it behind the rough saddle, waiting until Dan was well ahead before remounting. It would be less irritating to ride by herself.

It was early spring and though the landscape was desolate, there was freshness in the breeze. Coming finally to a fast running creek, Meagan let Red splay out and drink a hundred yards upstream of where Dan watered Blue.

"Go on and get your fill!" Dan called. "Next water's not 'till nightfall." Meagan pulled Red up so he would not drink too quickly. Dan and Blue splashed towards her through the shallow water.

"Have you been this way before?" she asked, prepared for another rude reply.

"Once. Coming the other way about three years ago."

"Coming from where?"

"Nowhere. And now I'm going back." He hesitated. "Look, about our misunderstanding the other day, the room and all."

"What misunderstanding? I think you were very clear."

"What I mean is, I don't usually do that sort of thing."

"I'm sorry, but I was there, and you did."

"Damn it, how *does* a body apologize to you? I'm sorry I took you for a Girl of the Line—but you're an aggravating woman, you know that?"

"Apology accepted," Meagan said, gathering Red's reins. "You're a pig. How much further?"

"Two days, not counting last night." Dan took off his hat to wipe his forehead. Beard stubble covered his lean, tan jaw; his intense brown eyes were slightly bloodshot from his recent drinking bout.

"You know, I've never seen you without your hat. How old are you?"

Dan crushed his hat back over his cropped light brown hair. "'Bout nineteen, if it's your business."

"I wouldn't have guessed. I'm almost eighteen, myself."

"Must be why you know so much. Anyhow, we should keep on. I was telling the truth, they're serious about horse thieves. Most fun they get in that town is stringing folks up."

"But they can't travel any faster than we can."

"Sure they can. They bring spare horses. You're riding mine."

"Oh." Meagan jumped up on Red and swung a leg over, groaning as her aching muscles stretched. "What about the saddle ... can we just add it to my debt?" She could not bring herself to ask him sweetly.

Dan snorted. "That'd be good money gone. No thanks. You just keep it cleaned up, I'll collect the saddle when I get Red back." He waded Blue across the stream and up the bank on the other side. A kind of truce had been declared.

———

True to his word, Dan rode far into the night before stopping. There wasn't much to making camp: they simply picketed the horses with a low stake and lay on thin bedrolls over the ground; but it was wonderful to dismount. Before Meagan could think what sort of creatures might find her to their liking, she was asleep.

The next day Dan shot a possum; when Meagan couldn't bring herself to eat it, he gave her a portion of jerky wrapped in leather. It was stored in butter-like grease and tasted delicious after a day and a half without food. Though it did not fill her, she felt light and energized.

The ride was a swaying journey across the open land, with stops at measured intervals to give the horses time to graze. It was, as Dan pointed out, a balance between going easy with light grazing or pushing to get into town for real rest. Occasionally they cantered the horses, and although Red's jog-trot was choppy, his canter was pure heaven—though the gait was not termed a canter here. In this place the four-beat stride was called by the relaxed word that described it perfectly: a *lope*.

Blue was the prettier of the two horses, a dark sorrel with only the smallest spot of white hair in the center of his forehead. *Flash*, Dan called it, bragging. "Now Blue, he thinks he's the big horse. I used to switch off riding, but Blue doesn't like taking turns. He gets downright mulish if you don't ride him regular. Red, he could take or leave it. Figures he's got a job and he's good at it, so it doesn't hurt his feelings to have some time off. And as you've seen, Red's pretty fast off his mark."

"It's like being shot from a cannon."

"Yeah. That little horse has got me out of a lot of trouble. Not that I like trouble, it just sorta comes my way. Blue, he could run faster but he holds his danged head up too high, a throwback from his early days as a ornery cuss. I mostly let him have his way and we get along fine."

Meagan nodded, watching the sorrel horse step nimbly over the rocky terrain. "So, why did you want to sell Red?"

"Now that was what you'd call a decision made in haste. If I didn't get out of that town, I was going to drink myself to death from boredom. Then I fell in a hole and drank my stake to prove it. I couldn't sell Blue—he ain't worth much on the open market and besides, it'd break his heart. But Red? Naw, Red's his own deal. Prime stock horse and a saleable commodity ... I do want him back, though. Want to deal a hand?"

They jogged on the trail still showing green, doomed to be dust by summer. Meagan would not have guessed they were near Dodge City until Dan raised his hand and pointed. She saw only a cross and thought it was a graveyard—until she saw it was actually the steeple of a church, buried among buildings so covered in dust they blended with the streets around them. A buzzing energy of shouting and sounds of construction drifted out to greet them.

"Do you know anyone here?" she asked.

"Maybe, don't know who all's here."

"This job that's waiting for you here ... what is it?"

"Naw, I couldn't work in Dodge *now*, I told that whole town I was coming here. A man shouldn't talk about what he's gonna do, he should just do it—something my daddy always said, dang him." He twisted his mouth, thinking. "The job *is* up north a ways, so it might come out all right. Courier work, and good pay too. First thing we got to do is find a livery, one off in the shadows somewhere. Word about our little skedaddle won't show up for a day or so and I'll be long gone by then."

She hesitated before asking, "Are you wanted for anything else?"

"Yeah, I stifled a loud-mouth girl outside Dodge City. What kind of question is that? No, I'm not wanted for anything else. Are *you?*"

The trail graduated to a road as it came into town. It was no improvement. The ruts were wet with filthy runoff that people jumped over, horses avoided and wagons churned through, splattering bystanders. Dan took the first road off the main street and rode along the town's outskirts.

"How about that one?" Meagan pointed to a comfortable establishment with a plank porch and hay piled neatly at one corner.

"Too fancy, too close to the road."

A short distance further they came to a sign announcing itself a "Publc Livry" over a painted arrow with drip marks showing the side entrance. The only indication of horses was a heavy manure odor. Dan shook his head and went on.

Finally, as town was receding into sparse and empty land, Dan pulled up outside a collection of shacks. One building was colored a handsome charcoal hue from a recent fire. Wisps of smoke curled into the air.

A brooding overseer sat on a barrel outside a small, intact building near the front of the yard, which featured an infinitesimal porch and window box of dead plants to indicate human habitation. An illegible poster featuring a disproportionate horse was tacked to the door.

"Have a fire?" Dan asked congenially.

"Green hay," the overseer replied absently. "Baled too soon."

Meagan had seen the blackened remains of such accidents, when damp hay fermented inside a bale to the point of spontaneous combustion.

"Got any good hay left for a couple horses?"

"Sure I do. I'm storing the rest inside with my wife." As if to underscore his statement, a woman's angry voice rose from inside the little house, well peppered with salty language and a clatter of pans.

Dan looked around and shrugged. "What do you think, Meagan? This place seems unlikely enough."

"I guess so, if the stalls are good. But where are we going to stay? I'm exhausted."

"That is the next item. We'll find something in a local hotel."

"I can pay for my own room, thanks."

"All right with me."

There is something about riding down the street on a prancing horse that makes you feel like something, even when you ain't a thing.

- Will Rogers (1879-1935)

Meagan had no idea how long the sun had been in her face, but she sat up in the bed with damp strands of hair clinging to her neck. For a moment everything was strange and unfamiliar, then the curtains drifting in a light breeze reminded her—they were the last thing she had seen the night before, blowing in the moonlight against the half-opened window. She rubbed her eyes and threw off the covers. It looked to be late morning and she was starving.

Dressing quickly, Meagan thought it strange Dan had not yet come by. The hotel seemed deserted as she walked down the wooden stairs into the front room that served as the lobby. A large mirror in an ornately-carved frame stood at the bottom of the stairs. Next to the mirror hung a vintage photograph—no, Meagan corrected herself, it was a modern, state-of-the-art photograph. Before her travels she had been under the unexamined impression that people from past times had been colorless—as if history itself had been black-and-white. It was odd to see the daguerreotype photograph sitting clean and fresh in its colorful frame, bright from dusting.

"May I help you?" asked a gentleman sitting at the front desk.

"Yes, please. I am staying upstairs. I came with a friend, Dan Beardon, and I was wondering which room was his."

"He left this morning."

Meagan felt her heart skip. "Excuse me?"

"He paid his bill and went on." The clerk showed no emotion, not even interest. He delivered such news often. "Will you be staying?"

In panic, Meagan hurried out into the sunlight. She tried to retrace their steps, making several starts before coming upon a familiar dark street. There it was, the scattering of buildings (one charred) and the proprietor sitting on his barrel as if he had never moved.

"Excuse me, sir, have you seen the man that was with me yesterday? We stabled our horses here last night."

"Yep. He came by, oh ... about an hour ago. Maybe more like two. Mornings go pretty fast."

Meagan's heart sank. How could she have been so stupid? Dan had given her every sign, he had even *told* her he was planning to get Red back. Then she saw something.

Red's unstolen head hung over his stall door, hay trailing from his mouth as he chewed. Meagan walked to look curiously in his stall. It was clean and dry, with fresh water and a stack of new hay. She heard a man's voice singing in a mournful croon. Meagan walked up quietly. It was Dan, standing in Blue's stall, brushing the horse in long strokes. Blue's ears were flicking in enjoyment. "Good morning," she said pleasantly in relief.

Dan glanced back. "Oh hello, didn't see you there. Good morning, yourself." He pulled the brush away and came out of the stall. "Glad you found your way over. I was fixing to go after you, guess I lost track. Sleep good?"

"Yes," Meagan answered nonchalantly, trying not to sound glad to see him. "Great, in fact. Amazing how nice a bed feels after sleeping on gravel."

"Yeah, it reminds me of back..." Dan trailed off, and broke into a grin. "I was thinking we'd go find something to eat. Then I want to head over to the post office and see what's doing."

Food was easy to find: most public houses were bars by night and restaurants by day. The meals were simple and heavy, paid for by the plate. Meagan had two.

Afterwards they walked through the town, past the trim clapboard stores and hotels. In one place a crowd had gathered, some seated stiffly on benches, others in small groups standing and talking. A few men were well-dressed and fast talking; most wore worker's clothes or the rags of a drifter. A small group of women in hoop dresses whispered in conversation.

Meagan looked for the attraction which drew the crowd, but all she saw was a small building whose front served as a bulletin board for flyers, cards and the occasional reprinted photograph. Some flyers announced events, or advertised *Help Wanted*—some expressed only the second word, with an identifying sketch.

"Why are all these people standing here?" Meagan asked.

"The post is probably late."

"The 'post?'"

Dan had stopped and was studying a flyer. He leaned closer, squinting. Meagan moved to look over his shoulder.

"This is the one," Dan said, pointing to a boxed advertisement. "Must still be hiring."

"That outfit's always hiring," claimed a gaunt man standing beside Dan. "Pay's good, but they can't keep horses or men."

"*That* is the job you want?" Meagan said, staring at the poster.

"Yep. Pays twenty a week, extra if I've got a spare horse."

"Twenty-five a week now, so I hear," interjected the bystander. "Something's fishy if they can't keep men at that pay."

Dan leaned closer to read. "Says there was a company official in town last week."

The bystander snorted. "Yeah, he was around. Got some boys all riled up and then got called away. Fishy, you ask me."

"Dan, wait," Meagan interrupted. "Are you serious? *This* is the company you were talking about?"

"I said yes, didn't I? Don't say you're going deaf too. Heard of it?"

"Yes, I have heard of the *Pony Express*."

"Well, good. Seems peculiar knowledge for a girl who don't know what a post office is, but who'm I to say?"

"A few boys wanting work went up to the headquarters in St. Joe," said the stranger. "Queer operation from what I seen."

"St. Joe? That's no good."

"Is it far?" Meagan asked.

Dan looked at her a moment, and broke into a grin. "Hell *yeah* it's far. You're the strangest thing I've ever come across. What, you looking to join up too?"

"I might," she said stubbornly.

"Or might not. They don't take women, and I don't blame them much."

Meagan crossed her arms. "That flyer doesn't say they won't take women."

"That's because it was written for sane people to read, and sane people know some things."

Cries started up and down the street and the crowd pressed forward. Dan looked up. "We'd best get on to avoid the crush, unless you got mail coming. Not that I would be surprised if you did." He strode off down the street, hands in pockets.

Meagan held back, watching Dan go. It was hard to know if he intended her to follow, the way he walked so quickly, head low and not looking back. *Should she just let him go?* Dan turned the corner and stopped, finally looking behind him. He cocked his head with the same expression as a dog confused by an odd sound. She hurried to catch him.

Dodge City was sprawling. There were no apparent rules on what or where to build—if a spot appealed to someone, he simply set to work with a hammer. Even so, there was already organization. They had entered town along the mercantile district, slept on the lower-rent side and eaten in the "entertainment" section. Judging from the smells, they were coming near the stockyards—the horse liveries were flowery by comparison. Meagan could see cattle lying in grassless pens with long fences segregating the herds. The cattle's woeful choir was punctuated by men's shouts.

"What are we doing here?" she asked.

"Don't know what *you're* doing, *I'm* looking for a job." Cowboys in chaps and crusted pants stood in groups around the pens. A few bosses were dressed in clean suits; Dan hailed one and announced he wanted a job.

The hailed man stopped and removed a cigar from his mouth. "Good to hear it, son. Talk to my manager over there." He pointed with his cigar.

"I will, sir. By the way, name's Dan Beardon ... yours?" Ignoring Dan's outstretched hand, the boss put the cigar back in his mouth and continued walking.

The indicated manager had small eyes that watered, giving him a beetle-like appearance. His glance darted to Meagan and back to Dan as they approached. "Can I he'p you?"

"Your boss sent me over."

"I need some swing riders. You might maybe rotate to flank, but that's all you get. Want it or not?"

"Where are you going?" Dan asked.

"Abilene, the new stockyards in Kansas. We be leaving in four days to meet up in Caldwell."

"Nothing sooner?"

"You got to get out of town?" The man's eyes darted. "Well, we had one pull out yesterday, big group heading to Medora, up in Dakota Territory. They'll make Gove by nightfall, about forty miles from here."

The names of long-dead or surpassed towns meant little to Meagan, but Dan seemed enlightened. "Too bad for them. I was laid up in Gove one winter. Bleak doesn't begin to describe it."

"They could always use drag riders if you'll do it."

"Be there by morning."

Beetle eyes flitted. "You ain't taking her, are you?"

Dan gave a short laugh. "Nope. She's stopping here."

"Wait a minute," Meagan protested. "Maybe I want a job too."

"I don't know, Miss." Beetle eyes looked her up and down. "Long days. Can you take the sun?"

"Oh, she likes the sun," Dan answered. "Stays in it all day. Listen to her talk a while if you don't believe me."

"I have a horse," Meagan said curtly.

The trail manager shrugged and looked her up and down. "No guarantee the boss will take her."

"Sounds like a sensible outfit. Who do I ask for, once I get to Gove?"

"Man named Lee. Like the General."

"What did that man mean?" Meagan asked as they walked away. "'Lee, like the General?'"

"Damned if I know. He was a peculiar old bug."

"Was he talking about Robert E. Lee?"

"Who in tarnation is Robert Ealey?"

Meagan tried to remember her history. 1861. "Is there a war going on?"

"Better not be. Folks talk, but that's all they do. Damn, woman! Try asking a reasonable question, just to change up."

"Ok. Why don't you want me to go to St. Joe?"

"I'm not going to St. Joe, I'm going to Gove. Weren't you listening?"

"I want to go, too."

"Really? The little ride here to Dodge just about did you, and now you want to trail all the way up to Dakota Territory?"

They walked in silence back to the horses. Meagan didn't want to be alone in this town: it was somewhere a person could disappear without anybody knowing or caring. They came to the little yard with the overseer sitting on his barrel watching the world pass. The horses nickered expectantly, heads over their doors.

Meagan stroked Red's blocky head while Dan pulled Blue out, ran a brush over the horse's dark coat, and saddled him. Red watched with interest, ears swiveling. Meagan said noth-

ing as she consoled herself. The local barrooms had dishes to
wash, surely, and she could ride Red whenever she wanted.
And someday soon, Red would take her home. Everything
would be fine, really it would. "So you've been on one of
these trail rides?" she asked casually.

"It ain't a trail ride, it's a cattle drive, and yeah I've been on
them. Problem is, these things don't go anywhere you'd
much want to be. Head north, mostly. Fatten the cattle up and
bring them to the railroads. Gotta feed you Eastern types,
who can't much do anything for yourselves." Dan stood a
moment holding Blue's reins. "I'm sorry, Meagan. It's only
that they wouldn't take you in Gove, probably. And this is a
lot better place than that, easy."

Yikes, Meagan almost said.

"A drive's no fun, especially riding drag. And the men
would be ... well, not the gentleman I am."

Meagan smiled and rolled her eyes. "What's riding drag
like?"

"Hell. Going to ask what that's like?"

Meagan laughed.

"Because I know, I had a preacher uncle. He ran a Gospel
mill down in Lexington." He stopped. "I'm sorry Meagan, I
am, but maybe this is better. There's gonna be people looking
for me."

"Have you forgotten they're looking for me, too?"

"Naw, woman, they ain't looking for you. It's me that's
been shooting my mouth off for the last month. I'm indelible.
My daddy always said a man should keep himself to himself,
and he's right, dang him."

"What about the money I owe you for Red? And how much
do you want for your saddle?"

Dan put his head back, letting his hat fall. "Tar*nation*. I'd
clean forgot how you got your hooks in Red. Now I've got to
sell a saddle or buy a horse."

"I've still got three dollars."

"Sure, and I'm taking your last three dollars on this earth.
All right! It's your way again—I was doing you a favor, but

you want to come, come on then. But I'm telling you right now, a cattle drive is no place for a woman, and sure no place for a lady."

"So now you think I'm a lady?" Meagan said, smiling. Dan tossed the reins over Blue's neck and led the horse out, cramming his hat on his head. She was almost sure she'd seen him blush.

They rode all that night, stopping only for food and water, finishing the final leg in the dark. Meagan did not complain until they came into Gove with the last of the night. "You're right, Dan. This place is worse than Dodge."

"This is the nice part."

The backs of sleeping cattle were visible like tiny mountain ranges across the rocky ground. Meagan slid off and stretched. Dan did the same, throwing her the stiff rope halter hanging from his saddle. Everything Dan needed he kept on his saddle: rope on the side, canteens on front rings, saddlebags on back. A bedroll padded the cantle.

"Where should we go to sign up?"

"Relax, I'll take care of it. I wouldn't be in any hurry." Dan stretched out on the ground as Meagan sat cross-legged, letting Red graze. "We didn't catch much shut-eye."

Dawn was imminent. The birds had already started their day, and the cattle were stirring. She jumped at a raucous clang that sounded like someone banging a frying pan with a heavy metal spoon, which someone was.

Dan stood stiffly. "So it begins. Stay here and I'll get us joined on. Boss doesn't need to see you're of the weaker sex."

"Gentler sex."

"And let's call you something different. How about calling you ... well, how 'bout Sagebrush? That's a good nickname."

"Sagebrush?"

"Yeah, like it? It don't sound like a guy or a girl."

"No, it sounds like a plant."

"Be right back."

It was half an hour before Dan returned. He seemed in a hurry. "Well get on, Sagebrush. Don't malinger your first day."

"We're hired? Just like that, and they didn't even want to meet me?"

"Nope, and as long as we're trailing he won't need to. Tuck your hair up somehow."

"All right, but I don't have a tie."

Dan pulled a piece of beef jerky from his saddlebag, stripped a strand off and tossed it to her. "There you go, Sagebrush, a hair tie and a handy meal too. Never know, those things might catch on back East."

"Why do you think I'm from back East?"

"You have to be. I've never seen anyone so citified. All prim and proper, just like society folk from college back home."

"I have no idea what 'citified' means ... you went to college?"

"I did. For a year." He looked at her importantly. "You don't know everything, do you?"

"Well I certainly didn't know *that*."

"A waste of time, my professors would agree."

"I didn't mean it that way, Dan. It just surprised me. Did the boss tell you how much the pay is?"

"See, right back to city talk. We're getting about forty dollars, far as we're going."

"What do you mean, 'far as we're going'?"

"They say the drive heads past Ogallala, near the Pony Express line. I figure we'll peel off and see what's what. Boss has no problem with that—they mostly need help through burr country."

"Burr country?"

"Lord, woman, you ask questions. Get on your horse. Now here's a spare bandanna."

Meagan held the filthy rag at arm's length. "What is *this* for?"

Dan chuckled.

A cowboy climbed aboard a bronc, which commenced to buck. The bronc caught a hind leg in one of the stirrups—whereupon the cowboy leaped out of the saddle. When the onlookers asked the cowboy what had happened, he replied, "Boys, when I looked down and saw that bronc's foot in the stirrup, I said to myself, hell, if he's getting on, I'd better get off."

- Anonymous

By noon Meagan believed she had made the biggest mistake of her life. She had expected to be sore, to be hot and hungry; she had expected the smell. She had not thought of the bugs.

The closely-bunched cattle were an insect's moveable feast, and despite her considerable experience with biting, buzzing insects, she had never seen anything to compare with these in size, quantity or ferocity. They buzzed or bit constantly, making the horses and cattle stamp and hitch. A swarm of ghostlike gnats danced a perpetual jig before her eyes.

And she had not expected the dust. Riding with the Mongols had been dusty, but the nomads trod grassland; the cattle were walking on dry clay. Perhaps it was the difference of the cow's cloven hoof to the horse's flat one, or the tight formation of the herd moving shoulder to shoulder, but the cattle raised more dust than she could have imagined. It clogged her eyes and nose and throat, and the bandanna was the only way to avoid choking. Dust crept into every crevice until her clothes were full of sand, and visibility was so poor she could see Dan's outline only dimly as he rode next to her. The cattle were apparitions in a cloud.

It had begun so gently, with sounds of cattle awakening and outriders silhouetted against the dawn sky. The smell of early campfires and hot biscuits wrapped around sausage and mugs of bitter coffee. Riders repacking saddles and filling canteens. Cowhands mounted up and went off to start the herd, waving hats to get the big animals on their feet and walking in the right direction.

"What should we be doing?" Meagan asked, watching the men at work.

"Stand right here until they move off."

"Then what do we do?"

"Eat dust."

Other riders had joined them in back of the herd, each with a piece of cloth tied around his head and over the bridge of his nose. When cattle moved forward, a fog of dust rose until it darkened the sky. It enveloped the herd with a sound like crackling static. Meagan scrambled to fit her bandanna even as dust began to coat the inside of her mouth.

Red and the other horses plodded on with their heads lowered, eyes slitted and ears back. Every hour Dan would motion to her to follow, and they would turn their horses out of the dust cloud into the open. They would shed their bandannas and gulp clean air, slapping at their clothes to toss off sheets of dust.

The horses looked as if they had been dipped in pale chocolate. Dan dismounted and went to each horse's head, upending his canteen in their mouths to flush them out in a muddy brown stream. He brushed their eyes and swabbed their noses.

"Should we let them graze?" Meagan asked

"No, makes too much spit. Cakes around the bit. Easier for them if their mouths are dry."

Blue tucked his belly and sneezed, blowing a trumpeting blast.

"Dan, I don't understand, what are we supposed to be doing ... just walk in dust?"

"Not much while the cattle are fresh. Later they tend to scatter and you gotta chase them, keep them going. Hopefully we won't have to do much of that."

"Hopefully?" Running in such dust seemed absolutely impossible. It would be like swimming in dirt.

It was five days to Benkelman before the push to Ogallala, notable mid-western towns of their day. There was occasional rotation, when drag riders shifted out to work the sides of the herd. Meagan enjoyed the change: there was much less dust, and she liked the sporadic short dashes to head off strays. But the coveted positions, the ones to which they would never ascend, were the jobs at the front of the drive, leading and scouting.

She dismounted each sundown with an inch of sand in her boot. 'Least you don't get sunburned riding drag,' was the conventional wisdom, but of course she did. Her skin lacked the men's leather consistency, and the brief rotations to the sides of the herd were plenty to redden any flesh that showed. Sunburn offered a new wrinkle of sensation; and even if it gave Dan a ruddy complexion, she was sure she looked like a scalded cat.

The one thing she truly loved about the job was the cow work. Much more than a vehicle for working around cattle, a good cow horse is an active and vital part of the job. Red was born to it and had the natural "cow sense" that made a gifted stock horse—he could see a running cow and know instinctively what to do, anticipating the animal's moves, matching its speed, spurting past and whirling to block it. The horse was easygoing to the point of nonchalance, but deadly serious when there was a job to do. On the ground, Red watched Meagan in a humorous, canny way that made her wonder how much of the famous cowboy ethos actually belonged to the cowhorse.

If Red was the athlete, Blue was the thinker. The sorrel excelled at watching and anticipating. Not as fast as the buckskin, Blue was quicker on the turns and kept himself where he needed to be. Even through heavy dust, Meagan could always recognize Dan and Blue, silhouettes running in short, tight strides, Blue's head raised high like a deer's.

A cattle herd of this size—stretching hundreds of yards wide—was its own entity, as edgy and panicky as a school of fish and always ready to turn back or change directions. There was a mood to the herd: either calm and moving happily, or fidgety, irritable, and prone to producing strays. Sometimes a mood had obvious reasons, such as a high wind or too-hard ground; the cows wanted to rest in hot afternoons, and in evenings they wanted to disperse. But some moods seemed to have no reason—especially the worst, when the shared feeling was suspicion and unpredictability. The herd was in such a mood the day Meagan truly understood the value of a good cow horse.

It was late in the morning, and there was much bellowing across the mass of unsettled cattle. A few aggravated steers began charging the horses. Meagan and Dan were called out of the dust to help with a water crossing in which the water was too *shallow*, instead of too deep.

The difficulty with crossing a shallow stream was that the cattle would snatch mouthfuls of water as they walked. With the number of cattle coming across, the herd actually drank the stream down to the sediment, leaving nothing for the last to drink.

One frustrated, thirsty steer broke in front of Meagan and turned back to the water. Red tensed instantly as two more steers turned to follow. The closest riders ran to block, heading off the followers and diverting them into the main herd. Meagan was alone when the instigating steer ducked and sprinted back toward the stream.

It was dangerous for the herd to see a steer in flight. The edge of the mass shifted as the rogue steer ran past, swiping at Red with his sharp longhorns. Red backed up, his muscles quivering. Meagan let the reins go slack as Dan had told her to do, sliding her hands up the buckskin's neck and holding tight to his mane. It was the signal Red waited for.

In four strides the buckskin was in full sprint. He adjusted his angle to come in front of the steer. The steer saw Red and instead of deflecting out—Meagan's guess—the steer ducked back toward the herd. Red slid almost in sitting position and rolled back over his haunches. The steer spun, running back to the stream, and Red sprinted forward again, outstripping the steer and again putting his hind end in the dust and whirling to face the cow. The cow feinted left, then right, determined to escape. Red lowered himself, feet splayed, pivoting right, then left. Meagan could not anticipate the lightening-fast direction changes of the steer, much less tell Red how to respond. The buckskin dipped and dodged, sprinted and braked like a crazy rollercoaster until the steer, demoralized, stopped and stood still.

She first thought the cow had hurt itself, but the animal simply turned and trotted obediently back into the herd. Later she learned the bovine will is not strong: a cow will simply give up if thwarted for any length of time. The cornerstone of handling cattle was a horse's ability to isolate an animal and keep him from his goal, thus rendering the cow docile.

The inevitable mistake came at the end of an especially grueling day of riding drag. Meagan had pulled up to unsaddle Red. Dan was still out, having agreed to help round up stragglers on the far side. She loosened Red's cinch and without thinking pulled off her hat, shaking her hair loose.

"Hey, lookie who's here! Come give us a little kiss, sweetheart!"

Meagan ignored the calls, angry with herself for being careless. Then one voice hit a nerve.

"You know why women like horses, don't you? It's the rubbing."

Meagan gritted her teeth as she dusted off, growing angrier as the men made their remarks. She took her canteen and sprinkled water delicately over one hand to clean it, then the other.

"Is he right about that, girlie?"

Studiously ignoring the men, Meagan poured water into a cupped hand and splashed it over her face. She reached for a clean cloth she kept in her saddlebag.

"Bet you like to ride, don't you, missy?"

Meagan had a sudden idea. She pulled her hair back theatrically, and then settled her eyes on the men. They grinned idiotically in unison. "I have an idea. I'll bet someone a saddle. Anyone good enough?"

The cowboys hit each other, whooping. One stepped forward and crooked an arm towards her. "Well, come on, little lady. I'll show you something!"

"I'd like to win it fair and square." There was much giggling among the onlookers. "Is that all right, cowboy?"

The man looked to his comrades for support.

Meagan smiled pleasantly. "Anyone who can ride a circle around the herd on my horse can keep my saddle. If he can't do it, I win his."

"What do you do then, girlie ... walk?"

Apologize to Dan and ride bareback. "Maybe I'll ride in the wagon," she answered with a coy shrug.

"I volunteer," said one of the hands. "The horse *is* a good one. Saw him after a stray a couple times."

"He's not worth a saddle though, Watty."

"Won't cost a saddle," the volunteer said gruffly. "Won't cost a thing." He walked forward with a slow, rolling gait. "If the lady wants to wagon it to Dakota, that's her business."

Meagan stood by Red and smiled at the volunteer. "Hello Mr. Watty. Where is the saddle?"

"I'm going to get it. Boys, don't let the little lady get the vapors."

He strode off and Meagan smiled at the others as they cackled and elbowed each other. The final workers rode up, among them Dan. "Hey!" called one of the cowhands, "you're just in time to see your girlfriend lose her horse to Watty."

Dan looked at Meagan, unmasked as a female. "Sounds unlikely."

"That's cuz you don't know Watty. He was breaking horses afore he could walk."

"I know *her* and I wouldn't do it."

"Oh no, you don't!" Watty shouted, striding back with a stock saddle propped on his hip. "She's made the bet and you ain't getting her out of it!"

Dan looked him up and down. "I was thinking to get *you* out of it, but go ahead."

Without a glance at Meagan, the cowboy strode up to Red and threw his saddle pad over the buckskin's back. Meagan whispered into Red's ear. "I need this favor, boy. I *don't* want him to ride you, but don't hurt him." The buckskin's ears twitched between Meagan and the unfamiliar hands smoothing a thick wool pad across his back.

"So, Sagebrush," Dan asked loudly. "What are you going to do with two saddles?"

"Sell one back to him," Meagan replied. "And don't look at me like that, Dan. They started it."

Watty brushed Meagan aside. "Step away. Thank you." He lifted his saddle over Red and settled it into place. "Horse stands quiet. Don't look outlawish to me." He watched for Red's reaction as he tightened the cinch. "Don't cinch him right you get wrinkles. Might make him jumpy, 'specially if he blows up." He was making reference to a habit of some horses to gulp air before being saddled, exhaling after girth tightening to leave the saddle dangerously loose. Watty brought a knee up into the horse's stomach. "Just making sure," he said casually. Red grunted and flattened his ears.

The volunteer grinned at his audience before shortening the reins to pull Red's head to the outside, forcing the buckskin to step toward him. Nonchalantly, Watty put his foot in the stirrup and glided a long leg over the saddle. He never looked at Meagan, but addressed the other cowhands. "Maybe I'll put my old horse back to second string. I've been needing another one."

At least, that seemed to be what Watty was going to say. He got as far the words "been needing" when Red leaped into the air, bowing his back and coming down flat-footed. It didn't unseat the man, but it stopped his conversation. Red spun in a short circle and hopped forward, planting his front legs and lifting his hind. Watty leaned back against the motion and Red came back down, repeating the stiff hop.

"*No!*" Meagan shouted over the whoops and whistles from the fence spectators. She had expected the simple sidestep Red had done before.

The rider encouraged Red to keep bucking by shouting and throwing his legs back and forth, trying to wear the horse down. Flecks of sweat were coming off Red's coat—after all, he had been out in the dust and heat all day. The buckskin gave a last fling of his hindquarters and stopped, head low and panting.

Watty turned the buckskin and dug his feet in, jogging back to the group, all teeth. "Well, boys, I'm just going to make that little circle around the herd now. I guess I got myself a new—" Red dropped a shoulder low and ducked hard to the right, digging into the ground and exploding in a sprint. All that was visible were the buckskin's pumping hindquarters and the back of the hollering cowboy, his hat flying up into the wind as if it had been shot off. Red skidded and pivoted to the side. The man followed his hat.

Dan whistled. "Girl, I don't know what you done to Red, but it's the handiest trick I ever saw."

Watty jumped up and brushed off his seat, walking back slowly and turning pink from the laughter and comments. Red jogged back to stand a few yards off, watching the cowboy warily. When Watty lunged, grabbing for the reins, the buckskin backed up just enough to stay out of reach.

Meagan walked quietly to Red and took the reins. "Thank you, boy. I'm sorry, I didn't think it would be so hard. I'll make it up to you. You've just earned all the treats I can find and *lots* of extra rubdowns."

Behind her, Watty began shaking his head and shouting he was cheated.

"Now, then..." Dan's voice had the tiniest edge. "The lady won fair. We all saw it. Best let it be."

Watty shouldered his way past the others and was gone.

Dan walked over to Meagan and Red. "Sleep easy tonight. No telling for sure, but I bet he'll want his saddle back."

"I wish I hadn't put Red through that. I was just so angry." Meagan ran her hand across the well-oiled leather. "At least the saddle looks like a good one."

"Yeah, it's ok. More'n okay, that's why I say sleep easy." Dan gave a short laugh. "If there's something else you want, tell me now so I can hand it over. Save us both the aggravation."

———

Besides the insects, another kind of pest could now be added to Meagan's list: the men in the company. Word had gotten out that a female was riding drag, and they came to pay their respects, as such. Dan cut off the more enthusiastic suitors, but mostly Meagan had to endure the attention. At dusk, she and Dan rode out onto the plains; he considered it less risky than the camp. Meagan thought it was considerate of him, and wholeheartedly agreed.

Meagan liked her new saddle. It was low, close to the horse and flexible. Red felt the difference too, and she realized the buckskin had been holding back. Now when Red headed a cow, it was like 'slipping on grease,' and he put a standstill on a cow in half the time. She was growing to love the swaying, low dips when Red dropped down and spread his forelegs, springing from side to side, as well as the breathtaking accelerations, "slide-kelly-slide" stops and wheeling rollbacks. Her situation was eased by the respect she gained for being a top cowhand—without, she admitted, much justification. Red was the real star, but as his only rider she shared in his glory.

In a show of kindness, Dan sold his extra saddle to Watty so he would not have to ride bareback. One late afternoon, coming out of the dust for a brief rest, Dan stopped and sniffed the air. "You feel anything different?"

"Yes, it's finally cooling off, thank goodness."

Dan swung down from Blue and pulled his canteen off, spitting out the first swig. He studied Blue carefully. The sorrel's ears were flicking in all directions. The horse backed a step and swished his tail.

"Oh, damn." Dan scanned the horizon. The sky was clear except for dust clouds on the north horizon. "Damn, *damn*. Drink up, Meagan. Blue says we have a storm coming. I'm going to ride around and tell the camp."

Riding back, it did seem to Meagan a restlessness had fallen on the herd. It was nearing dusk, time to bed down the herd, but the cattle were growing agitated, glancing from side to side and moving faster. Red's steps were choppy and she had to keep him under close rein.

Twilight came quickly. A breeze picked up, bringing in a damp, ozone scent. Flashes of light ran across the darkening horizon. Dan loped into view; Blue's head was high and there was froth on his hindquarters. Dan pointed at the northern sky, dimming with the last light of sunset into shades of sickly green. "They'll likely stampede. If they do, get over to the left side. Cattle run to the right, and we'll want to circle them into each other."

A cowhand pulled up behind Blue on a ragged pale dun. "Dang, I hate to ride at night," he bawled, wiping his face on a sleeve. "Once't we bedded down in a dry lake bed when a Norther blew in and mixed the tumbleweeds up with the cows—chased a damned tumbleweed near's a mile 'fore I roped it!"

Men were hurrying to hide metal in the wagons. A low groaning sound rolled across the herd. Pricks of light began to flicker, tiny sparks in the darkening band overhead. Meagan looked at the bottom edge of the horizon and saw it was alive with flashes of lightning.

Currents within the herd began to flow toward the edges. Long, low rumbling passed overhead, fading into the stamping sounds of running cattle. A wind gust cleared the air of dust and scattered cold droplets like stinging bites. Lightning lit the sea of running backs, suspending the moment. The highlighted cattle seemed to hover in the air, surprised, moving again as a long splitting sound ended in a boom.

The riders let their horses run out in tight strides. The far right edge of the herd was spreading fast and loose, like lava. The cattle were flowing around Meagan and Red, building to panic. Cattle bumped them from behind. The buckskin stiffened and whinnied, shaking beneath her. Dim shapes were all she could see, images looming into vision and passing. Men's shouts rose above the thunder and hooves, punctuating the chaos. The stampede was taking her away, and there was nothing to do but run with the herd or be trampled.

Meagan and Red ran through the dark, dodging through gaps, guided by nothing but the margin of panicked cattle around her. Red was pushed from behind and for a terrified second Meagan felt the horse stumble. She opened Red up, letting him pull into the clear and run before the herd. Lightning flickered in all directions, striking across the sky and into the herd, giving glimpses of running shapes frozen in terror. Curling tendrils of St. Elmo's Fire spit across the longhorns, played over Red's ears and down the reins. Strays ran crossfire as she let Red find his way.

She saw dark shapes of mounted cowhands galloping in a line to circle the herd. Red whinnied into the storm, a high trembling whistle that was snatched and lost. The horse veered to the left and Meagan felt her reins being pulled. A dark rider had Red's bridle and was guiding the buckskin away from the herd. Lighting flickered and Meagan saw Dan holding Blue's reins tight in one hand, his arm outstretched to guide Red with the other.

Dan's mood was poor the next morning. Upending his second cup of coffee, he made a face at his plate. "Powerful sorry outfit when the beans are tougher than the beef. After last night and *this* grub pile, they expect me and Blue to pop strays all day."

"Should I go, Dan? I'd love to get out of the dust for a day."

"Naw, leave it to Blue and me. Red's no brush popper. You need a horse that can smell out a cow without losing his head, and Blue is good at it. You can help pull cactus needles out of us tonight."

A tiny puff of dust on the horizon caught Meagan's eye. It grew like smoke from a locomotive's stack. "Look there, Dan. Something's coming." As the puff came closer, she could make out the shape of a galloping horse, a fleck against the cloud it was making. The lone rider streaked across the barren landscape, chased by nothing, and crossed far in front of the herd without stopping. Then he was diminishing in the distance, and gone.

"Dang me, dang me—get a rope and hang me!" Dan threw down his plate and stood up. "Hell, *we* don't have to brush pop *or* chew dust. I clean forgot in all this fun: that was the Pony Express! Stay here. I'm getting our pay."

He rode off as Meagan waited, watching the cattle and dust move on without her. Somehow she had expected music or cheering for the famous Pony Express, something more than a speck running through silent country.

When Dan reappeared, he handed her a single gold coin. "Here's your pay. Ten dollars. Want to make a payment on your means of transportation?"

Meagan turned the coin over in her hands: a Liberty head was on one side, a stylized Eagle on the other. If she brought it back to her own time, it would be of astronomically higher value.

"Well, Sagebrush? Is the gory hand of greed striking now?"

"No. Sorry." She reluctantly deposited the coin back into Dan's outstretched palm. "Now I've paid you twenty."

"And twenty more will do it," he said cheerfully, mounting up. She followed, and together they trotted in the direction of the lone courier.

Fine steeds, like true friends, are few,
even if to the eye of the inexperienced they are many.
-Al Mutannabbi, 9th century A.D.

THE PONY EXPRESS station was even more underwhelming than the appearance of its riders. The entire enterprise was a leaning shed built beside a ramshackle pen, holding a single saddled horse whose bridle hung from the saddle horn. Meagan and Dan actually trotted past the outpost, at first mistaking it for an old farmer's shack. Only the horse's brand made Dan stop. "Wait, that horse was Government Issue, and I don't think the Army would call *that* a fort."

Meagan had expected an office of buzzing activity, tense riders and stalls filled with fit horses. After all, the Pony Express was the day's fastest communication, a relay of horses that carried mail across the continent between St. Joseph to Sacramento in three days—an unheard-of speed. The building seemed deserted: the shack's step was a wooden half-barrel turned upside down. Peering inside they could see the worn soles of two boots, crossed and propped on a crate. Dan knocked against the door frame.

"Tarnation!" A hat popped up as the boots dropped down. "*Tarnation!* Who is it? Answer quick or I start shooting!"

"Hold on there! Nothing's the matter, just two riders coming by. Is this the Pony Express?"

The occupant half-rose, a gun in his hand. "What're you all, sightseers?"

"Naw, we're looking to join up."

"Yeah? Do I look like a hiring boss? Head up to St. Joe and let me sleep."

"Is there a—"

The click of a gun being cocked interrupted the question.

Dan looked at Meagan. "Man's serious about his rest."

They moved the horses to a set of trees a short distance from the station. Dan stamped around it. "Snakes," he said simply as he did it. "So what'd you think of it?"

Meagan winced. "It's a little smaller than I thought."

"Damn disappointing, that's what it is. Might as well spend the night, though. The horses need rest. We can catch up with the drive tomorrow. Sure hate to get back in that dust. Blue's catching a cough."

They made camp quickly. Cinches were loosened, bedrolls were tossed down, and a fire was started with newfangled, state-of-the art-technology called *lucifers*: match sticks. To sit against a tree with water boiling for coffee was priceless luxury.

"What made you want to join the Pony Express?" Meagan asked.

"Pay."

"Simple as that? No other reason?"

"Simple as that. No other reason."

"What I mean, Dan, is whether you have plans beyond that?"

"'Course I have. Man's got to have plans. They're a step down from dreams, more realistic."

"You have a dream?"

"Yeah. Used to anyway, then it changed on me and left me stranded out here." He leaned to fumble with the leather coffee pouch and poured grounds into the water. "I left home to prove I was as stupid as my daddy said I was, so really I'm quite a success. Back then there was talk about gold in the West, and I lit out to make my fortune. As you can see, I haven't exactly built an empire."

"Where did you go?"

"Everywhere, nowhere. Same place really. Mostly trying to make enough money to get back home to Kentucky."

"You have money and a horse, why don't you just go back?"

"Why thank you, Meagan, I hadn't thought of that. Just go back, you say, and me puzzling and puzzling." He stood and stretched. "I'm gonna talk to Blue about your suggestion."

They both heard galloping hoofbeats at the same time. Dan pulled his gun from his saddle and squatted. A lone rider traveling at a hand gallop gave out a high-pitched cry as he pulled up at the station—he was off his horse and untying his saddlebag before any motion came from the shack. The rider gave his call again, and a few moments later the man from inside the shack led out the government-branded horse. Saddle pads with bundles of mail sewn into each corner were transferred to the fresh horse and secured. In seconds, the government-issue horse was packed, mounted and away.

"We'll see if this one's any friendlier," Dan muttered, walking back toward the shack. Meagan filled her tin mug with the bitter coffee and followed.

The rider pulled his saddle off and carried it in both hands, bridle and reins slung over his shoulder. His hat, now hanging from the saddle horn, had left his hair plastered in a ring around his head. His horse was a lean brown-and-white pinto mare. Her coat was curled with sweat and she was breathing hard, flanks tucking and dropping.

Meagan could see the rider was just a boy, gaunt and freckled. Setting his tack outside the shack, the boy put a halter on his horse and led her into the pen. He allowed his mare a sip of water before taking the bucket out and closing the gate. Meagan held out the tin of hot coffee.

"Thank you," the boy said as he took it, shaking from exertion. "I'm obliged to you, ma'am. All's they leave in here is hard tack the rats will leave alone, or a salt stick of something, maybe." The boy set the water pail back inside the horse's pen briefly, letting the pinto take a more few sips. "Coffee's good." He looked at Meagan shyly. "You make it?"

"No, I did," said Dan curtly. "She can't cook worth a damn."

"Thanks for bringing it, ma'am." The boy went around the shack and came back with a flake of hay. He leaned it against the side of the pen, talking as he worked. "This run weren't too bad. Second one since last night. Buffalo's running up north a bit. That's good—draws Indians off."

"You have trouble with Indians?" Dan asked seriously.

"Nothing but. They's burned out a station last month when I was on the west run. Came up to find it a smoking ruin. Horse gone, rider gone. Said he was killed but I don't know. Seems strange they wouldn't of left him. They don't usually take a body. I had to run the next leg too, twenty-five miles in all. Chrissy just about had it with that run, even going as easy as we could. You got to be careful not to run your horse to death—you *can*, you know. Horse will just be running fine, you stop and the horse still seems fine, but he just won't cool off. I saw a horse die that way once and I don't ever want to see it again."

"Chrissy is your horse?" Meagan asked.

The boy looked down, embarrassed. "Yes, ma'am. Named her after a calf I got on my birthday when I turned ten."

"How old are you now?"

"Just about fifteen ma'am. I'm doing this to keep from farming. Rather be on a horse than behind it, I guess."

"How's the pay?" Dan asked. "I heard it's gone to twenty-five."

"It can go to thirty-five—don't matter if you don't see it." The boy glanced sheepishly at Meagan as he spoke. "Some say the company only keeps the riders it does because we're waiting on pay. Rain or shine the mail goes, but conditions have to be exactly right to get paid for it." The boy went into the pen and felt his horse's chest. He came out and gave the mare a longer drink. "My daddy told me not to do it, so I did," the boy said matter-of-factly. "Right sorry about it now, and when they pay me I'm heading down to the Butterfield line. Stagecoaches needing escorts. Say pay's not as good but it's regular. You looking to join up?"

Dan shrugged.

"Poor idea, you ask me. I'd head to Butterfield, south of here, like I'm doing. More sociable than this and you don't get shot at near's much."

"How far to the next station?"

"Twelve miles to the next relay, either way. The *big* main station east is about fifty miles. You just ride to the next relay, twice a day. Lope along, not too hard. Gets real hot later on, I hear—it would, summer in Colorado. Beats the damn snow, I say." The boy opened the gate a final time and set the pail inside, throwing the flake of hay into a corner. "She's pretty well cooled off now," he said shyly to Meagan. "I see your horses standing by that tree. Which is yours, ma'am?"

"She doesn't have a horse," Dan answered. "She's buying one from me, and she's awful slow pay."

"I won't make a lady pay me for a horse, if she wants it."

Meagan winked at the boy. "That's because you're a gentleman."

"Shows what you know about ladies, boy," Dan snapped. "Shouldn't you be getting some sleep? Your partner seemed real set on it."

"Yeah. We've had to work both runs, 'count of the war."

"War?" Dan stared at the boy.

"Ain't you heard? It's been going on near three months now. Not much has happened, and some say nothing will. But they's formed a Confederacy and stopped being part of the Union."

"Confederacy of what?"

"I don't know, but the whole country's taking sides. The Carolinas and Georgia are going to make their own country, they say, and all the Southern states are joining. They say they's got as much right to start a country as we did against the Brits. Yanks say it ain't so, and the Rebels are going to show them. Don't you hear nothing?"

Dan ran his fingers through his hair. "I guess not. Which side is Kentucky?"

"Don't know." The boy squinted at him. "You a Reb?"

"I guess that's what I'm asking, boy."

"Maybe you're my enemy."

"That's ridiculous. Do I look like your enemy?"

The boy shrugged. "My friend Cuddy says any Johnny Reb's the enemy."

"Well, your friend is a blamed fool. Now point us to the nearest town."

The boy hesitated before glancing at Meagan and making up his mind. "Cheyenne's that way, Fort Laramie's north of it. Either is about three days. Less if you're in a hurry, I guess."

"Much obliged, boy." He turned and walked back to the horses. Meagan said goodbye to the young rider and hurried to catch Dan.

"That boy would shoot me dead if his friend Cuddy said I was a Rebel," Dan said in disgust. "No wonder we got wars."

"I thought we were letting the horses rest, Dan. What about Blue's cough?"

"The horses can rest later on. You heard it, these shacks are regular Indian attractions. If you want, you can stay here with the boy. It's a free country, so I've heard. Ain't read the papers lately but it might still be."

"Daniel Beardon, I believe you're upset that boy paid attention to me." Oddly, Meagan found herself enjoying his consternation.

"Oh, please, woman." Dan threw a saddle pad over Blue's back. The gelding swished his tail and stamped to show displeasure at having his grazing cut short. "Easy there, Blue. War's on, everybody's got to do his part."

"Where are we going?" Meagan asked.

"Hell if I know. Guess the Fort's better if there's Indian trouble around."

"You really didn't know a war was coming?"

"No, it hasn't made the rounds of the polite company I keep. Do *you* know anything about it?"

Meagan thought about what to say about the Civil War. "I just know that it's a bad one."

"Oh, a *bad* war? Here I was setting store on it being a good one. Is Kentucky joining this Confederacy? You know that?"

Meagan shook her head. "I don't remem—I don't know."

"Course not. You know a lot of peculiar damn things, but not one that could matter to a body."

There is no secret so close as that between a rider and his horse.
                                        - R. S. Surtees (1803-64)

WIDE PLAINS STRETCHED endlessly before them, slopes rolling across the ground in shallow waves. All directions were open and the sensation of pure freedom was exhilarating—and frightening.

"Look," Dan pointed.

Meagan scanned the empty horizon. "I don't see anything."

"That smoke, there, against the rise."

She squinted. "I guess..."

"No guessing about it. It's smoke all right."

Meagan conceded. "Who could it be?"

"*That's* the guessing part. Fire burns about the same for everybody. Best way's to go see. Sure would hate if it was Indians, though."

"Wait, Dan, I have an idea. Let's ride around that hill and look without being in the open."

"I ain't got this far in life doing things thataway," Dan said, taking Blue into a lope. The alleged smoke began to show more clearly as they topped one rise and glided down the other side. Dan pulled Blue up abruptly. He was grinning. "Look, cattle's been through here!" He pointed down at a patty of manure spread like a plate in the bending grass. "*Fresh.*"

"At least you've found something to put you in a good mood."

"Don't you know this means a decent meal? Come on!"

At the words "decent meal," regardless of context, Meagan's stomach leapt to life and began a lively conversation. Stews, steaks, butter and bread seemed to float in the smoke ahead. "Easy, Red—*oh!*" Meagan did not see the man until Red shied, swinging suddenly around with ears forward: an older gentleman, perhaps in his fifties, sat against a scrub tree with his knees propped. "I'm sorry, sir. I didn't see you there."

"Then why did you stop?" he asked in a petulant voice, making a shooing gesture. "You are standing in front of the hillside I'm sketching."

"I'm sorry." Meagan urged Red forward out of the way.

"I have to draw this in late-afternoon light," the man explained, studiously sketching. "I have been trying to finish for days, and I simply must have the correct sun. It is a study in shadows."

"Well hello, mister," Dan said, coming back on Blue. "I guess I just rode past you."

"Yes. Thank you for that. Pray continue."

Dan looked at Meagan.

"Which are you?" the sitting gentleman asked in a bored voice. "Traders, buffalo hunters, bullwackers, stagecoach drivers, trappers, gamblers, miners, settlers, homesteaders..." he looked up. "Please, stop me anytime."

"None of that. We came up with a cattle drive to Dakota territory."

"Migrant workers," he said, looking back to his sketch.

Dan set his jaw and turned Blue back toward the smoke.

"Tell them to set a place for you," the seated man called, still preoccupied with his sketch. "Say Anderson sent you."

The last ridge dropped into a shallow valley ringed by hills. Fences outlined a dozen pens, making a crossword puzzle of paddocks and outbuildings. Smoke rose from a long rowhouse. Buildings and fences, picturesque at a distance, became cracked and dilapidated upon closer inspection.

A few cowhands perched like crows along the corral fence. No one seemed to notice as Dan and Meagan loped up and stopped. Dan had to speak to gain their attention. "Afternoon, all. We're wondering if it might be possible to work off some food and a place to stay?"

"Might be," said one, talking to his boot.

"Anything's possible," opined another.

One of the hands slid off the rail fence and wearily walked up to them. "Can you rope?"

"Indifferent," Dan shrugged. "I can head, heel and cut, though..."

The cowboy leaned over and looked at the ground a while before spitting. "Need a roper. Got calves coming in."

"Anderson says to set us a plate."

"Anderson can kiss my ass." Chuckles from the fence greeted the remark.

A young man walked by, his hat pulled too low to see his features. He carried a rope across his hip and chaps that seemed sanded down to fine linen. Ducking between the rails in the fence, he approached the corral's only occupant: a nondescript, dingy bay horse with a bristling mane, bearing a ragged, beaten saddle. Calmly the cowboy circled his rope once and let it fly. The horse swerved, running to the other end of the pen as the cowboy quietly pulled his rope back for another throw. On his next attempt, the rope settled over the horse's neck.

The horse bolted while the cowboy dug in and skied through the dirt until the animal came to a stop, whirled, and ran the other direction. The spectators on the fence hooted and shouted, waving hats. The horse shied away from them as he ran back and forth, the cowboy in tow.

The horse stopped and stood, sides heaving, as the cowboy picked himself from the dirt and walked towards him, winding his rope as he came. Again the animal flinched and bolted, and again the young man sat down to let the horse pull him across the corral. The cowboy was able to come gradually closer each time before the scared animal broke and ran.

When it finally happened, it was fast: suddenly the cowboy was up in the saddle. Spreading his feet under the weight, the horse stood trembling but did not move. Disappointed sounds of derision came from the fence rail, mocking the rider and calling names until the cowboy—rope coiled in one hand—wound his fingers in the horse's mane and smacked the horse on the flank. The horse started forward with a jerk, trotting a few steps and kicking up with the tail-swishing hop a green horse makes from annoyance. The effective remedy for such crow-hopping is to urge the horse forward calmly. Instead, the cowboy opened his legs and raised the rope high, bringing both down hard.

The horse flattened his ears and tensed. If given the opportunity, some horses prove especially talented at throwing a rider—this horse was an example. The reluctant mount planted his front feet and his hindquarters rose high. The cowboy stayed on, but this was merely a prelude. Tucking his head, the horse did what is descriptively called "breaking in half," throwing his back end high and hard, expertly snapping with so much force that his front hooves came off the ground in a head stand.

The contest is not uneven: equine joints are limited to moving only forward and back. In comparison, a bull is a more challenging ride because a bovine's anatomy allows spinning and changing direction. Once a horse starts bucking, the rider's best strategy is to lean back.

The cowboy slipped forward on landing, however, and on the next buck he made an arc through the air. The horse continued a series of bucking flip flops without him. Giving a last contemptuous kick toward the men on the rail, the horse trotted to the opposite end of the arena. The fallen rider lay a moment in the dust before wearily standing to catcalls and insults. Yet, when he suggested another might try the mustang, the other cowhands only looked from one to another. No one came off the fence.

"That, Meagan, is called *passing the buck*," Dan said quietly, then spoke up. "Not to interrupt, gentlemen, but have we reached an agreement? Just for a few nights, and then we'll move on."

"I just *told* you," one of the hands said gruffly. "The only thing we need is a roper. Can you or can't you?"

"Well, that's a mite complicated. See, this little woman is sitting on my old roping horse. He'll stop on a quarter and give you change—problem is, no one can ride him except *her*."

Several cowboys on the fence turned with sparked interest.

"You mean, she can ride the horse but you can't?"

"I believe I would have said that if it were my meaning. To repeat myself, that woman, that one right there, *she* is the only one that can ride *that* particular horse." All eyes went to Red, who stood calmly swatting flies.

"Dan..." Meagan whispered.

"Just a moment, my dear." Dan was warming into a carnival barker's singsong. "Gentlemen, I believe my lovely partner has a suggestion. A sort of wager. Anyone who can ride the lady's horse can have ..." He glanced at Meagan's scowl. "My saddle. If not, we stay and help out a bit—meals free."

"Who's to say the horse is any good?" scoffed one of the men.

"Excellent question. In answer, my lovely partner will offer a demonstration."

"Dan!"

"If you'd excuse me gentlemen, the little lady is calling."

"Have you lost your mind?" Meagan hissed, retreating out of immediate earshot. "I don't want to gamble with Red anymore. I was sorry I did it last time. I told you that."

"Trick was good enough on me, it'll do for them. Anyway, I'm just trying to get a safe place for us to rest and something to eat. Red'll be fine."

"I don't think it's a good idea. They look pretty good."

"Pretty good at flying through the air. Trust me, Meagan, I know a thing about bucking. There's a skill to throwing a rider and Red's done some thinking about it. Ain't you, Red?" Dan leaned over and rubbed the buckskin's neck. "And don't forget you still owe me twenty more dollars. Patience, free of charge."

"You should have asked me first. It will cost you ten dollars, for room and board."

"Ten dollars! Whoa, Meggie, look around at the quality of the establishment. It ain't worth ... oh, fine. A man's got to eat."

"So, Dan, only I owe you ten more dollars after this. And please, don't ever call me Meggie."

"Wonderful. Can we get on with it?"

Several cowhands tipped their hats to Meagan as she and Dan rejoined the others. "Go on, dear," Dan said warmly, "show the nice gentlemen how good a roper Red is. Here, take mine."

Meagan looked at Dan in alarm: he was handing out his coiled rope while giving her a wide smile. "I don't know how to rope," she whispered. "And don't I need a cow, anyway?"

"Naw," Dan said softly. "There's nothing to it. Start Red off in a run, throw the rope over his head and stop. You can do that, can't you?" He handed her the rope. "For ten dollars?" Then he raised his voice loud enough for the others to hear, "That's sweet, darling, but not now."

Men snickered as they opened the gate to an empty pen. Meagan irritably jogged Red inside.

"Go on, sweetheart," Dan called. "Make me proud."

Meagan set her jaw and ignored him. The stiff rope felt strange in her hand as she held it out sideways for Red to see. The gesture was unnecessary: from the moment Red saw the rope being passed to his rider, he had been alert and jigging.

Meagan knew almost nothing about roping, but she had seen it done: horse runs, rider throws. Easy enough. She braced herself and slid the reins up Red's neck. Wind tore at her as she leaned into the blast of speed, conscious of the men blurring past her. Swinging her arm awkwardly, she threw the rope—and before she even started to pull on the reins Red sat into the ground, sliding to a gravity-defying, dirt-spraying stop. Meagan collided with the buckskin's thick neck and fell over the front of her saddle.

Draped across the front of her horse until she could regain her seat, Meagan felt her ears redden at the jeering laughter. Red walked stiffly in disapproval, dismayed to have his rider so ineptly dislodged. Jogging back to the others, spitting coarse horsehair, Meagan wondered why a horse's silky-looking mane had the texture of steel wool.

"Heck, she can't ride," commented one of the men.

"Nothing wrong with that horse, needs a real hand is all."

Meagan rode out of the arena and up to Dan, flashing him an icy glare.

"Why, you make it look easy, Sagebrush!" Dan said cheerfully.

"You might have mentioned Red was going to stop when I threw the rope," she hissed.

"Heck, you did fine," Dan said, whispering. "Now they think anyone can ride that horse better than you."

It was decided that a quiet, hard-faced cowhand would be the one to try Red. Meagan had a flash of worry as he calmly led the buckskin to the center of the ring. Thorough and workmanlike, the cowboy took no chances and lengthened the stirrups to suit himself. He called another man to hold the buckskin and stepped up into the stirrup. Before he could throw his other leg over, Red abruptly swung around and dropped the would-be rider to the ground. Meagan closed her eyes in relief. It was a wonderful anticlimax.

Others thought differently. "That weren't nothing," one of the cowhands said. "Horse's just a little skittish is all."

"Sorry, boys," Dan said. "A wager's a wager."

"And cheating's *cheating!* That wasn't fair—the horse didn't buck at all!"

"No one said the horse had to buck."

Meagan could hear the tone of the group turning angry as she ran out and took up Red's reins. The fallen rider was up, a cold expression on his face. "That horse ain't got nothing. You all running some kind of game?"

"We don't much care for cheaters," called another. "Maybe you all can just head out."

"Maybe leave the horse, though..." added one of the men, testing.

"Yeah, maybe just leave the horse." Affirmations came from the others, and some jumped from the fence to move toward Meagan and Red. They were stopped by the sound of a gunshot.

Everyone froze, including Meagan and Dan. A petulant voice broke the silence. "My word, what is this? Such acrimony in God's country." It was the gentleman with the sketchpad, now sitting straight on a pale dun horse. He watched from the side of the corral with reins in one hand, and casually fingered a pistol. Groans from several men and their resumption of their seats on the rail showed they knew who he was. "So," the man asked again, "what is *this?*"

"Nothing, Anderson."

"I distinctly heard someone mention a wager. I love wagers. Tell me."

"We are seeking the hospitality of the place for a few nights," Dan explained. "We were coming to terms."

"Oh? I should give the men more credit. *Hospitality!* What will they surprise me with next?"

Meagan led Red forward. "Hello sir, I am Meagan Roberts. Thank you for coming just now." The gentleman's expression was pleasant, but without recognition. "We met up there," she prodded. "You were drawing under a tree."

"Oh, yes. Though I would hardly call that a meeting. I never break concentration during sketches, but I do remember some people coming by. I am Anderson, and it is grand to meet you both. Where shall we house you two—are you married?" He noted Meagan's quick, violent shake of her head: "Very well, we'll find something suitable."

"Can I see the sketch, sir?" she asked politely.

"Why, certainly! Are you a connoisseur of the arts?"

"If it's just the same," Dan interrupted, "I'd like to unsaddle the horses before we do any confabbing."

"Oh," Anderson said coolly, twisting in the saddle, "since you were still seated, it hadn't occurred to me there was a question about your mount's comfort. Very well, follow me."

"Just point the way," Meagan said curtly. "He'll find it."

"I seem to have intruded on a quarrel." Anderson slid down from his horse, ending no higher than Meagan's chest though he stood ramrod straight. "There's no reason for unpleasantness, I'll take you to separate quarters. Then we can talk and your gentleman friend can unpack. Have we exchanged formal introductions?"

"Oh, excuse me! My name is Meagan Roberts, and *that* is Dan Beardon."

"Pleased to be acquainted, Miss Roberts, Mr. Beardon," he said, making short bow to each. "I'm Anderson Morgan Keffield III, Major, Second New York."

"Nice to meet you, Major Keffield. Aren't you a bit far from your unit?"

"This is confabbing," Dan pointed out. He had dismounted and was leaning on Blue's shoulder with a bored expression.

Anderson leaned toward Meagan. "Your paramour *is* impatient, isn't he?"

"Yes. And he isn't my paramour, either." She and the Major walked slowly in conversation, leading their horses while Dan and Blue trailed silently behind.

"Right there, Miss Roberts." Anderson pointed to a spare unpainted box of a building. "The office would suit a young lady better than the barracks. It's private and cleaner. We'll move a cot inside." He turned to Dan and pointed to a low, dark structure. "Yours, sir, is that building."

"Fine," Dan said, sliding off Blue.

"I would take a top bunk. Fewer insects. It's not the most commodious, but it is something."

"Should have gold basins and hot towels, price I'm paying," Dan grumbled.

"And where are you two heading?" Anderson asked him civilly.

"Fort Laramie is our idea," Dan said, loosening Blue's girth. "Trying to stay away from Indians. She's along until she pays me for that horse."

"How *gallant*. But you needn't worry about Indians. Fort Laramie is just over a days' ride northwest. The ranch is practically in its shadow because its cattle supply their troops."

"Good to hear. Been through there once myself, my first time going to California."

"Yes, it gets a lot of that. I thought I would go to California myself, as I am on a tour of the military outposts, but I've recently been recalled. The war, you see. I have been dallying here too long, but in truth I hate to leave. The men here are in desperate need of horsemanship! I stay for the horses' sake."

"There really is a war?"

"So they say, but no one's fighting. Probably won't, if the secessionists aren't too stubborn. I daresay this new President Lincoln seems a bit of a bumpkin. Makes a bad impression."

"Which side is Kentucky on?"

"No one can say," Anderson shrugged. "It's undecided yet. Tennessee seceded, so perhaps Kentucky will go with."

Dan heaved his saddle off Blue. "Damn frustrating. I'd like to know which side I'm on."

"I want to see your sketch, Anderson," Meagan urged.

Pleased, the man went briskly to his horse and dug in a leather satchel until he pulled out four rolls of paper. He carefully unrolled them one at a time. "It's a study of the canyon at different times, see ... dawn, mid-day, late afternoon and dusk."

"Oh, I *do* see. What is that?"

"A hawk. I made the shadow longer to indicate speed. Here, you can take it as a present."

"Really? I mean, I do like it, but it's part of your study. I can't."

"You can and you must. These regions yield so few art enthusiasts. I feel I must encourage culture wherever possible."

Smiling, Meagan walked into her new, spare quarters and spread it against a wall. "It's wonderful, Anderson. It makes it so homey in here!"

Anderson beamed in gratitude. He called to Dan, who was bent over, cleaning Blue's hooves, "I'm close by if you have difficulties. Keep a watch out for Meagan!"

"Good advice, Anderson, though it's a little late now."

Show me your horse and I will tell you what you are.

- English Proverb

"HAND ME THE TONGS," Anderson said briskly, bent over a horse's hoof held between his knees. A bystanding cowhand passed long-handled metal pliers, resembling ice tongs, for Anderson to test the hoof. He closed the tongs and clamped the hoof, moved the tongs, and clamped again; the horse suddenly flinched and tried to move his hoof. "There's your problem." Anderson set the hoof down and stood straight. "Stone bruise. It could be abscessed. You've been riding him after I advised against it, haven't you?"

"He didn't seem so bad," the owner grumbled.

"Well, he rebruised it and he's going to be lame for a good while."

"Should I put him down?"

"You can be glad your employer isn't so free to dispose of you," Anderson sniffed. "When the blacksmith from Laramie comes by in a week or so, have him open the abscess. Keep the horse in a dry pen for a week, let him out to range for the summer and he'll be good as he was. Is this is within your capacity?"

The owner looked sheepish and shrugged.

"Anderson, while you're at it," Dan asked, "do you think you could look at Blue? He took up a cough on the ride up and can't shake it."

"I'll look at him." Anderson patted the stone-bruised horse and moved on. "Have you tried a neck poultice?"

The relationship between Anderson Morgan Keffield III and the ranch cowmen was strained. However, though his difference from the others was pronounced and unmistakable, and though some laughed and ridiculed Anderson to each other, all sought his advice. "It's disgraceful," he complained to Meagan privately. "These men's attitude about riding is the same as their attitude about bedtime activities, that it only needs to be good for one party."

"*Anderson!*"

"Well, it's true. They won't even allow me to work with their rough stock anymore. After I schooled a few of their more troublesome projects, I believe the enlightened remark was, 'Durn, they won't buck no way. He done plumb ruin't 'em!'"

A cavalry man to the core, Anderson was utterly convinced that, in matters of horsemanship, there was always a right way to do things—and that is how they should be done. "It's no good allowing everyone to go his own way, willy-nilly," he would lecture. "Effective equitation must have order. A disorganized cavalry is a defeated cavalry. Poor horsemanship is not only slovenly and primitive, it is an insult to the animal."

Something else explained the respect the others had for Anderson: he was known to be a crack shot.

——————

Meagan accepted Anderson's invitation to tea. Their chosen spot was on a nearby hillside that surveyed the ranch grounds. At noon a flood of cattle arrived to be ushered into the long fences and chutes. Like water flowing through channels, cattle filled the enclosures as the cowhands moved among them on horseback, swimming above the current, directing. Utilitarian "western" tack made utter sense in this environment of rough wooden rails and bumping cattle, where long hours required a padded, comfortable saddle. If the horse could not jump or gallop as freely under such heavy equipment, it was not an important sacrifice: other extreme athletics were needed for the job.

One cowhand on a brown-and-white pinto horse had been working the edges of the herd all afternoon. His horse was "nappy," or reluctant to go forward. Several times the horse stalled, churning backwards and wringing his tail as the cowboy swatted the animal's rump. A small group of other riders stood watching, shouting advice. In a fit of temper, the cowboy jumped off and kicked the horse in the chest.

"What are you doing, my good man?" Anderson called out mildly.

"This pinto horse has about worn me out!"

"Do you suppose kicking him in the chest will provide the instruction?"

"What do you suggest, I git the horse a cup of tea and ask all polite like?"

"Asking is good, but don't be ridiculous. A book would be much better. Many horses benefit from a good reading to."

The other riders laughed. Anderson took a sip and set his cup down. "Loosen his girth and secure the horse. I'll attend to him shortly."

Dan came up the hillside, carrying a neatly-tied burlap sack. "Afternoon, everyone."

"Afternoon, Daniel. Care for some tea?"

"No thanks, Major. I was wondering if I could steal Meagan from you."

"Certainly." Anderson turned to Meagan with high eyebrows. "Steal away."

"Excuse me," she protested. "Where am I being stolen away to?"

"Just up there by the trees. I've brought some food for us."

Anderson nodded approvingly. "A picnic under the trees I have immortalized in ink."

"The very ones, Anderson," Dan agreed congenially. "Meagan, will you come?"

"Let me see." She stood and dusted herself off. "What do you have, is it a surprise? Oh, look, it *is* a surprise—*beef.*"

Neither spoke on the walk to the trees except in general terms of general things: the weather, the horses, the food. Dan set his sack down and pulled out a makeshift dinner cloth, spreading it in the shade under the trees. The main course was charred, its usual sin, but the fresh air compensated.

"I like it here," Meagan said, contented. "I mean, except for some of the people."

"I like it everywhere except for the people," Dan answered, setting out the camp's hard rolls that were impossible to eat without dunking. "I came out here to get away, but wherever people are it's just the same."

"I thought you came for gold."

"That too, I guess. Don't really know. I told everyone I wanted to make my fortune, and maybe I believed it. I think I just wanted to get away to think my own thoughts, but it's hard to live the way you want to live, even out here." Dan stared at the open horizon for a moment, and lay back. "All this is going to change anyway. People aren't going to leave this open country alone. I'm thinking about going back, maybe."

"How old were you when you left?"

"Sixteen. Got started at Transylvania University, but I didn't like school much."

"Sixteen seems pretty young."

"Seemed about right. What about you, when did you leave home?"

"Fifteen, but that was different."

Dan chortled. He leaned up on an elbow and met her eyes. "Yeah, 'course it was."

Meagan looked away, suddenly embarrassed. "Maybe you *should* go back home, Dan. War makes everything different."

"Maybe. I can say it does. I hate to go back without a stake of my own. They won't ever let me forget that." Dan lay back again. "That's what I'm fighting, I think. I want to go home but I'm afraid to." A wasp swooped to his forehead—he swatted it away, but it caught in his clothes. He leaped to his feet, brushing himself. "Ow, dang it. *Ow!* Blamed thing got right under my arm!"

"You want me to look at it?"

"No, I'll get some iodine from the cook." Another wasp buzzed by and they scattered. Meagan hurried back, pulling the picnic cloth from under the tree. She quickly packed everything.

They talked more easily on the way back, with Dan waving his stung arm in circles. It occurred to Meagan that she felt lighter than usual, and had an almost floating sensation. They passed Anderson in one of the fields, sitting ramrod straight on the troublesome, nappy pinto. He was reading aloud from an open book in his hand.

Meagan woke in the night. She lay still and listened, not sure what had awoken her, until a high-pitched squeal came from the horse pens. Throwing a blanket over her shoulders, she stepped outside her barricaded quarters. The landscape was harsh in the white moonlight. Shouts and sounds of arguing were coming from Red's pen—and then a gunshot.

She ran across the cold ground, ignoring rocks and burrs until she was against the fence. Red stood trembling and white-eyed in the center of the pen; two figures stood with him. A noose was looped around the buckskin's neck. In shock she called out, *"What are you doing?"* One of the figures was bending down, and when he straightened she recognized his stiff form. "Anderson! What happened? Is Red all right? I heard a gunshot."

"Major Keffield is pretty loose with his gun," answered the second man.

"I find it communicates things quite well," Anderson said curtly. "Some don't understand otherwise. No need to fret, Meagan, your horse is more frightened than injured. Our boys thought they'd try a little moonlight ride on your horse. No one seemed to enjoy it very much. I would guess two hands won't be showing up for work in the morning."

"They'll show if they want to eat," the other growled.

"Indeed, sound policy. Meagan, after failing to achieve satisfaction, it seems our good boys decided to punish the horse," Anderson finished dismissively. "We have accounted for a dislocated shoulder in one, and a broken leg in the other."

"Not to mention the hand with a shot-up backside. You can't just come out here and start shooting, Anderson."

"That overstates the situation. The gentleman will soon be back to what is normal for his variety. I am quite happy to submit to judicial proceedings."

"What judicial proceedings?" the second man snorted. "Where do you think you are, New York?"

"My mistake. It must be the conversation."

After the men had gone, Meagan went over Red carefully with her hands. The horse had welts around his neck from the rope. Meagan gently loosened it. The buckskin flinched as she lifted the noose free.

"I'm sorry, Red," she told the horse, "it's my fault." Holding the rope, stroking him softly, she let herself cry; at first for Red, then about more ... the horse accepted her touch and his eyes grew distant again, soft and calm. She reached up and put her face against his neck, letting her tears run down the coarse hair.

———

Meagan sat on a log outside Red's pen until dawn, huddled with her blanket high around her ears and tucked under her bare feet. Red nibbled his hay as if nothing had happened.

"Good morning," Dan said cheerfully, coming out of the grayness. "Thought you'd still be asleep."

"Some of the men tried to ride Red last night. Gave us all a scare."

"How is he?" Dan went to the pen. The buckskin carried his mouthful of hay to the fence and nuzzled Dan.

"Okay, I think. He has welts on his neck and his right foreleg has a scratch, but he seems fine now."

Dan looked at her. "I'll be right back."

Gripping her knees, Meagan burrowed her head in the blanket. Another day was ahead, time to get up and dressed. She could hear stirrings of the workers and livestock.

Dan returned and held out a mug. "Here, have some coffee," he said gently, and sat beside her. The mug was hot, and she held it in both hands. Bitter grounds floated in the black liquid, but she liked it. It belonged with the cold desert morning and the musty, frayed blanket.

"I'm sorry it happened, Meagan."

"I should never have made riding him a game. I knew better."

"Maybe we shouldn't have." He reached up and brushed back Meagan's hair. She felt his hard callused hand, so warm. She leaned against it. She smelled his coffee and tobacco breath, and turned in time to meet his kiss. It surprised her— she kept her mouth closed, and then slowly responded.

"*Hello!* We're up early, I see." Anderson tramped briskly past them and over to the pen. "The animal looks quite recovered. I was a bit worried about that foreleg, but I see he's putting weight on it."

Both Meagan and Dan were up. Meagan pulled her blanket tighter. "Sorry, we didn't see you, Anderson."

"Am I interrupting?"

"No," Dan and Meagan said together.

"Anderson, I didn't thank you for last night," Meagan hurried to say. "I told you, Dan, didn't I, that Major Keffield helped Red last night? Before I got here. He shot one of the men."

"Really? Oh. That was mighty nice, Anderson, thank you."

"Flesh wound. I can't abide abuse of dumb animals. Now they wish to take my firearm." He wrinkled his nose. "I'm not going to allow that, so it seems I'll be leaving in the morning. Things do get tense after gunfire."

Dan nodded politely. "Are you heading to Fort Laramie?"

"Yes, for a couple of days. A stagecoach to Kansas City passes through. From there I will return East to resume my commission."

"Oh." Dan nodded again. He and Meagan avoided looking at each other, standing well apart. "Well, I'm sure there's breakfast cooking somewhere. Meagan, care for some?"

"Yes, I'll be along in a moment."

Dan excused himself. Anderson stood a moment watching him go.

"Thank you again, Anderson," she said uncomfortably.

"Think nothing of it, my dear. I am glad to see things are progressing with Daniel."

"It's nothing, Anderson. He was just being nice."

The cavalryman smiled, his eyes bright.

"Anderson, stop. I was going to say, since you are leaving in the morning, maybe we could all go together."

"Fine idea! I'd love the company. In the meantime, I've been called to look at some horses. I find it astonishing that a man can depend on horses for his livelihood and not know a thing about them."

Meagan excused herself. She felt as if she had been thrown from a horse. She could still taste the coffee and smell the tobacco from Dan's kiss. It was her first real kiss and it had been so gentle ... *no*, she wouldn't let herself dwell on it. It was ridiculous. There was no future with Dan; she could be gone at any moment. She had made a mistake, but she would fix it. The next time it came up, Meagan would tell Dan she wanted to remain just friends.

<hr>

The following day, Dan was up before Meagan as usual, knocking on her door with a cracked mug of coffee. He made no mention of the kiss, nor did he make any more advances. At first Meagan was happy to be relieved of the need to reject him. On second thought, she felt a gentleman would at least have said *something*.

Anderson was up early on his tall dun horse, ready to start. As Meagan and Dan mounted, a herd of cattle surged down a slope toward the pens. Riders loped in beside the cattle, forming a corridor, as others stayed back to keep the herd together.

"Say, isn't that the horse from yesterday?" Dan pointed to a brown-and-white pinto. The horse made a dash to intercept a stray before falling back into an easy lope.

"He's not balking at all." Meagan called to Anderson. "Did he like you reading to him?"

"No, it wasn't to his taste. I read him Thackeray all afternoon, and I believe it engendered in the horse a dislike for contemporary literature."

Meagan smiled, watching the pinto horse eagerly gallop down the slope, happy to be doing something, *anything,* other than standing in one place and listening to Romantic classics.

Anderson picked up his reins and moved into a good clip on his rangy dun, setting a vigorous pace. Meagan opened Red's stride to follow.

"You ride well, Meagan," Anderson commented.

"How about me?" Dan asked.

"Don't ask for what you don't want to hear, Daniel. But for that, praising one is not faulting the other. Riding has many levels."

Dan scoffed. "That so? Name one."

"I will name three. The first is becoming used to the horse's motion and staying on. Since you haven't fallen off in my presence, Daniel, I assume you have mastered that. The second level is being aware of the horse's comfort and efforts, and to ride accordingly, allowing the horse to work without interference. You also seem to do that quite well.

"It is the third level of riding, however, that is the most subtle and difficult. It is to sense the horse as yourself, making his balance your balance, to know what the horse will do an instant before he does and influence him invisibly."

"And Meagan can do that?" Dan guffawed. "Go on. Have you seen how she ropes?"

"I've seen how she rides," Anderson said crisply. "That was what we were speaking about, wasn't it?"

Meagan stuck out her tongue at Dan. "Thank you, Anderson." Dan glowered back, setting his jaw to suppress a smile.

The first part of the ride crossed a wide plain, but by late afternoon the rises were steeper and more frequent. Anderson pointed into the hazy distance. "If it were clear you could

just see the Fort by now. We'll have to camp outside tonight.
They will be closed before we get there."

"The Fort closes?"

"They bar the gates at dusk. Most of the itinerants stay outside. It's a bit rugged, but patrols circle the area. It's safe
enough."

They ate from the saddle as they rode, and Anderson produced a flask. Meagan passed—the fumes were enough to
warn her away—but Dan took a long draught. "So you heading back to the front lines, Major?" he asked, eyes watering.

"No. No more cavalry for me. Purely criminal to be using
horses anymore. It's outdated. What is the point of running a
horse against a cannonball?"

"Been doing it in Europe. It must work out all right."

"Horses can't talk, Daniel, but it is bad. Horrible. I should
know, I did requisition for my cavalry unit. Every cavalry
manual from every nation says the same thing: kill or maim
the horse."

Fort Laramie rose from the landscape as they rode closer.
They arrived at twilight to see makeshift campsites overflowing with travelers from east and west. Hollow-eyed children
stared from the sides of wagons stowed next to picketed
teams of oxen, horses, donkeys and mules. Lean dogs ran
through the camps. "I suggest we find an open spot," Anderson advised. "The water troughs are on the other side."

"Let's picket them out on the edge, away from the crowd."
Dan slid off Blue. The sorrel ducked his head and hitched his
sides in a dry cough.

Anderson went to the horse and felt the animal's chest.
Blue ridged his stomach and issued a dry blast. "That cough
isn't any better, Daniel. Have you been steaming him as I in-
structed?"

"Every night, Anderson. I think it's getting worse."

Meagan watched two settlers struggling with a large
wooden wheel. The wagon it had supported was leaning to
one side, propped precariously on a tilted log. A mother sat
nearby with a baby hugging her neck and another one playing in the dirt beside her.

Anderson frowned at the scene. "Looks to be a broken axle. It's a shame, but anyone on the trail is only a mishap away from failure. It's been that way for a hundred years."

"What'll they do?" Meagan asked.

"Turn back, or buy another if they have money. Or stay here. The Fort's population is made of families stranded with broken axles or sick oxen."

"I always heard my great-great-grandparents first brought oxen to California, and then went back for the horses. I thought it was just something they said."

"Your great-great-*grand*parents you say?" Anderson nodded, a bit dubious. "Well, it is one thing to *ride* to California, Meagan, on horseback you can travel fast, and it's easy to jog off the trail to find grass. It's something else to have horses *pull* you across the country. Long, slow days in the sun will kill them. Working horses won't last on thin grass and water. You need oxen for desert miles."

Voices and music drifted in from the falling darkness. Campfires began to surround them, some big and blazing, others small and flickering. Babies cried in the dark. Dan and Anderson squatted by the fire, not talking but simply staring. "A gypsy once told me to be careful about looking into a fire," Meagan told them. "Something could be looking back."

Anderson clucked. "The trails do grow some tall tales. Where would you see a gypsy, Meagan?"

"Don't get her started, Anderson. She'll trip you up," Dan warned. "My word on that."

"Nonsense! The closest thing to a gypsy found in this part of the world are the horse thieves they haul out to be hanged," Anderson replied.

"Gypsies are not thieves," Meagan retorted. "That's just a mean *gadjo* myth."

"A what?"

"I warned you, Anderson. Best let it go."

Meagan smiled and looked at Dan's silhouette in the flickering light. He continued to stare into the fire.

> *[Rad] byp on recyde rinca gehwylcum/sefte...*
> *(Riding seems very easy to every warrior while he is indoors...)*
> *- The Rune Poem (Ancient)*

THE CAMPS BEGAN to stir early the next morning. As Meagan rose, the looming outline of Fort Laramie showed in the cool light of dawn. She picked up her clothes bundle and hurried behind a neighbor's hung laundry to change, anxious to see if Blue's condition had improved. Coming to the spot where they had picketed the horses, she found Dan standing with his head down. In alarm she looked for the sleek sorrel horse. Blue was nowhere to be seen.

"Dan," she said fearfully, laying a hand on his shoulder. "Is Blue ... ?"

"He's gone."

"Oh *Dan*. I'm *so* sorry."

"Me too. My worst fear came true."

Others were milling about looking stricken, and Meagan didn't see her buckskin. "Wait—where is *Red?*"

"With the rest of them, I guess," he said darkly. "Our horses, plus some others that were picketed close by. They're saying it was Arapaho. Anderson went to the Fort to see if the Army will send out a party."

It took a moment for Meagan to understand they were without horses and without money, here, in the worst place— where people were trapped because they lacked transportation out. "What about the saddles?"

"Well, of *course* they took *those!*" Dan spat. "They don't even *use* saddles, that's just how ornery they are. I had the saddles stored between me and Anderson—hell you'd think he'd be finicky about sleep like everything else—but he snores loud enough to muffle gunfire!"

The camp was soon alive with talk of the stolen horses. Anderson returned with two official-looking people who asked many questions and, when they were finished, made it clear there was nothing Fort personnel would do.

"Then what the *hell* are we standing here for?" Dan snorted. "We've got our horses to find."

"All descriptions of Indian theft must be listed in the Army's records," the official informed Dan. "I've heard no report of violence, which would be a treaty violation. The matter will require negotiation."

"*Neg-o-ti-a-tion* ... so *that's* how people get stuck out here! Anderson, are there any Indian guides or suchlike in that Fort?"

"Some traders, probably."

"If they're Indian, they'll do. Let's go."

"One moment," the official said. "I'm not quite done."

"That's fine, you can stay." Dan walked off toward the Fort gates with Meagan behind, leaving Anderson to finish the report.

"Dan, where are you going?" she asked.

"Our horses were stolen by Indians, I'm going to get another one to find them!"

"How do you know for sure it was Indians?"

"Meagan, they sneaked up to an Army fort, took a dozen horses—with saddles—and didn't alert a dog. Trust me, it was Indians."

The gates to Fort Laramie did not open with the light as they had closed with the darkness, and it took several minutes of calling before sentries swung open the timber gates. Anderson rejoined them, and Dan walked through the gates calling out: "Hello! We need a good Indian guide! Come one, come all, we got cash!"

"*Dan*," Meagan whispered fiercely. "It's too early ... why don't we ask around first? You're going to insult anyone that might help us, yelling like that."

"Strange, but I'm not all that concerned about insulting Indians just now. Hell, you *can't* insult them except by not having horses to steal."

Anderson broke in. "Daniel, I'm in agreement with Meagan. I have some connections, and I'd rather take someone recommended to us."

"Oh, yes, do find us a 'recommended' Indian."

"Calm him down, Meagan. I'll find out what I can."

As Anderson left, Meagan turned to Dan. He held up a hand. "Don't start. I'm calm as I'm likely to get."

"Hey, mister!"

Meagan and Dan turned to see a scrawny settler, dusty and rumpled from a night of sleeping on the ground. He approached and spoke in close confidence: "I once't had a horse taken by savages. Damn thieves is all they are, them reds. Me and some others are setting up a search group and heading after them. Want to come with us?"

"Partner—excuse me, could you stand downwind?—you go on ahead. I'm going straight to the source."

"Hell, them reds ain't gonna listen to reason!"

"Who said anything about reason? I aim to *buy* them off."

"Mister, if you don't mind my saying, that's just plug stupid. Injuns'd sooner kill then look at you."

"Naw, that would be the excuse the Fort needs and they know it. I want my horse back and I've got the pay."

"Best come with us. If we don't find no horses at least we'll send a few on to meet their Great Spirit, if you catch my meaning."

"I'm telling you *no*," Dan replied irritably. "I just want my horses, no murdering."

"You *gotta* kill them! Them reds are killers."

"Yeah? Miraculous how we don't get along better, isn't it? People are mostly dangerous when you're shooting at them."

The man's black eyes looked small and lively in his leathery face. He watched Dan warily without speaking.

"Anderson, tell him we have a reward for the horses," Dan said impatiently.

"He speaks English, Dan," Meagan prompted. "Tell him yourself."

Black eyes fixed on Dan. "One dollar a day."

"No!" Dan stormed. "I've got no intention of running around this blasted prairie for weeks. It's four dollars when you find them, if you find them, and that's *all*."

"Six."

"Five."

The Indian nodded. Meagan stepped in front of Dan before he could say anything else. "Pardon him, please, he's just upset. My name is Meagan Roberts. What is your name?"

"Tonawa."

"Hello, Tonawa. What does that mean, by the way?"

The native looked blankly at her. "Means Tonawa." He bowed slightly and departed.

Dan let out a low whistle. "My goodness but she's friendly."

"I don't see the point in being rude, Dan. You act as if *he* stole the horses, and a few minutes ago you were defending Indians."

"That was for show. I hold the private opinion they're all murdering thieves."

Meagan grimaced. "Help me, Anderson. Talk some sense into him."

"In my experience, Meagan, opinions held on the subject of Indians are inconsistent in the best of men."

Dan snorted. "So imagine how it is with *me*."

Tonawa reappeared with a pouch and a plain poncho. As the guide led them toward one of the Fort's entrances, Meagan tried not to look at the settler's grimy faces moving with downcast eyes past the gray buildings—or the cleaner, blanker faces of the uniformed soldiers.

A cry came from behind them. "Sentries! Stop that man!" In a rush, Meagan's group was flanked on all sides by soldiers.

An official sounding voice called, "Is a Major Anderson Keffield present?"

Anderson pursed his lips. "Hello, Kirtland."

"You will address me as Lieutenant *Colonel!*"

"Certainly, Kirtland. Habit."

The other soldier's face flushed. "You are under arrest!"

"You lack novelty, Kirtland. What is it this time?"

"Sentries—take this man to the stockade! Make certain he is unarmed!" A rush of uniforms grabbed Anderson from each side. Anderson looked back as he was hurried away, giving Meagan a last look. She was sure she saw him wink.

Dan whistled. "Our little traveling party is suffering attrition. What do you think Anderson did?"

"I don't know. Should we follow him to find out?"

"No, wait until we come back. At least we know where *he* is."

The sun climbed steadily, and there were few travelers on the trail. Walking on foot felt strange after weeks of riding horseback, and to Meagan it seemed they moved slowly and awkwardly, making no progress toward a destination.

Shortly before noon, the guide turned onto a small path that wound through scrub brush and ended on a ridge overlooking a steep valley. Along the valley floor were well-tended, compact buildings.

"Wait. Stay." Tonawa turned and disappeared into the brush.

"What'd you think, Meagan?" Dan asked, peering after him. "Are they planning out an ambush? Maybe this wasn't such a good idea."

"Maybe now isn't the time to think about that," she answered testily.

"That's it, keep dealing the guff. You're gonna feel pretty silly tied to a stake."

"I hear they spare women and children."

"Old wives' tale. They take the women first, 'specially the talky ones."

Tonawa soon reappeared with another, younger Indian of dark, well-weathered complexion. "This Paisha. Scout. Buffalo near. Paisha know buffalo, know Arapaho. Pay Paisha also." To all this, Paisha nodded vigorously.

"Now wait a second, what does *that* all mean?" Dan fumed. "Can we get our horses back or not?"

Paisha nodded again, adding gestures for emphasis. "We Arapaho ask. If not Arapaho need, horses returning you."

"Oh, if that's all. See, I wasn't even thinking how *they* might need our horses. I'll add a dollar for him, Tonawa, but no more."

The original guide did not change expression. "Paisha speak to Arapaho. Then you speak." Tonawa turned into the brush, holding back a branch and indicating for the others to follow. Stepping carefully down the slope through the branchy undergrowth, they emerged near the base of the valley. The village seemed still and quiet, but as Meagan watched she realized the tiny settlement was alive with activity of women at their crafts and children quietly playing.

Sudden shouts rose from the empty ridge above them. Every face looked up as Indian riders burst into view along the top of the valley's wall, their horses stretched out in a gallop. Long manes whipped back like flames against the clear sky. The riders swept from view, and Meagan's first panicked thought was that the village was under attack. Warriors were coming to do what all horseback warriors did: kill and pillage. Yet ... no one seemed to care.

Dan closed his hand on hers and pulled. "Come on Meggie, let's go back before they find us."

"Wait, Dan. Look at them." Every person in the village was alert, watching the riders calmly. There was admiration on the faces, excitement and some smiles. "They aren't afraid."

The cries started again, coming closer as the riders broke into view once more. They streamed across the line of the ridge—and suddenly the riders vanished as if winked out of existence. The riderless horses galloped on across the ridge. Wheeling and circling, the riders reappeared in the instant of turning. Again the riders ran the ridge, and again disappeared to leave only the horse's silhouettes. The villagers watched the exhibition as the horses ran along the ridge, sometimes with riders, sometimes not.

Meagan had read about Indian riders who could slip down the side of a horse at a full run, hooking a foot across the horse's back and an arm over its neck. Such a rider could shoot underneath his mount's neck, using the animal's body as a shield.

The riders made a final whooping pass. A cheer went up from the village. The exhibition—or demonstration of force— was over.

"Showing off, that's all," Dan said, swallowing hard. "I never did like trick riding much."

The sun's horse is a yellow stallion, a blue stallion,
a black stallion; the sun's horse has come out to us.

- Apache ceremonial song

THEIR INDIAN GUIDES led Meagan and Dan into the village, where they were received by the leaders as other tribe members gawked. Unfortunately, it was soon apparent that most of the Arapaho's horses were participating in a buffalo-hunting party ... and could be gone for weeks. The hopeful news was that the hunters had departed only hours before, and might be close enough to locate.

The sun was high as the group set out once more to find the Arapaho hunting party. The rocky ground was hot, and Meagan and Dan struggled to keep up with their Indian guides Paisha and Tonawa. The barren landscape became bleaker with the miles. Heat rose in thermal waves.

A rumbling vibration grew around them as the afternoon wore on, as if the rocks were simmering beneath the surface. Dusk was approaching when they rounded a hillside formation to see buffalo spread before the setting sun like a black lake, reaching from horizon to horizon. The edges of the herd rippled as tribesmen on horseback plunged into the herd and back out like ospreys fishing in a dark sea.

Beside the rock formation was an Indian camp which suddenly reminded Meagan of the Mongolians under Genghis Khan. Men squatted around small fires while a few women worked in gathered groups. The people, the camp, the horses—they *were* nomads. The spirit of the Horde was alive on the prairie. Unwittingly, the white settlers had recreated and rearmed him: the American Indian's empathy with ani-

mals made them formidable horse people within a generation. But these nomads would have no time to unite, no time
to conquer. It was an ancient spark blazing into life to be
quickly extinguished, leaving the meek to inherit the earth.

Paisha went alone into a circle of natives. After brief discussion, commanding voices were raised and Arapaho began
departing the camp. Tonawa wordlessly pushed Meagan and
Dan forward, and two tribesmen rose to meet them as they
walked into the camp. One took a step toward Meagan, peering closely at her. His face bore the deep lines and ruddy
ochre of a life lived in wind and sun: he was aged but not old.
The man's hair was black and his strong hairless chest was exposed under his tunic. He retreated into a conversation with
other tribe members. Black eyes kept returning to the pale
people.

"Meggie," Dan whispered, "over there."

Meagan took in a sharp breath when she looked. She could
barely recognize the three horses being led toward the camp
in full war paint. Blue had a series of feathers plaited into his
mane and tail, and Anderson's lanky mount bore lines drawn
in red and white. Black lines ran down the front of Red's tan
legs. Painted white circles surrounded each horse's eye.

The elder tribesman watched Meagan intently. He gestured
until she understood they wanted her to mount Red. The
buckskin raised his head as Meagan approached. He wore a
simple thong around his head and a hackamore loop; there
was no mouthpiece. She traced the paint on the buckskin's
coat as Red lipped her hand in greeting. Looking back at Dan
and the silent nomads, Meagan jumped on Red and threw her
leg over.

A hushed murmur went through the men. Several stood.

Meagan picked up the loop of reins that circled Red's neck
and moved him forward into a jogging trot. As she did, sudden hoof beats rushed behind her. Another rider streaked
past at close range, howling a taunt, trying to provoke. Red
tensed, and without thinking Meagan slid the reins to the top
of his neck and held on as the ground melted in a blast of
wind. Red caught and breezed past the taunting rider.

In a few seconds, the hottest edge of the impossible rush dissipated and released them to skim across the open slope. They galloped along the sea of buffalo, past tribesmen on horseback riding the edges of the herd. To be on a horse in its own element was like soaring. Meagan circled Red in a lope back to the camp as if gliding to earth.

All the Arapaho were on their feet as Meagan pulled Red into a halt and slid off. Talk rumbled among them. Dan took Meagan's hand and held it tightly as the elders approached. Gesturing to Red and back to her, one of leaders spoke and the guide Paisha interpreted. "Return you Great Spirit."

On a signal from their elder, other Arapaho tribesmen led Anderson's horse and Blue forward. Impulsively, Meagan went to Red's forelock and pulled a few strands with her fingers. Twisting the hair into a small braid, Meagan held it out to the tribe elder standing before her. He did not take the forelock hair immediately, but when he did, the man's lined face creased into a smile.

"What was that all about?" Dan whispered as they took the horses.

"Let's just go," Meagan told him softly.

———

"I'd say that was close," Dan said in relief as they rode out of earshot. "Didn't know if they were going to cooperate at first." He was ponying Anderson's mount with a short lead. The pale dun gelding towered over Blue but was a perfect gentleman and kept the pace Dan set. "Nice touch at the end, that little braid you gave them. I think that was the trick that got our saddles back."

When Meagan said nothing, Dan whistled cheerfully and patted Blue. "Good to be back up, isn't it? Feels like your legs are cut off without a horse. Ever wonder whether the animal was set down here on earth for people to ride? I mean, horses do seem custom-made for the job. For one thing, it's passing strange a horse has no feeling in his mane. You can pull and pull, won't hurt them at all. If they had hair like ours, heck, that would have stopped progress in its tracks, first time a body got a little loose and had to grab on."

Meagan remained quiet. If the Indians had recognized the Great Horse—and she had no doubt they had—it was still nothing she wanted to tell Dan. She did not want to see that dubious look of disbelief. Not from him.

"Oh, come *on*, Meggie. Say something. We got our horses back and with a good wash they'll be back to normal." It was full darkness. The moon was rising and lighting the open landscape. Dan pulled to a halt. "Hold up a minute."

Meagan stopped Red.

"Are you still scared?" he asked. "I was, you know. Scared, I mean."

"No ... I will be fine, Dan."

"You haven't said much since we left."

"I'm sorry, it's just..." She stopped and shrugged. The incident had left her introspective, and a little, inexplicably sad.

Dan cleared his throat. "I think I know. They're going to kill the Indians off. We all know it. It's a winning issue—the newspapers want it, politicians run on it, and no one has a chance against *that* kind of heartlessness. I should have shut my mouth about Indians, thieves or not. I'd wager you're a born abolitionist—don't tell me, we'd start an argument— you're soft on people, I see it. The world needs that, more'n the other kind. So I'm glad you are. You're right, and I'm sorry."

"Dan, it wasn't that. Though I'm glad to hear you say it."

"Now slide down and let the horses rest. We're almost back to the Fort, and there is something I've been wanting to make right."

Meagan swung her leg over and was about to slide to the ground when she felt Dan's arm around her waist. He half pulled, half carried her down, and as she turned his hand went behind her head and pulled her close into a kiss.

———

That night Meagan and Dan camped with the horses as close to the Fort's walls as they could manage. Stretching out on rough blankets, they lay on the ground, stared at the stars and talked. She drifted off, waiting for an answer from Dan about something, happy knowing they had no schedule to keep. At long last, she could sleep in...

Shouts woke her an hour before dawn. "Clear the area! All non-military personnel are to vacate the perimeter!"

Meagan opened her eyes to see soldiers in uniforms standing in the early pre-dawn. Colors were not yet visible, only shades.

"All non-military, up and out! Livestock not removed from this area will be confiscated!"

Panicked civilians swirled among the dark uniforms to comply. Dan stood groggily and stretched. Meagan hugged her knees as she waited for her head to clear.

"What's this about?" Dan asked a soldier.

"Regiment coming in!" he barked. "General's orders. All civilians are to clear Fort perimeter south." The uniform walked on, shouting commands.

Meagan yawned. "If you get the horses, Dan, I'll get everything ready."

Dan disappeared among the increasing number of uniforms. Meagan stretched and stood. People around her were rushing in the predawn light, beating oxen to get them to rise and stowing their gear in wagons or onto pack animals. She bent to wrap the bedrolls tightly as Dan had shown her, stacking their belongings together.

The uniforms around her were coloring to blue when Dan emerged from the crowd leading their mounts, a horse in each hand. "Good news!" he called, grinning. "I think Blue's cough is gone!"

"Really? Let me listen." Meagan put her ear on the sorrel's side. "Where's Anderson's horse?"

"I have to go back and get him. Poor old boy, they really did him up, didn't they? All red-and-white stripes. There's a crowd just gawking. Not that *these* two didn't get their share of looks." Dan grimaced at their two horses. The mane feathers were mostly gone, but both animals were still covered in

Indian war paint. The white circles around Red's eyes looked clownish in the gray light. "I want to wash them clean before we do anything else."

"You know, Dan, I think Blue *does* sound better." She couldn't hear even a wheeze.

"Yep, the ol' Indian cure. It's a dandy if you don't mind the stealing part."

Meagan lifted her heavy saddle off its pad and set it pommel-side down over the bedrolls. She had just picked up her saddle blanket and started toward Red when she heard a loud voice.

"Look here, Captain! We got ourselves some real live Indian ponies." A uniform walked forward and gave Blue a hearty slap. The sorrel gelding cocked back his ears. "This one here's even got feathers!"

Dan reached up and plucked a stray tuft from Blue's mane. "Missed one. Thought I got them all."

"What'd you do, steal these horses from some old Indian?"

Dan bristled at the tone. "It was the other way 'round, actually. We got them back ourselves, no thanks to *this* outfit."

The soldier eyed Dan a moment. "Get Lieutenant Colonel Foster," he said to another uniform, then squinted to look more carefully at Red. "You say your horses were with Indians, and you just went out and took them back?"

"Yeah. That's pretty much the story of it."

"Seems strange."

"Can't say I'd argue." Dan met the man's gaze steadily as another soldier strode up. The new man's uniform showed more contrasting colors on his chest than the first's.

"Lieutenant Colonel Foster, sir. I thought you'd want to see this."

The officer gave the horses a quick glance. "How did they get here? These are Indian war horses."

"Looks that way, doesn't it, sir? I can't think why they'd be painted up otherwise."

Foster fixed expressionless eyes on Dan. "Where'd you get these animals?"

"One in Sacramento, the other Silver City. Can't recall seeing a tepee either time."

The first soldier snorted. "He took them from some Indians, sir. That's what he told me."

"*No*," Dan replied testily, "what I said was Indians *stole* them, and I went to get them *back*. No thanks to—"

Meagan put her hand on Dan's shoulder. "We came back late last night," she told the soldiers respectfully. "We haven't had time to wash the paint off."

"Are you aware horses of Indian tribes in conflict with the U.S. government are subject to requisition?" the officer asked with detached calm.

"Now these don't look much like Indian ponies, do they?" Dan asked, mocking. "I mean, look at them. They're much too raggedy."

"Sir, these are our horses," Meagan said sincerely. "They have never belonged to an Indian tribe, we can assure you."

"Can't you tell a decent cow horse when you see one?"

"Dan—" Meagan said evenly.

"I'll not be accused of having a damned Indian horse! Go find Anderson, *he'll* tell you where these horses came from!"

"Who did you say?" asked the Lieutenant Colonel, interested.

"Anderson Keffield. He's a Major! He'll have something to say about this."

"Do you mean Major Anderson Morgan Keffield, the Third?"

"That's him. The big painted-up thoroughbred dun on the picket is his." Dan hesitated when he saw Meagan's tense expression. "Ask him. Anderson can straighten this out."

The Lieutenant Colonel and several others broke into grins. "Anderson *Keffield*. Why didn't you say so?" Foster turned to the soldiers around him. "Boys, take these horses to the pens. Tell the men they were requisitioned courtesy of Anderson Keffield. You'll find another horse up on the picket—what was that description ... 'big painted-up dun?' Take him, too. And the saddles."

"The *hell* you will!" Dan said hotly.

"Dan..." Meagan put her hand on his arm to restrain him. Six rifles were out, trained on her and Dan. Soldiers pried the lead ropes from Dan's stunned hands. The captain tipped his hat as the horses were taken away.

Dan stood watching the horses as they disappeared from view. "Do you believe this, Meagan? Do our horses have 'public property' written on them somewhere?"

"We've got to find Anderson."

"Oh, that a fact? Anderson isn't exactly popular 'round these parts, if I'm reading it right. *He* got us into this."

No, Meagan almost said, *your mouth got us into this.* Instead, she walked to a nearby uniform. "Excuse me," she asked politely. "Can you point me to the Fort's jail?"

—————

Anderson was facing out his one window when Meagan and Dan were allowed inside. A cot claimed one side of the cell, and a desk took up the other.

"Nice place you got here, Anderson," Dan said sarcastically. "What's the charge?"

"Politics, Daniel." Anderson turned to them, arms crossed. His countenance was pale and drawn. "I'll be out in a week, once I have a superior speak with the little Lieutenant about my duties elsewhere."

"So you *do* know the Colonel. That's good, because he sure seemed to know you."

"Yes he does. I think it would have been better to have left my name out of this matter, Daniel."

"Now you tell us. This cockeyed little dustup cost us our horses!"

"I was legally detained, Daniel. Any fool would know better than to say my name to the people who arrested me."

"Any fool, or just my variety?"

"Perhaps you could explain to me why the horses were still in Indian markings?"

"Slow down, Andy. We didn't have a scrub brush and basin handy."

"Anderson! The name is *Anderson!*"

"Stop it, *both* of you," Meagan interrupted. "Anderson, whatever the horses looked like, it was hardly an excuse to steal them."

"Confiscate, Meagan. That is the word for stealing when it's a government action. And you'll be interested to discover it is quite a *good* excuse, actually. The matter is out of my hands."

"Sorry to trouble you, then." Dan put his hat back on. "Andy."

"And thank *you*, Danny, for having my horse sent over to the rotting New Jersey *Third*. I'd rather he was left with the *Indians!*"

Dan slammed the door behind him.

"That's not fair, Anderson," Meagan protested. "Our horses were taken, too. We didn't know there was some kind of grudge here."

Anderson sat on the edge of his desk. "I know, Meagan. It *is* my fault, actually. This started three years ago, when I was cavalry requisition for the Ninth New York. We were stationed in Washington, and my job was to keep the troops mounted. I had a devil of a time keeping sound horses under the thoughtless clods, and when a load of horses passed through Washington for Foster's regiment, I had them 'reassigned' to my own. A simple matter of paperwork. I'm not proud. I was a cocky little clerk, and now I'm making us all pay the price. As you see, Kirtland hasn't forgotten."

"Can you get them back?"

"Considering things as they are—politics, bureaucracy, no friends here, a highly agitated commander..." He looked at her. "In short, no. I can't."

"We are free citizens. You could testify for us."

"To whom? It's wartime, dear Meagan, and war gives people excuses to do things. I have no influence here. I am being reassigned myself. To Fort Benton up north, Kirtland hopes, but he will be disappointed."

"They took your sketch. It was in my saddlebag," Meagan said quietly. "I'll miss it."

"Thank you, Meagan." The man's voice was tight.

"I'm worried about Red. Is there anything we can do?"

Anderson put his hands behind his back. "I know how you feel, Meagan. I'm going to miss my old Richmond terribly. Did you know my mount's name was Richmond?"

"No, sir, I didn't."

"I got him on assignment there. I was at the rail yard watching the remounts being sent out. I remember hearing people laughing, so of course I went to see. There is so little to laugh about in the Army, you take your opportunities. People were standing in a circle around a tall, thin horse going on the last car. Someone had painted words across his ribs: *'Bound for the Knacker's.'*" Anderson stood quickly and walked back to the window. "I hear there was much laughing when they brought the horse in wearing Indian paint. I truly hate that."

"Anderson, I am so sorry."

"A man can get damned attached." He remained looking away, standing straight as if at attention. "Noble creatures. Never ask for more than good treatment and decent food. On occasion they save us."

"I know, Anderson. Women can get pretty attached, too."

"He won't last. Richmond hates gunfire. At least he won't be heartbroken from betrayal: I've heard it said dogs believe men to be gods, but cavalry horses know us better." There was a pause, and Anderson turned. His eyes were rimmed in red but he spoke evenly. "I can offer you credit at the trading store here for some new clothes and effects. Please agree, it is the least I can do for the trouble this has caused you and Daniel. A coach comes through every two weeks on the way to Fort Riley. From there you can get a line to Kansas City, and wherever else you wish to go."

"I think we might go to Kentucky. Dan says that. And I'd like to find the horses."

"If you ever have word of—well, unlikely. You will be reimbursed in full for the horses and equipment. I've already had the necessary papers filed on your behalf. That I can still do."

"I will let you know if hear about Richmond. Thank you, Anderson."

He turned back to the window. "God bless."

———

Meagan was conscious of the eyes upon her as the soldiers let her pass. She walked with the military escort among the pens until she found her buckskin in a group of horses, huddled beside the rough, split-rail fence.

She was nervous, but had to come for Red's sake. Meagan waited as the pen's gate was unlatched and opened for her. She walked slowly to Red. He had been washed clean and his mane was pulled short. A fresh, livid U.S. Government brand festered on his shoulder. He nickered softly as she stroked his neck, then bumped her with his nose.

"Hello, boy," she said gently, letting the buckskin sniff her hair. "Now, Red, listen to me: I want you to be a good boy for the cavalry riders. When others try to ride you, just let them. They ... have my permission."

Meagan was not sure what she expected. Red did not look at her with special understanding. He simply cocked a hind foot and hung his head, preparing for a doze. She patted her cowhorse a final time, kissing him on the neck and turning without looking back. A guard opened the last gate for her, and all eyes followed as she walked out of the cavalry yard.

———

Lieutenant Colonel Foster's regiment pulled out amid shouting and dust, passing outside Meagan's open window. She sat in the room's one chair, watching the cavalcade pass between the clean plaid curtains of her rented room. Hooves beat an undercurrent to the military drums.

She watched for Red without wanting to see him, fearfully studying each buckskin as it passed. She had lain awake thinking about the gypsy woman's warning to stay with the Great Horse. Somehow she had to find a way to follow the regiment, but as the riders filed past on their way to the open prairie, Meagan could only watch the horses leave, and with them her only means to go home.

Then there was Dan. Not since the brash, betraying chariot driver Braedin had she felt an irrational pull towards a man, but her emotions in Rome had been a glimmer of what she felt now. After the past few days of quiet time alone with Dan, she found herself wondering if her lightheaded mood was falling in love. Her feelings bore the hallmarks explained in love songs back home, and regardless of her internal discussion, whichever angle it took, she could not stop thinking of him. The ancients might say she had caught the insane-making illness of romantic love. A bad case, it seemed.

She bit her lip, thinking the timing could not be more inconvenient. Even if Dan was aggravating and difficult, or had once seemed so, home felt less distant than before and the world a far friendlier place. Her journeys with the Great Horse were as mysterious as ever, and now her feelings for Dan were confusing the issue. Maybe she should take a chance and tell him everything...

There was a knock at the door. It cracked. "You decent?" Dan peeked behind the door.

"At least you asked this time." Meagan stood. "I am."

Dan stood sheepishly, fingering his hat. He looked down at it. "Just had it pressed."

"Looks nice."

"Yeah, thought I should. Want to look my best. After all, my family's not seen me in three years." He glanced at the window. "Did you see the horses? I think I saw Blue, but I didn't look too hard, you know?"

"I do." Now was the time. "Dan, do you know when Red was born? I mean, was it morning ... dawn maybe?"

Dan shrugged. "Heck, I don't know. Red was just a stock horse I found in Sacramento. Bought him at auction. My kind of horse, all full of himself like I wanted to be."

"So you don't know who owned him before?"

"Naw, an old man sold him to me out back before the bidding. Said he was good luck and I should have him. Good sales line I thought."

"I ask because I have to tell you something."

"Well, go on, Meggie."

Meagan smiled, thinking how much she once hated that nickname—now, on Dan's lips, she (almost) loved it. "There is a legend I want to tell you. It's about a horse, an angel."

"A *horse* angel?

"He comes to help people, and inspire them. Now listen, Dan, this is important. There are three ways to know a Great Horse. First is that they are born at dawn. The second is, no one else can ride a Great Horse without the owner's permission." Meagan hesitated, thinking of the third rule, that only a Great Horse's owner would believe the legend.

Dan walked up and took her hand. "I'm listening. What's the third way?"

Suddenly she couldn't tell him. He would only think her eccentric, if not crazy—she would not risk it. "Never mind, Dan. The third way is if they sprout wings and fly on a full moon. Ever seen one of those?"

"No," Dan chuckled. "Can't say I have, unless I was flying pretty high myself. Seen strange things on camp moonshine. What brought that up? You said it was important."

"I know, but it's not. It was just something I was thinking about."

"Okay, if you are finished, I have news, Miss Roberts. Our coach pulls out at noon sharp."

"What coach?"

"Butterfield Express, special to Kansas City. Isn't that the one Anderson recommended?" Dan held out two printed stubs of cardboard.

"Dan! How did you get them? The clerk said everything was booked!"

He shrugged modestly. "It's surprising the hand some people hold when they're sitting inside a bottle of whiskey. I know. I've done it. And it's a damned disgrace, if you want my opinion."

People on horses look better than they are.
People in cars look worse than they are.

- Marya Mannes (1904-90)

O<small>F ALL THE</small> modes of travel Meagan had experienced, nothing equaled the misery of a stagecoach. The cramped interior was a stifling box of heat. Moldering fabric snips fluttered over tiny side windows collecting grit and smell. The hapless passengers jammed along the insides or battled back to back in the dreaded center seat. In answer to Dan's flippant question about who else in the coach—besides himself and Meagan—had known a bath within the year, one fellow traveler spit tobacco juice on the bare floor of the coach so it tilted and ran in rivulets between everyone's feet.

There were no roads: the stagecoach ran over the raw plains using landmarks to stay on course and avoid the most treacherous ground. The vehicle had nothing in the way of springs or other mechanical device to absorb shock, and the oversized wheels allowed the horses to pull the coach over sizeable rocks without stopping as the passengers careened back and forth inside.

Five minutes into the journey Meagan thought it unbearable. Seventeen hours and two horse changes later she staggered from the coach and nearly fell to her knees on the hard ground. One of the passengers, a woman who had been ill the last hours of the trip, was laid flat upon the dirt. Dan emerged gripping the stagecoach's door frame for balance.

The stagecoach driver hopped down and surveyed his distressed passengers. "We'll be stopped here to rest the horses about two hours," he said gruffly. "Walk around, get something to eat."

Passengers moaned at the suggestion.

"Dan," Meagan said. "I can't get back in that thing."

"I agree." He called to the driver. "Where are we, good sir?"

"Not rightly sure the place has a name."

"That's a comfort," Dan mumbled.

"The middle of nowhere. I know it well."

"I'd say we should rest a day or so and find a better coach, Meggie, but I don't know if there *are* any better. That one's as good as I've seen. At least the floorboards had drains."

Meagan shuddered. Local workers had come up and were undoing the horses' harnesses with an air of leisure. She went to them. "Excuse me, do you know where could we find something to eat?"

"No place," said one worker calmly, intent on the harness. "Leastways, not for outsiders. Not since the war started."

"You must mean the Yankees, but I don't know if that applies to us."

"It don't matter, ma'am. Union, Confeds, we're sick of the damn thing. Our whole town seceded last month."

"What do you mean, the town 'seceded'?"

"Just that. We declared independence from North and South, *both!*"

"That makes no sense," Dan argued. "A town doesn't secede."

"This one did. Walk into town, you'll see. Southern bunch tried to ride in here the other day, most likely thinking about all the livestock they was going to take in service of Their Cause. Took a right amount of convincing to make them see different—fact a couple fellows *died* unconvinced. They's up at the cemetery. Killed by lead poisoning, you might say."

"Oh," Meagan said, turning back to the stagecoach.

Everything was wonderfully peaceful and silent. Meagan opened her eyes and saw blue sky: something was very wrong. She sat up, realizing what was different. The world had stopped moving; the buggy she rode had come to a halt.

"Daniel, your lady friend is awake!" A young gentleman sat cross-legged on a blanket outside the buggy, calm amidst the struggle between his tight jacket and the exuberant, frilly white shirt it was trying to strangle. Lying next to him, on his back, was Dan. The unfamiliar man introduced himself pleasantly. "Hello, I am Arthur Metchamp. We met in Louisville."

"She was passed out from heat, I told you," said Dan wearily. "The final leg just about killed us."

"Yes, yes, I know. Here ma'am, have some wine."

Dan lurched to his feet. "She doesn't need wine, you fop, she needs water! Hand me that mug." He walked a bit unsteadily to the side of the buggy. "Here, Meggie, drink it slow."

She took a gulp, rested, took another. The world spun if she moved too quickly. "Who is he?" she whispered between drinks.

"Name's Arty. Arthur. An old friend from Transylvania University, before I quit and departed for points west. His family owns trotters. I saw him at the station and he's giving us a ride home."

"That's nice of him. Where are we?"

"Not far outside Louisville. We'll take it easy and get to Lexington tomorrow afternoon."

Arthur stood and brushed himself. "Introduce me again, Daniel. You say she's forgotten."

"Meagan, Arthur. Arthur, Meagan."

"Pleased to meet you, Meagan ... I didn't catch your family's name?"

Meagan saw that Arthur was studying her faded, stained gingham dress. She hesitated to open a discussion about family. "You must excuse me," she said politely. "It has been a difficult few days. I'm not feeling terribly well."

"Certainly ... and I'm sorry, the last name?"

"She didn't say, Arty. She isn't feeling well, or didn't you catch that, either?"

"Anything we should know?" Arthur simpered.

Dan glared at Arthur until the man retired to his blanket, then squatted down to lean against the buggy's wheel. "Just like old times."

———

Kentucky is a territory of many geographies, lying between the Appalachians and the Mississippi river. In the push across the continent, the earliest settlers faced a nearly insurmountable obstacle in the mountains of Appalachia until 1775, when Daniel Boone followed the track laid by Thomas Walker, and blazed the opening that was to be known as the Cumberland Gap. Settlers poured through heading for the wide open spaces of the West. Seeing the fertile green miles of Kentucky, many decided to stop right there.

The soil and climate were ideal for raising tobacco, and the grain it produced fermented into uniquely mellow bourbon. The soil and climate were perfect for something else: horses.

Kentucky winters are cold enough to kill parasites but not so severe as to cause hardship. Heavy spring rains bring grass for long days of grazing and galloping, and autumn sees harvests of good hay and grain—but it is a coincidence of nature that makes one part of Kentucky like nowhere else on earth. The grass of central Kentucky is a uniquely lush, deep green cover called bluegrass. Many settlers first coming through Kentucky moved on, suspicious of the oddly-colored grass. Later, science would unravel the peculiar mineral blend that produces this color, but from the beginning it was clear that bluegrass imparted a special quality to the mares and foals bred on it. Within a few generations, Kentucky's famous bluegrass entered history.

Meagan had never seen bluegrass in person. She looked carefully from the coach, but nothing about the groundcover seemed unusual. That evening they stayed at a tiny, deserted inn, and the next day took to the road early. The grass she saw was thick and green, the same as good grass everywhere. The uniqueness of bluegrass must be only a legend, she thought, and settled back in the buggy, disappointed. She

dozed, and later in the morning half-opened her eyes and noticed that shadows had fallen across the fields. "How much
further, Dan? Are we going to beat the rain?"

Arthur and Dan turned. "What are you talking about,
Meggie? It's a clear day."

She opened her eyes fully and looked up. It was true—the
sun was bright overhead. Only wisps of clouds scuffed the
sky. Meagan looked again at the fields bathed in the strong
sun: the grass was inviting, dark and cool, as if shaded. Bluegrass.

"Do you like it?" Dan asked. "Some don't."

"It *is* different! I *love* it." She should have known better than
to dismiss a legend.

He grinned. "Good. We aren't far now."

"Not far at all," Arthur piped in. "Just over the next hill is
my family's place. We'll stop in and let them take a look at
you."

"No thanks, Arty, if you don't mind," Dan protested. "I
think I should go home first."

"No, we should stop," Arthur insisted. "Mother would
want to be the first to greet you back home."

"Arty," Dan said firmly, "I insist."

The driver gripped his reins more tightly. "My horse needs
rest, and I'm sure Mother has something to send your father.
It won't take a minute."

"Then we'll walk."

"Now that would cause a stir, having you *walk* home after
your big adventure."

Meagan leaned forward to interrupt. "Arthur, please. I
must appeal to your gallantry in this matter. You understand."

"No," he said obstinately. "Mother will want to meet you."

"Surely she would understand the need to refresh before
meeting Dan's friends." Arthur hesitated, and Meagan placed
her hand on his shoulder. "Being a Californian, I've heard so
much about the honor of Southern gentlemen—*oh!*" She

snatched her hand away. "Dan, have I made a mistake? I assumed Metcamp was a good name."

"Indeed we are, ma'am," Arthur said, flustered. "It's one of the oldest names in Kentucky."

"Oh, that is a relief." Meagan settled back. "Then I've said enough. Thank you, and I promise to visit as soon as I am able. I shall have to write father immediately, and my uncle in Philadelphia too, about what charming and generous friends Dan has...." Meagan continued chattering away pleasantly, ignoring Dan's amused expression. She did notice that they passed Arthur's hill without stopping.

"Look at the foals!" Meagan exclaimed, leaning out the buggy's side. Low-bellied broodmares grazed next to their foals in fenced meadows. Some babies lay down; others whisked their stub tails as they nursed or leapt in short dashes across the grass. "Does your family have horses, Arthur?"

"Of course," Arthur said, sounding offended. "Walkers and trotters, blood horses. That was before the war—those are the last of our broodmares. No one has many horses since the cavalry came through. They paid Mother half their worth or less, and it was that or nothing."

Dan whistled low. "So are we part of this Confederacy, Arty?"

"It's hard to say. Even Mother isn't sure which way we'll go. Some want to join the Rebs, but they confiscated so many horses the politicians won't do it. Some think we will end split in half like Virginia."

"So we're not rebels yet?"

"No, not yet."

Rail fences zigzagged across gentle hilltops. Not many fields were cultivated; a few pastures held small herds of mares and foals, or were private pens for solitary stallions. In every group at least one horse stood, head high, watching the buggy pass.

Atop one hill were several low, lodge-type houses nestled in close rows together. "Those are curing houses for tobacco,"

Dan explained. "They're only used during the season, the rest of the time it's left to the rats." A roof appeared. As they climbed the hill, the roof grew into a rambling house with a lattice porch running around it. Wisteria and honeysuckle vines covered the sides. Trees of dogwood, laurel and chinaberry shaded the home, and a well-tended dirt road wound up to and around it.

"Is that a plantation house?" Meagan commented. "It's beautiful!"

"Doesn't grow enough to call it a plantation," Dan told her. "Raises horses, mostly. Or did."

"Do you know who lives there?"

"We'll see, I guess. I used to call it home."

The buggy swung off the main dirt road onto a private one lined with matching pairs of trees, making a looping turnaround before the main house. Dan jumped down and turned to help Meagan.

Before accepting his assistance, she lay her hand lightly on the driver's shoulder. "Thank you *so* much, Arthur. I expect you'll be seeing us soon."

"I expect," he said glumly, watching Meagan disembark. "Mother will be disappointed."

Dan shook his hand. "Thanks for the ride, Arty. Much obliged. I'd ask you inside, but you know Dad." Arthur nodded and lifted the driving reins. As the buggy moved off, Dan said to Meagan, "I almost hate to disappoint the old dandy. He was looking forward to showing off the prodigal son's return."

"Help me, Dan, there's no mirror. Should I put it up or leave it down?" Meagan gathered her hair, turned in each direction, and let it fall. It was long now, almost to the middle of her back; the last time it had been cut was in a salon at Versailles. "I want to make a good impression on your father. What does he like?"

"As if I have any idea. It looks fine that way."

They walked up the stone path, past metal statuettes of horse heads painted black. Dan crossed the porch in steady, slow steps. At the door, he reached up and lifted the heavy knocker. Hesitating a moment, he let it drop and clasped his hands behind his back. Before the door opened, he leaned over to Meagan and whispered, "You look wonderful."

"*Land o'Goshen!* Mighty Moses hallelujah! It's the lost tribes of Israel standing on my porch!"

"Afternoon, Sojourner." Dan smiled as he took Meagan's hand and stepped into the house. He kissed the thin, gray-haired black woman on the cheek. "It's good to see you."

She opened her arms and hugged Dan, then pushed him away. "None of that, child! You want my waterworks going so I won't scold you like you need scolding." The woman dabbed her eyes. "I say, you are as dusty and dry as an old piece of hoof. Something been gnawing on you? What excuse you giving old Sojourner for keeping away so long?"

"Just got a bit lost out there, ma'am."

"Child, we all is lost 'til we find our home in the Kingdom. Now who is this?"

Meagan felt herself pinned by clear, dark-as-obsidian eyes.

"This is my traveling companion, Miss Meagan Roberts."

"She your wife, Daniel?"

"No, ma'am."

"I *see* ... she your betrothed?"

"She won't say, ma'am."

"She better say, she want to come under *this* roof!"

Dan laughed and kissed the woman's cheek again. "Thank you for being just the same. Meagan, this is Sojourner. She keeps the house and gives us the run of it, mostly."

"Daniel Beardon, did you tell your father you were coming?"

"No. I came when we heard of the war."

"You a little late." Sojourner gave Dan a significant look. "You gonna stay?"

"I might, if Dad will have me."

"Oh, he'll have you. Maybe just your head, but he'll have you."

"Where is Mother?"

"Europe, she and your sister both. They went on a tour last fall and now your daddy won't let them come home until this war is over. Speaking about your daddy, he's laid up in the smoking room talking trash and horses." The woman paused, her dark eyes dancing. "You want me to tell him who's here?"

"No, I'd better go in myself."

"Ambush him, you mean. I think that's a good idea, child."

Dan held out his hand to Meagan. He had hardly taken a step when Sojourner's stern voice stopped him. "You aren't planning to walk through *this* house in *those* boots, Daniel. I hope I'm not seeing *that*." Dan nodded, bending down to pull each off. Meagan looked at her own worn shoes. "Don't you be fussing about that, young Miss," Sojourner said sharply, fixing Meagan with a piercing look. "You got enough to worry about without meeting Mr. Beardon in your bare feet. Just follow Daniel on into the lion's den."

Dan tightened his hand around Meagan's, leading her past the entry way into a large open hall. "That was the easy part," he said softly.

"I like her," Meagan whispered. "She missed you a lot."

"She won't like you for a while, probably. Sojourner is hard on strangers. She gets grumpy but remember it's only an act. Mostly."

Men's voices were coming from an archway set off from the front hall entrance. Dan's grip tensed as they walked to the open double-doors. Through the entrance Meagan could see a dead fireplace behind a long desk stacked with books and papers. "Wait here," Dan whispered, and walked through the doorway.

"Hello, Dad."

Conversation stopped. Two older gentlemen in coats stood in the center of the room; each man's remaining hair was a shock of white. One came forward, a stout figure with a fleshy, weathered face set on large shoulders, larger than Dan's. His expression was blank. All Meagan could see of Dan was the back of his head, and she wondered what was passing between them. But the gentleman did not stop, and when he reached Dan he hugged him. "Son," he said simply. They embraced a long moment before separating. The older man gripped Dan's arms, looking intently into his face. "You're thin, son. Are you all right?"

"I am. I'm great actually. I've brought someone for you to meet."

Meagan stepped into the open. Trying her hardest not to blush, she immediately turned bright red. Dan's father stepped back and looked at her for an awkward moment. She came forward and extended her hand. "Meagan Roberts, sir. I am so pleased to meet you."

Mr. Beardon clasped her hand reluctantly. "Is this your wife, Daniel?"

"No, sir, not yet. I would like her to be. I've asked her."

The man's expression became grim. He turned toward his associate, showing his back. "Is she pregnant?"

"No, sir. Nor did she come to be insulted."

The elder Beardon turned back to inspect Meagan. He looked her up and down. "You could have married any girl in the county, son. You know that."

"Are you asking me to leave?" Dan asked heatedly.

"Not exactly the homecoming you expected, is it? *Son.*"

"I'd say it's about exactly the homecoming I expected."

The man drew a breath. "Fair enough, Daniel. This wasn't the welcome I planned to give you, the Lord knows. My apologies to your lady friend. Let me finish with my partner and we'll talk at dinner. Tell Sojourner to set two more plates. You know where your room is, your friend can stay in your sister's." Clasping his hands behind his back, the elder Beardon looked at his son silently for a moment. "Glad to have you back, son. I hope you are."

"Thank you, Dad." Dan took Meagan's arm and they walked out. "That's done," he whispered in relief. "I'm sorry about that. It went better than I thought."

She pushed away her feelings about the cool reception. "Your father said he's glad to have you back, Dan."

"We'll see. Time opens all wounds."

Sojourner met them before the base of a wide staircase. "Well, you staying?"

"We've been invited, for now. Meagan's going to stay in Lucille's room."

"Heaven has mercy. Come on, then." Sojourner walked up the stairs, leading. When they reached the top, Meagan felt a cool hand circle her wrist. "Go on, Daniel. Your room is where you left it. I'll take care of *her*." She waved Dan away and nodded to Meagan. "Come on, girl, Miss Lucille's room is this way. Don't be watching him like a cat spying a mouse."

Meagan was surprised by the vise grip and strength with which she was propelled down the hallway and thrust into a sunny room. Lace curtains blew in the breeze from a half-open but shuttered window. The pink bedspread and cluttered vanity table announced the space to be a young woman's room.

"I'll know what you touch," Sojourner warned.

"Of course." Meagan wanted to rub her arm but refused to give the woman the satisfaction. Sojourner stood, hands on hips, as Meagan sat delicately at the vanity table, trying to ignore the harsh reflection. "I'll need to wash up," she said pleasantly. "Are there towels?"

"Yes there're towels."

"Oh," Meagan smiled, starting to get up. "I'll get them. Tell me where."

"*I'll* get you a pitcher and *a* towel. Don't want you bumping all over this house." Sojourner walked briskly out of the room.

Meagan knew she was being slighted but didn't care. Right now her thoughts were filled with happy images of herself and Daniel together. Her heart was light and she felt foolish, gloriously so. Like a balloon tugging a string, her heart's only direction was up to the sun.

She leaned into the mirror. The face that looked back was hardly familiar. Could she really be only seventeen ... or was it eighteen now? Her skin was dusky brown, stretched over hollow cheeks. She lifted her hair and pulled it back: her grandmother's reflection stared back, as if from one of the cracked photographs stored carefully in her mother's closet. Meagan dropped her hair quickly. Her chest constricted and she put both hands on the vanity top to breathe for a moment. Eighteen now, surely. She would have to award herself another birthday.

Sojourner came back into the room with a chipped, painted pitcher. A single small towel draped over her shoulder. "What you doing, young Miss? Looks like you seen a ghost." Setting the container down hard on the vanity, the woman slapped the towel over it and swirled out, leaving scents of talcum and rosewater in her wake.

"Thank you," she said softly. Bringing the pitcher to the open window, Meagan poured water over the towel and wrung it out. She dabbed the cloth on her face, neck and arms, her only skin allowed exposure to the air.

The question Meagan was avoiding was quietly waiting: *how should she answer Dan's proposal of marriage?* He had made it on a stagecoach platform outside Louisville. They had just arrived at the station when he circled her with his arms and whispered it. Every part of her had been sore and her stomach had been shouting for food, so she had commented on his timing and made a joke. He had taken her hands between his and kissed them. They sat down to rest a moment. Apparently she had fainted; she remembered little more until waking in Arthur's buggy.

The proposal had taken her by surprise. Even now she felt light-headed to think of it. She had left Fort Laramie intending to travel with Dan to his home and then to go on to find Red, the Great Horse, who had traveled East with the cavalry. Searching for a horse in the middle of war was plainly ridiculous, but she thought she had no choice.

Now, suddenly, she was confused. She could marry Dan, and a part of her wanted to consider it. She was *not* making a choice between him and her family—was she to tramp across the Old South hoping to find the Great Horse, wandering through camps and battlefields, a penniless woman, alone? There were no easy answers, and though she missed home, those memories were becoming the hollow ache of something long lost, like an old regret.

The substitution of the internal combustion engine for the horse marked a very gloomy milestone in the progress of mankind.
- Sir Winston Churchill (1874-1965)

THE SUN WAS still above the treetops when Sojourner knocked to announce dinner. Meagan frowned at her reflection a last time—there was only so much to be done with a hairbrush and wet cloth. A newly-shaven Dan waited on the stair landing. Scents of rubbing alcohol and mint were strong on him.

"You look nice," she smiled.

"You too. How are you and Sojourner getting on?"

"Famously." Meagan did not want to add to the tense atmosphere. "Let's hurry, I'm starved."

Mr. Beardon was already seated when they came in. He rose and said curtly, "It's just us, young lady, sit anywhere. We don't stand on ceremony around here."

Dan held Meagan's chair, quite ceremoniously she thought. "I love your house, Mr. Beardon," she said politely.

"I don't care much for it myself. Would find something else if Lexington weren't getting so crowded. Dan, tell her this place used to be nice and quiet!"

"As the grave. I don't see much signs of this war, Dad. Have we picked a side yet?"

Mr. Beardon snorted. "There aren't signs because this war is nothing but an excuse for politicians and their friends to steal our property! And as far as what side I'm taking, I'm taking the side of plain common citizens against the damned military traipsing in and lifting our good bloodstock—*that's* my side!"

"I *know*, it's awful," Meagan said sympathetically. "We had trouble ourselves."

"It's outrageous!" Mr. Beardon's fist hit the table. "They see a fit, well-blooded horse and offer a pittance, telling me it's being recognized or whatever they say."

"Requisitioned, Dad. They took our horses, too."

"It's an outrage!"

"Did they take many?" Dan asked, concerned.

"About all of them, son," the elder gentleman growled. "Don't know which is worse, the North begging for my horses or the South demanding them. They cleaned out the county! It's enough to make a man take up arms in his old age! *Yes*, Kentucky has taken a side, which is to say *leave our horses alone* and we'll stay out! I've always said, young lady, and Dan will tell you—bluegrass doesn't look right without a horse on it. *That's* my Cause!"

"Which horses did they take, Dad?"

"Easier to say which they didn't! We sent a few we could to Canada—the army left me only two plow horses, our Cleveland carriage team and my Saddler, High Boy, and I had to pull favors just to keep *him*. The finest blood in the state and they wanted him to pull a damned army wagon! The military has *no* respect for decent life, I tell them myself!"

Sojourner entered with a plate of bread rolls, clucking at Mr. Beardon's raised voice. "You just hush now and eat something," she said gruffly. "All we hear lately is 'bout this war and your horses, and it's not fitting conversation for the table. It hurts the digestion."

Meagan took an offered roll from Sojourner. She was being careful to not wolf the excellent meal of greens, ham and potatoes, letting the others talk.

"Did they take the trotters, too?" Dan asked.

Mr. Beardon hesitated. "Yes, the trotters, too," he said finally.

"More horses!" Sojourner clucked, moving around the table. "The Lord in Heaven sees my burden. What *I* want to know is, how did you pick this woman, Daniel?"

"Off the ground," Dan said.

Meagan choked on her mouthful of greens.

Dan held up a glass, smiling. "And she was dropped from Heaven as far as I'm concerned."

Sojourner and Mr. Beardon exchanged a glance. Meagan gave Dan a furious look.

"She looks it. Dropped I mean," Sojourner sniffed. "Leastways, she did when she got here."

"We had a long trip," Dan replied testily. "And that will be enough, Sojourner." The woman resumed her duties, grumbling as she shuffled to the sideboard.

"Where *are* you from, young lady?" Mr. Beardon asked, not impolitely.

"California, sir. The southern part of the state. My father is a ... a farmer."

Sojourner and the elder Beardon exchanged another look as silence fell over the table. "California is the land of sin, as I hear it," Sojourner mumbled as she gathered plates. "All this *rush* for gold, they says. It ain't Christian."

"The meal was excellent, thank you." Meagan folded her napkin. She decided for propriety's sake against asking for seconds—and thirds. "Mr. Beardon, whenever you have a chance I would love to see your horses, the ones you have left. My mother was a horsewoman."

"Your *mother?*" Mr. Beardon chuckled. "Daniel, you take Miss Roberts around. I've got work to do."

"I've heard about the Walkers here," Meagan pressed. "I didn't know Kentucky had Walking horses, I've only heard about ones from Tennessee."

"Then you haven't seen a Walker at all, young lady!" Mr. Beardon leaned forward, brows knit. "And you say you know horses?"

"I plead ignorance about Walkers, sir," Meagan said quickly. "But I would love to be educated."

"Then you shall be!" Mr. Beardon pushed back his chair and rose. "Come along young Miss, and see what a horse from Kentucky looks like!"

Sojourner harrumphed loudly in annoyance and departed the room.

The faint smell of hay drifted through the airy stables. Mr. Beardon huffed down the deserted main aisle and proudly swung open a stall door as Dan haltered its occupant. *"This* is a Kentucky Saddler, young lady! Let your eyes feast."

With Dan leading him forward, a chestnut with a dark red mane and tail made a stately exit from his darkened stall. The last rays of the day's sun burnished the horse's coat. An honest sixteen-one hands high, the horse gave the impression of even greater height by his regal head carriage.

Meagan had never heard of the Kentucky Saddler. She knew about only two gaited breeds—Tennessee Walkers and Saddlebreds—which were high-stepping horses valued for their smooth and flashy way of going. Status symbols of their day, gaited horses were luxury transportation, bred to carry a rider in style. These horses possessed the three natural gaits—walk, trot and gallop—and two "man-made" ways of going. One artificial gait was called the *rack*, a free-stepping, circular pattern of footfalls. The rack was the optimum in rider comfort and, important for status, the distinctive movement was identifiable from a distance.

"His name is High Boy, out of High Tide by Boy Allegheny," Mr. Beardon narrated. "Has his mother's fine temper and his father's presence. Daniel remembers."

"He looks good, Dad. I had forgotten about High Tide's colt. He wasn't even green broke last time I saw him."

"Won the Lexington trophy and was second in the Louisville State Fair." He looked at Meagan triumphantly. "What do you think of your Tennessee Walker now?"

"This horse is *very* handsome, Mr. Beardon. I'm impressed!"

"Handsome? Ride him with a cup of tea in your hand and you'll never spill a drop! He'll go all day, too. You say your mother knows horses. Let's see what she taught you. Go ahead, try to fault him."

"Pardon me?"

"That's right. I'll stand him here in what's left of the light and let you find some fault in the horse ... if you can."

"No, really I can't, Mr. Beardon. I don't know proper Kentucky Saddler conformation."

"Good conformation is universal. Go ahead, I insist. Show us what California teaches its daughters."

She took a deep breath. "Okay ... well, he has a flat croup, but I suppose that is for action. Good slope to his shoulder."

The man frowned. "That's no fault, dear."

"I really don't—"

"Dan, I'm disappointed to see you chose a woman who doesn't know horses."

Meagan was stung by the slight. "Very well, sir. He's got straight pasterns," she said finally, and walked to the horse's side. "And he's thick in the throatlatch. His forehead is bowed." She ran a hand down a foreleg. "Some old splints on the inside cannon bone, too high to be forging." She caught the stiff expression on Mr. Beardon's face and quickly stepped back. "But there's nothing to fault on his topline, and I can't place anything off in his quarters. Absolutely perfect behind, where it counts." She stood close to the suddenly silent older man, examining. "How did you breed such a long shoulder with such a refined head?"

"His mother had the shoulder. There's thoroughbred blood back in her maternal grandmother's side." Then he glanced at Dan and chuckled. "Well, Miss Roberts has us dead to rights. I asked for it, didn't I, son?"

"You did, sir."

Mr. Beardon studied Meagan a moment. "I might like this woman. Here, let's put the horse up. I have something to show you."

Meagan and Dan followed Mr. Beardon on a short uphill walk to a huddled set of low-roofed dark buildings. The tobacco sheds were the last buildings on the farm to receive the failing light, and long shadows stretched down the bluegrass slope. Mr. Beardon pulled open a short door and ducked inside. "Come, get all the way in. I've got to shut the door before I light a lantern."

Meagan stepped inside expecting the musty smell of tar and dried tobacco, but was met with the living, clean scent of hay and manure. Nickers went up and down in the darkness. A lantern was lit, revealing a row of horse heads poking from makeshift pens lining the building's center.

"What is *this?*" Dan asked.

"My legacy and your inheritance, son. Some of us had words with the politicians we try to help now and again. I had to sell the Army some stock, but I hid the best right here."

Dan walked down the row and whistled. "How do you keep it secret?"

"It's not hard, son. I don't have many interested in my sheds. Everyone knows I can't cure a decent tobacco wad."

"Contraband on the hoof. Hey, these are trotters! I thought you said they were all sold."

Mr. Beardon hesitated. "Sorry, son," he said sheepishly, embarrassed. "I didn't want to make explanations just then."

"I see. Who is this?" Dan stopped before a stall which held a sleek, long-necked horse watching them nervously.

"Two-year-old, out of Dart."

"Oh, where is Dart?" Dan perked up, looking.

"Gone. I couldn't keep the ones people knew about, just the yearlings and two-year-olds."

"Sarsaparilla?"

"Gone."

"Lasso?"

"Gone. All sold north to Canadian breeders. Better than having them slaughtered in some field so a caterwauling bunch of politicians can profit—*aye!* No, son, I can't let myself."

"It's such a *waste*," Dan said under his breath. "Your connections couldn't save them?"

"War-fever is a strange affliction, son."

"You know, the Union cavalry confiscated our own horses—two of them."

"I'm owed a few favors," the elder Beardon said charitably. "Let me know where the horses are and I'll see what I can do."

"They went with Kirtland Foster's regiment, I don't know where exactly." Looking down the aisle, Dan ran his fingers through his hair. "I hate seeing our bloodstock like this. I can't believe the cavalry cleaned us out."

"It's happened all over the county," Mr. Beardon answered defensively. "Of course, you weren't here to make it any different, were you, son?"

A horse's refined head poked out of a stall, and Meagan rubbed the velvet-soft nostrils. "Who's this?" she asked, hoping to forestall an argument. "She's cute."

"Name's Marilu, out of Clementine by Abdullah. Remember Abdullah, son ... the Taylor's sire?"

"Never did much, as I remember."

"Three years is a long time away to say such things, Daniel. Abdullah sired some right croppers. Neighbors had a colt by him that almost broke two minutes in his maiden." Mr. Beardon looked slyly at Meagan. "If you like this filly, Miss, why don't you come see her? Tomorrow night me and some others are having a match race down at Siler's shed around midnight."

"Oh, I'd love to!"

"Why midnight?" Dan asked.

"That's what it's come to, Daniel. Honest men forced to gather by night to enjoy the good things in life."

———

Meagan could not remember a finer day. It had actually begun the night before with a long bath, featuring the ageless luxury of hot water. Meagan lounged until the water cooled, then rose and wrapped herself in an enormous clean towel that went around her twice. She actually felt feminine. The water she left behind was tea brown.

She had slept until mid-morning, and not from exhaustion but for the pure pleasure of it. Finally she had arisen to dress, and went downstairs to hear that Dan was still asleep.

Sojourner was predictably gruff in her greeting. She had bumped and clanged about the kitchen making Meagan a late breakfast, but in the end served up rich chicory coffee, thick bacon slabs, jam on fresh biscuits and eggs brown from the ham grease in which they were cooked. "Mr. Beardon says you're welcome to Lucille's clothes," the woman said disapprovingly. "I 'spect you'll find something that suits. Mr. Beardon says a carriage will be by for you and Daniel 'round about eleven o'clock tonight. I don't ask why and don't want to know."

"Could it be any louder down here?" Daniel complained grumpily, coming in with his hair sticking up on one side of his head. "Or was that artillery fire?"

"You just *shush,*" Sojourner snapped. "Decent folk don't come down at noon, neither. I swear you acted better when you was in diapers."

The day had continued with a wardrobe expansion. Dan's absent sister, Lucille, possessed an extra room for her clothing; Sojourner made it clear she was unhappy about opening it to a stranger. Looking down the rows of pegged racks, Meagan saw wire hoops in various sizes hanging along one wall. "I don't know, Sojourner ... maybe a light dress, something comfortable?"

"Miss Lucille don't have comfortable clothes."

Meagan pointed to a simple printed cotton dress. "How about *this* one?"

"That's nothing Miss *Lucille* would step out the door wearing."

In the end Meagan found a serviceable gray dress she could wear with small hoops, which hung attractively from her bodice to her feet. Meagan stood passively as Sojourner applied the bewildering layers of clothing: first the inner pantalets and chemise, then the restricting corset and its covering camisole, on to the petticoat and hoop skirt and *over* petticoats—two of those—and finally the blouse and skirt. The ensemble was topped with a matching bonnet and blue ribbon, and thus was Meagan transformed into a proper Southern belle, almost helplessly ensconced in fabric.

Dan had surprised her with a picnic, and they spent a lazy afternoon under a tree watching the remnants of a once-thriving breeding farm: three gangly foals bouncing around their grazing mothers; slender-legged hopes for the future. Together they had watched the sunset from a carriage and visited the hidden horses after dark, and finally came to eat and drink, arriving in the main dining room.

"I think the thing I missed *most* was your cooking, Sojo!" Dan grinned as he held up a forkful of fried cornmeal cake. "And don't Miss Roberts look *passing* nice in that dress?"

"Passing something," the woman grumbled. "Don't know about nice."

Meagan laughed.

"Don't know what you laughing at girl, 'cept maybe you're feeling your wine, I guess."

"Is it true you knew Dan when he was in diapers?"

"Did. He was a squirmy worm, yes he was. Didn't like wearing nothing—a jay bird's got more modesty. Never *did* listen. Don't be looking like that at *me*, Daniel Beardon. I whup the hide right off you and stuff it with goat straw, you look at me like that. There that girl goes, laughing again. Who-ee, you two are a pair."

A sound from outside had Dan on his feet. "Come on, Meagan. Love to reminiscence more, Sojourner, but we have to go."

"I don't know and I don't want to know," was the gruff reply. "Put my usual on Marilu."

A black carriage awaited them outside. Two bright lanterns hung in the front of the cab. Dan stepped aboard and turned to assist Meagan. Once she was up, the driver clucked to his horses and the coach moved into the night, gliding behind a team of shadows.

Dan sat close to Meagan. The night was warm and soft breezes flowed around them. As they rounded an embankment a blazing bonfire came into view, set inside many smaller lights sparkling from lanterns. The carriage pulled to a stop. "Call me Charon!" the driver called, taking a bottle from the floorboard for a swig before setting back into the night.

"Meagan, you *did* come!" Mr. Beardon emerged beaming from the shadows. "Capital! Daniel, meet some friends of mine."

A group stood talking in the firelight. Meagan could smell horses and hear their soft sounds, but only murky shapes could be seen in the darkness.

"Here, Blalock, you remember my son, Daniel."

"Ah! I heard he was back. Carol Metcamp's son, Arthur, brought him from Louisville. Said he hadn't fare to get home, and that he had some road wench along with him."

Meagan froze at the words.

"What did you say, Mr. Blalock?" Dan's hand tightened around Meagan's. "I should warn that you are standing before both *her* and my *father!*"

"Oh, I did not mean to offend. I was passing idle conversation."

"Idle enough for an early grave!"

"Daniel!" Mr. Beardon exclaimed.

"I think we can agree," Meagan said quickly, "Mr. Blalock's words lacked a certain tact, but please, Dan, let's enjoy the night. We came to see the horses, remember?" As shocked as she was by the insult, she did not like to see a fighting impulse in Dan. She had seen enough of violence to know it settled little and tended to escalate.

"Very well," said Mr. Blalock, holding up a glass. "To the horses."

Dan struck the glass from the man's hand; heads turned as it shattered on the ground.

"*Daniel!*" Meagan said hotly.

"Leave us be, Meagan. This is a man's business."

"Actually it's a fool's business, if we're splitting hairs."

"Go, Meagan." Dan turned, and even in the firelight Meagan could read danger in his face. She backed a step. His temper was unpleasantly reminding her of a certain arrogant chariot driver.

"Come, dear," said the elder Beardon quietly. "Let's go make our wagers."

Meagan looked archly at Dan before putting her hand on Mr. Beardon's arm. She prodded him forward. "Lead on."

Together they walked toward a ring of lanterns. Dark forms of horses and people stood within the light. "Pay no mind to Daniel," Mr. Beardon consoled her. "He is like all youth today, so brash and full of themselves. This war wasn't *all* the fault of old men. Now, Meagan, there she is—my Marilu! Tell me she isn't a beauty." Mr. Beardon reached up and proudly patted his horse. Even in the unsteady yellow light, Meagan could see the filly fidgeting like a darting minnow. A trim sulky was brought forward.

"I love the trotters," Mr. Beardon sighed. "Something is very civilized about them, like a good wine or fine music. I've got five on Marilu for Dan and myself. And Sojourner, she never misses a bet. Would you like the same?"

"I'm afraid I only have, well, let me see..."

"No, no, dear. It's my treat. Five?"

"Why yes, Mr. Beardon. I would like that, thank you."

"Very good. It so happens Marilu is trotting tonight because of *you*, my dear. I was deciding between her and a maiden filly, but you decided it for me. Oh, don't look at me that way. I am utterly superstitious. There is no other sensible way to place a bet on a horse."

"Where are they racing?"

"They start on the other side of the pasture—see the trail of lanterns? They follow that around and end up here." Mr. Beardon pointed to the swirling bonfire.

Marilu pranced as the poles of the sulkies were dropped over her and fastened. The lifeless contraption animated, quivering with energy. Handlers held the horses as the drivers mounted and took up the reins. One by one they passed before the fire, a montage of man, horse and machine gliding through the light.

"You see, young lady," Mr. Beardon explained, "the shaft angle has direct bearing on the load and speed at which a horse can pull it. Twelve degrees is optimal for a racing sulky. At that angle, a horse can generally pull about six times its own weight."

"So Marilu is about what, nine hundred pounds?"

"If that, the tight shape she's in. We keep the sulky as light as possible—*hello* son!" Mr. Beardon welcomed the approaching figure of Dan. "You're back in one piece, I see!"

"Yes. I think I straightened that out." He reached for Meagan's hand, but she moved away. "What's this about? Don't make a scene, Meggie."

"I don't intend to," she said coolly, "as long as you keep your hands to yourself."

"Not exactly the hero's welcome for saving your honor."

"My honor is in no need of saving, thank you. Except maybe the honor of being heard. Mr. Beardon, how will we know when the race begins?"

"Fine with me, Meggie, be like that!" Dan retorted. "Yes, Mr. Beardon. How *will* we know?"

"The judge will put his lantern up when he is ready to start. It will be out there, near the first light. They should be coming into position any time now. Watch close—Marilu is fast off the mark and she can stay the distance. Only trouble is, if she gets bumped too hard she loses heart. She's just a wee little thing." Mr. Beardon pointed to the path of yellow pinpoints leading to the bonfire. "The drivers follow the lanterns. It's not the horses that have trouble, of course. They see like it was midday."

"What exactly is the problem, Meagan?" Dan interrupted. "Was I supposed to let the remark go by?"

"Yes." She answered simply. "Mr. Beardon, who is driving Marilu, or did you say already?"

"One of my grooms, with hands soft as a kitten. My Marilu needs soft hands."

"Meagan, I am trying to talk to you."

"As I recall, it is none of my business," she told Dan briskly. "What could a woman say that possibly mattered?"

"Oh, stop. You just don't know how people can be."

"No I do, and that is why I asked you to stop. I don't need you to fight my battles, but I *do* need you to listen to me."

"I am the *man* here, you are to listen to *me.*"

Meagan turned to his father. "Mr. Beardon, is that the judges' lantern?"

"So it is."

She ignored Dan and strained to see the sulkies, but there were only dim shifting shadows. The crowd around her leaned, waiting. Then the judge's lantern swung, and cheers came from across the darkness.

The race's progress first showed only in the flickering of light as the horses passed the lanterns. Gradually the sounds of squeaking harnesses and clopping hooves grew as the shadowy image of a many-headed beast spilled into view, spinning wheels and flying legs flashing in graceful syncopation. The field swung toward the bonfire and into the homestretch. The sound of pattering hoofs swept past like a hard rain. The crowd's voice rose with the final drive, reached its peak and fell away.

"Too close!" Mr. Beardon called, squinting. "Needs a sharper eye than mine to call the winner!"

"Then we're in trouble, leaving it to Judge Harbor."

"What do you mean by that, son?"

Dan shrugged. "Nothing. You yourself say Harbor is as straight as a grapevine and righteous as an alley cat."

"I never did! The Judge is an old friend!"

"He wasn't when I left ... or have you already paid to make sure Harbor sees it 'correctly?' In that case, let me collect my winnings now."

"That's some accusation—you know, son, you've never understood how the world works."

"Oh I do, I just don't think it's how it *should* work. I almost choked to hear what 'honest' folks your friends are."

"Excuse me," Meagan said, leaving the arguing men and walking into the darkness to wait for the carriage.

"You can't live in the real world! Your failing is..." were the last words Meagan heard before leaving.

Four things greater than all things are:
Women and Horses and Power and War.

- Rudyard Kipling (1865-1936)

"Stand still, child. My old eyes ain't good enough to keep up with your squirming."

Meagan tried not to flinch, but Sojourner had stuck her with so many pins she could hardly keep from it. Her formal dress was beginning to take shape, literally. She thought it a strange custom to come to a party in one dress and change into another, but it was expected.

She had enlisted Sojourner's help by asking for it at the breakfast table in front of Mr. Beardon: a cheap ploy recognized as such by both herself and Sojourner. It was necessary, however, for Mr. Beardon had made the party an obligatory event and insisted on Meagan's presence. Lucille's ball dresses were a bewilderment of hoops, bows, wraps and ties. Meagan could only imagine what she would emerge wearing if she had to guess.

Already Meagan had learned one truism: never, *ever* incense the person lacing up one's corset. From Sojourner's first determined tug Meagan felt her innards squish into unlikely new forms. She finally straightened, blinking and gasping in a mildly dissociative state, believing the famous delicacy of Southern belles might be explained by the cessation of circulation. And now, the pins.

"I said stand *still*, girl!"

"I'm trying to keep from getting blood everywhere."

"Oh this child, dear Lord! Job had never the trials she gives me."

"*Ow*, Sojourner! Can't you tell the difference between me and the *cloth?*"

"I could swear it's like you never wore a proper dress before." Sojourner paused. Meagan held her gaze calmly. "Oh, *child*. You are good."

"You are doing a wonderful job, Sojourner. Let's keep going."

"If I walked myself out of here, you'd be up the creek, wouldn't you, child?"

"I would take that big bow right there and slap it around my middle and walk downstairs in it. Just like I am. And Dan would think it was funny, so don't give me any ideas."

Sojourner stared for a moment. Meagan could see her struggling to keep from smiling. "Oh, you would too. I can see it."

"So you see, the Beardon honor is at stake."

"It is at that." Sojourner clucked. "You two are quite a pair, Miss Meagan, I will say." Sudden tears welled in the woman's eyes.

Meagan's irritation melted with them. "I'm sorry, Sojourner, I don't mean to be difficult. I really am trying."

The woman shushed her, and rummaged among the ribbons. "I know you are, child. I am just thinking about my Daniel. The Good Lord knows how precious that boy is to me. His daddy was so hard on him, and I always hoped he'd find his happiness 'round the bend."

"I hope to take as good care of Daniel as you'd want me to, Sojourner." Meagan smiled kindly. "I brought him home, didn't I?"

"Yes. Yes, you did." Something seemed to let go within her strong constitution, and dark streaks ran down the woman's cheeks, instant rivers. "Land o' Goshen, if you two aren't in conspiracy to make me a leaky old woman in my golden years. *Shame* on you!" Sojourner shuffled back to Meagan. "Let me play you out an inch, Miss Meagan, you looking a little bug-eyed. Just shame on you *both!*" The woman set to

work on the back of Meagan's garment. As the pressure released, Meagan could imagine the hissing of a deflating tire.

"*Thank* you, Sojourner." She breathed a moment for the
pleasure of it.

"Maybe there weren't anyplace around here to sow oats as
wild as my Daniel had to sow. I say the Lord knows what
He's doing." Sojourner's rare smile lit Meagan's world with
the promise of peace. She was not yet in the fiercely loyal
woman's inner circle, but was now a candidate.

"I hope so, Sojourner." Meagan held up her arms for the final phase. The woman's strong hands carefully pulled a silk
garment over Meagan's head and down over her waist so it
spread across the hoops. The finished ensemble radiated light
blue in all directions, with a contrasting royal-blue bodice
above. "Please, could you give me the brush and those velvet
ribbons? I can't get within reach of anything." Sojourner
wordlessly handed them over, and Meagan wound the ribbon into her own hair, deftly making long braids on each side
of her head. With the ribbon ends hanging down, she pulled
the rest of her hair back and into a tight bun.

"What is that you're doing, child?" Sojourner asked, be-
mused.

"Just trying something. Please bring some pins and hold
these braids up. Higher, please. There." Meagan pinned her
free hair into place, then gathered the lowest braids and
wound them in loops, crossing them into the 'X' hairstyle she
remembered from Versailles. Pulling the remaining braids
tightly around the base, she asked for the mirror and held it
before her. The result was not as symmetrical as a salon hair-
dresser would have made, but enough to be suitable.

Sojourner made a low whistling sound. "I've never seen
that before."

"Do you like it?"

"Can't say I don't, 'cept I can't remember when I seen a
woman's hair fancier than her dress. No, child, I believe it
looks right pretty. Now, let me finish up the back and show

you how to walk around without knocking over peoples and furniture. Stand *still*."

Meagan had not wanted to attend the formal party, but Mr. Beardon had been so insistent—and Dan so persistently sweet and apologetic—that she finally agreed. She was learning that Dan's soft side could make her agree to anything, although that was something she would admit only to herself. Breathing deeply and listening to the sounds of the gathering crowd below, she almost wished she had not said yes. The murmuring conversations below sounded like a bubbling shark tank.

I have been in worse places before, she told herself. But this was different, this time it *truly* mattered. Besides Dan, she loved Kentucky and the people, and for the first time in her travels she felt she really belonged. She was actually thinking of staying to become Mrs. Daniel Beardon. The very sound stirred excitement in her, as if she'd heard the name before—was she excited, or afraid?

A liveried attendant came to the door. "Miss Roberts, the others are assembling for the entrance."

Meagan turned to thank Sojourner with a nervous knot in her stomach. She felt like a suited astronaut in her hoop skirts and rustling undergarments. Music stopped as the women filed to the top of the staircase to descend to the party as they were announced. Meagan followed the others down the dark hallway corridor, and suddenly she was next, alone in the light at the top of the stairs. Hoop dresses below were blossoms in a garden of black and silver appointments.

"Introducing Miss Meagan Roberts of California, guest of Daniel Beardon."

Meagan realized that she could not see the stairs, and there was no way to reach the handrail past her skirts. Gritting her teeth, she stepped off into space. Every step was an act of faith. She felt the stairs one by one, nearly missing several. She resisted the urge to jump when she got close to the bottom, but made herself step confidently until she joined the dark suits and brilliantly-colored dresses below.

Dan stepped forward and held out his arm. *"Meagan.* You look fit!"

"Dan. Women want to be beautiful, not *fit."*

"I wasn't finished."

"Daniel! I've been looking everywhere. This must be your new friend!" A stately woman with peacock feathers streaming from her headdress beamed at Meagan. "My, but you are lovely, dear—a *vision!* I'm Claire Meriwether. I've heard so much about you from Daniel's father! We had a late foaling and I missed the Jamboree, so it's wonderful to finally meet!"

Dan gripped Meagan's hand as the woman drifted off. "She's an old friend and a true horsewoman," he whispered. "Her late husband raised some of the finest Walkers in Lexington until the South helped themselves for The Cause. Put her right out of business, and now she has only a few carriage horses. She had to sell her home and rents her own former guest house."

Meagan walked with Daniel through the crowd. For all the disaster to come, she thought the guests were remarkably unconcerned about war. Only the slightest signs of deprivations due to the conflict were visible: wildflowers were featured rather than imports, wine was served only on request, and the ice was carefully tended.

They walked into a large portrait gallery with a piano, where a woman in a long violet gown was playing to a circle of men.

"I'll get our drinks," Dan whispered, excusing himself.

What struck Meagan most about the hanging portraits was that they were all of horses. Nondescript jockeys or drivers were optionally painted in, or not. Small plaques hung below each, and Meagan walked closer to read one.

"Fleet Circus!" toasted a portly gentleman coming to stand underneath the picture. "Big winner in Eastern contests, bred right here in Lexington."

"Oh? I can't read the year..."

"1848. A good year for horses, and whiskey too. What is your name, young lady?"

"Meagan Roberts, sir, and yours?"

"Kyle Blakey, at your service."

"Hello, Mr. Blakey," Dan interrupted politely, drinks in hand. He was accompanied by a freshly starched Arthur Metcamp, the young man who had given them a buggy ride from Louisville.

"Hello, Miss Roberts," Arthur said warmly.

"Why hello, Arthur! You look *well*. How is your mother?"

"Mother is not feeling well. I think we will be leaving early."

"I am so sorry. You know, Daniel has been pressing me to arrange a time for us to visit." Meagan avoided Dan's pained expression. "Perhaps an afternoon next week?"

"I will ask Mother."

"Please do."

"Everyone, here's to our young Daniel Beardon!" Kyle Blakey toasted. "The wanderer doth return!"

Dan took Meagan's hand. "Mr. Blakey, I would like you to meet my friend, Meagan Roberts. She is visiting from California."

"You don't say! Good work, my boy. I wouldn't leave her alone if I were you." Kyle Blakey gestured to two ladies passing. "Vera, Christina, come and see our young man all grown up!"

"Daniel *Beardon* ... my, you *have* grown!"

"How have you been, Mrs. Wheeler, Mrs. Brody?"

"Never mind us, you must have *tales*."

"I would like you to meet Miss Roberts. Meagan, these are two of my mother's dearest friends."

"Christina, just look at her—Miss Roberts, just look at you! I saw you coming down and I was struck, simply *struck!* I love that dress ... it is Lucille's, isn't it?"

"*Vera!*" the second woman exclaimed. "Hush now, she will think us catty." She took Meagan aside. "Dear, your hairstyle is all the talk. Is it new from Paris? Please, I *must* know!"

"Thank you, it is a French style, yes."

"I knew it! It is stunning. The very latest fashion, I suppose?" The woman beamed. "And, oh Heavens, I've heard you love horses! You will *adore* Lexington, dear."

"Yes ma'am, I think I will."

"Daniel's mother will be *so* excited to meet you when she returns. You will love her, Meagan, simply love her. You *must* visit, both of you."

"Meagan, there you are!" The crowd parted to let the elder Beardon pass. "Daniel took you away before I could come over. Excuse me son, let me borrow Miss Roberts for a moment."

Meagan was pulled toward a group of men circling the piano. "I have some old friends for you to meet," Mr. Beardon confided. "Daniel would never introduce them—he doesn't approve—but they will adore you. I'm afraid Daniel has always been rather difficult when it comes to my associates." He squeezed her hand. "It's hard, my dear, having your boy leave and come back a man. I hope you will make allowances for my behavior."

A soldier in a crisp blue uniform stepped in front of them. "Beardon, you rascal. Who are you gallivanting with, now the missus is safely overseas?"

"Now watch what you're saying about my son's delightful lady friend!"

"Pardon me, ma'am," the soldier bowed. "I meant no disrespect."

"This is Frank Dalley, Meagan, a colonel in a visiting Union regiment. Since this is a party, we have to call them 'Confederates' or the 'Union.'" The names I usually say would be unfitting for a social occasion."

Meagan allowed her hand to be taken and kissed, and tried not to smile at the seriousness. "Pleased to meet you."

"Colonel Dally, *why* haven't you gotten the Confederates out of Kentucky?" Mr. Beardon thundered. "Now I hear they've taken to raiding! Plundering, that's all it is!"

"Southern rabble. We'll fix them." The officer bowed humbly to Meagan. "Don't worry your pretty head about *that*, young lady."

"Which side is going to win, Colonel?" demanded Mr. Beardon. "That's what I want to know!" Conversation in the vicinity stopped.

"Why the Union, of course, sir."

"Balderdash! I ask a Confederate and they swear it's the South."

"Maybe we could ask an impartial jury," answered the Colonel. He smiled at Meagan. "Perhaps our lovely belle has an opinion ... ?"

The conversation paused as Meagan hesitated before the expectant faces. The moment seemed suddenly filled with import. *Could she possibly save bloodshed and destruction ... could this even be the purpose for her travels?* She took a steadying breath and said politely. "I can only be honest, gentlemen. I believe victory belongs to those who *don't* fight." The faces around her flinched as if stung. She hurried to explain: "In my experience, the greatness of a civilization is measured by its restraint from war, not its fighting of it."

The response quickly doused her hopes. A few guests smiled politely, but most looked as if seeing a virulent pox; a weakening agent. Conversation hurried to mend the tear in accepted decorum.

"Oh, you speak from *experience*, young lady. Do say."

"Pretty heads seldom make sense."

"*Women.* If the world was only so simple."

Meagan felt chastened to have thought she might temper a force so ancient and irresistible as war fever as it raged.

The Colonel was magnanimous. "Speaking of fighting, General Foster's regiment is camped out with his whole cavalry in Powell County, three days from here in Bakerstown. He should put an end to the raiding for you."

"Excuse me, sir," Meagan asked quickly. "Did you say General Foster? Is that Kirtland Foster, by any chance?"

"Yes, ma'am. New Jersey regiment, just back from Indian fighting out west. Do you know the General?"

"Oh, slightly. He has some horses of ours."

"That's a shame, ma'am. They are fixing to throw the whole division into a grinder..."

The conversation continued but Meagan heard nothing more. If the Great Horse was killed ... *how could she ever see home again?* She looked at Dan, who was watching her across the room, smiling. He came up and took her hand. She could hardly say it, but Kirtland Foster's regiment was three days away and now everything was different.

Crickets played loudly from all sides as Meagan rocked. She was huddled in a cane-back chair, wrapped in a bed blanket. The party had been a long succession of names and faces, but the night had gone wonderfully and she had been welcomed as a kindred spirit. Women vowed to copy her Versailles hairstyle at the big Derby race being held in Louisville next spring.

She hugged her knees tighter. The Great Horse was three days to the east, and now she felt empty, a ghost, again a woman without a home. Irrationally she *knew* she wanted to be with Dan, but she was not ready to let go of her family. She told herself she didn't have to choose: if she brought Red back to Lexington, she could let the Great Horse decide.

There was a gentle knock on her door. "Meggie?" Dan cracked the door. "Your light was on."

"Come in." She watched as he entered.

"Are you crying?" He knelt beside the chair and brushed back her hair. "What's wrong? Did someone say something at the party?"

Meagan put her head against his shoulder. "No, and please don't go off shooting anybody."

"About that, Meggie. I'm sorry about the other night. I should have listened to you. Yes, we men are beasts. It's how the world is, I guess."

"Please don't say that, Dan. The world is not only one thing." He surprised her by only gritting his teeth and falling silent. "I'm sorry too, Dan. I know you were trying to defend my honor, but I've seen..." She pushed specific remembrances away. "I've seen enough fighting, that's all. I don't suppose you could have known that."

"I'm finding I don't know a lot of things, Meggie." Dan was quieter as he spoke. "Meeting you is something different I never knew before. So remind me of that and I'll listen to you. It's possible there's something else I don't know, I guess. Unlikely as it seems."

"That was nice, thank you, Dan." She straightened and looked at him seriously. "The other thing is about our horses. Their cavalry thing or whatever is in Kentucky. Bakerstown they said."

"Yes, I heard. Out by Middle Creek. But that doesn't mean they still have our horses, or that we *could* get them back even if they did. Do you know where Bakerstown is?"

"No, but..." She hesitated. "I *have* to find Red."

"Meggie, listen. This is our home now. Those horses are gone. I hate it too, but that's how it is."

"They're not gone." She swallowed, suddenly scared. "They can't be. That couldn't happen yet."

Dan took a long breath. "Maybe I should stop talking a minute." He leaned closer and kissed her hair gently. For a long time they were quiet, listening to the crickets. "There's something I always liked about the West," he said finally, softly. "You could always get a horse if you had to. It's called 'walking down a mustang.'

"Nothing to it, if you have the time. Horses are careful about watering places, so if you follow he gets too jumpy to drink. At first the horse gallops off, tail up and making fun of you. You just follow his tracks. The first three days are hardest, when you try not to lose him. By the fourth day, the horse's head is down but you just keep walking, following him. By the sixth day, the mustang's so thirsty he can't stand it, and when he comes to water you finally let him drink his fill. A horse will overdo, naturally, and then he's done for, so sluggish and sleepy you can just go on up and lasso him easy."

"You did that? I'm impressed, Dan."

"No, I got to the third day and drank too much at a stream myself, and lay there sick the rest of the day, on my back looking up at the sun."

Meagan laughed. "Why are you telling me this?"

"No reason. I think I just like reminding myself I was somewhere else once. Did something different. All this talk about trotters and politics ... it's like I never left."

"I used to try to forget about home so I wouldn't miss it so much. Now I try to remember."

"Do you want to go home, Meggie?" When she only looked down, he added quietly, "time goes fast, doesn't it? It sort of creeps by every day, and then..."

"I know." Meagan reached out and touched his hand softly. "We are a lot alike, Dan. Maybe you hate to hear it."

"Yeah. No one can tell me anything either." He chuckled. "I was on my way to being nice and disreputable when you showed up. Now I'm stuck here, farm and all." He grasped her hand firmly. "And I would, I *would* like you to be a part of it."

Meagan looked away.

Dan said quietly, "It's alright, Meggie. Tell me."

"I ... don't know if I can."

"Well I do, Meggie." Dan squeezed her hand. "We'll be okay. Maybe you're just nervous like me, and have never been asked? "

"Once..." She remembered Horace's poetic proposal on the steps to the Emperor's platform. On the steps to disaster. She gripped his hand back. "I just don't know how much time we would have."

"Heck, Meggie, none of us know that. For however long it is, I want to be with you. I've been crazy about you since I set eyes on ... well, no." He looked down. "That would be telling one. Fact is you were damn aggravating. I guess it was fall in love or bust."

"That's very sweet."

"But that was the old Dan and now it's the new Daniel. Respectable farmer and gentleman, friend to all and a studious foe. All that. I want the normal life now, like I never did before."

"Me, too," she said softly. "I always have."

"So say yes. And we will go get the horses. Heck, Red is special, so maybe it will work out."

She turned to him. "What do you mean, Red is 'special?'"

"Oh, Red is one-of-a-kind. You know, he once gave *me* the eye before he did you."

"The 'eye'?"

"Sure. Red ran off and found you, so I guess he chose. I had every fortune-teller from Sacramento to Texas tell me that horse was Luck itself. Yeah, *hard* luck ... never won a hand again. Though, come to think, I *did* quit drinking and playing cards once I was stony broke and had to stop." He grinned. "That there's a damn miracle."

"Do you mean," she asked slowly, "that you *know* Red is a Great Horse?"

"Sure he is, don't you think so?"

Meagan looked at him curiously. "I do. I didn't know you did."

"I mean, I don't hold much truck with fortune-tellers and superstition. Folks have a hard enough time associating me with the Temperance Movement as it is. I figure horses are special—Red's just a little more so, I guess. 'Course I think Blue's pretty special, too."

"You were selling Red, though."

"Now that was a desperate act by a desperate man. I needed my card luck back somehow, or thought I did, and I wasn't much but a pain and irritant to the horse anyway."

"So you know about the legend?"

"The legend of the drunk cowboy who fell off his horse?"

She smiled. She still could not tell if Dan was serious. "No, the legend of the Great Horse."

"See, this is just the kind of moonshine talk that starts a person to thinking about plucking horses out of cavalry in the middle of a war. Oh but you're going to go anyway, Meggie, I have no doubt. It's daft—but I sure wouldn't mind seeing the boys again." He frowned in the dim lamplight. "If it is that important to you, we'll go together."

———

Long after Dan had gone to his room, Meagan remained staring at the starry night sky. Her heart was torn; she was discovering the serious meaning of love-sick. Love and logic seemed to be enemies.

As romantic as it sounded, she did not believe the purpose of her journey was to live in Civil War Kentucky. She questioned how she would accept living in the 19th Century. The incident of Dan's recent altercation caused her worry. She knew he was only defending her "honor" as he saw it: that was how men of his day behaved. Yet this willful world and these people were shortly to face the downside of the glorification of force, and not just the horrors of brutality and death, but also disease, hunger, poverty and degradation. *How would it affect her and Dan?* Again love and logic, if not enemies, seemed at best estranged friends.

She made her decision before dawn. She would say yes to Dan. That was the answer in her heart, and he would never understand her refusal. As for going home, she would try to find Red and then let the Great Horse decide.

Slowly she got up from the rocking chair. Methodically lighting a lantern, she folded her blanket and sat before the mirror. As soon as her eyes were no longer red, she would go to Dan. Every moment she could spend with him was precious.

I know Kilpatrick is one hell of a damned fool,
but I want just that sort of man to command my cavalry.
- General William T. Sherman (1820-91)

THE CLAPBOARD BUILDING'S fading sign read: *Bank of Bakerstown*. The tiny town had the misfortune to be accessible to both Northern and Southern armies: it would pay with its existence. Now the abandoned bank housed foreign correspondents and other reporters of the war effort. As Kentucky residents—a still undecided and neutral state—Meagan and Dan were allowed to join the journalists. They were near a place known by the indeterminate name of "Middle Creek."

"Pile your stuff in the corner!" a cigar-smoking man called out conversationally as they entered, throwing a playing card on a barrel top. "Nobody will take nothing, we're all friends here!"

"Y'all from Appalachia?" asked another, looking Meagan up and down. "There's a woman came yesterday down from the mountains, spitting tobacco and looking to join up. Said her husband lit South at first sign of war and she's aiming to find him. Said she could shoot better'n he could anyhow."

"We're from here in Kentucky," Dan said, flinging down his bedroll. "And my wife doesn't spit tobacco, except maybe on Sundays."

"Good Ol' Kentuck!" The speaker squinted. "Say, why you here anyway? You don't have to join up. Kentucky ain't made up its mind if it's Yank or Johnny Reb."

Dan replied with the easy familiarity of a complete stranger. "We're here to find a couple horses that were requisitioned by the cavalry. This was as close as they'd let us get to the camp."

"Well you're almost atop it. Did you say you're looking for a horse in the cavalry? That'll be a trick. Cavalry goes through horses like a cow through cabbage."

Dan possessed a letter from the Mayor of Lexington, his father's friend, requesting the return of the two horses. It was an unusual document, but topical. The war was deepening, and the Union needed Kentucky's allegiance, or at least neutrality: the military had become very careful about taking horses from Kentuckians.

Of course it would have been pure scandal for Meagan and Dan to travel together unchaperoned before their marriage. Arriving from parts unknown was one thing, but it was entirely another to traipse off together, unmarried, with half of Fayette County watching and gossiping.

The marriage had been a brief ceremony with only Dan's beaming father and a few smiling friends, and Sojourner with her "waterworks" in full operation. The simple gold band still felt strange on Meagan's finger; it had been Daniel's grandmother's ring. Stranger still was the feeling of the cold derringer Dan had given her that was now strapped to her thigh.

"Don't get too comfortable," a red-faced journalist announced as he entered the room. "McGallister's spies just alerted our division. Southern militia's coming up from Chattanooga." Cardplayers jumped to their feet. There was a general scrambling for gear.

"Where you all headed?" Dan asked a man furiously tucking paper into a satchel. "Running away or running to see?"

"To the Overlook to watch the battle. Come on if you want to see it." Meagan nodded tightly to Dan. He clenched his jaw but agreed.

The edge of the ruined town ended in wooded forest. Dan and Meagan followed the journalists down well-stamped earth paths. They passed soldiers crouching on the ground, soldiers in trees, soldiers sitting on cold cannons with blank faces. They came abruptly upon the main force of the Foster regiment, stationed in underbrush of the woods above a wide, cleared field. Crowded together, visible in the dappled sun under the trees, stood rank upon rank of mounted cavalry.

"Dan, look!" Meagan pointed to the shadowy rows of horses. Beyond, journalists were hustling toward canvas tents pitched on a bluff over the open field. Someone tugged gently at her sleeve. She turned to see a familiar boy looking shyly down at his oversized boots.

"Hello, ma'am."

"How *are* you! Why ... how did you get here?"

"Chrissy and me came out with the regiment. We do courier duties, ma'am."

Dan looked him up and down. "Well, boy, what happened to the Pony Express?"

"I cleared out when I heard about Foster's regiment heading East and looking for riders. Cuddy Burke and I joined together." The boy looked over his shoulder. The hair visible below his tight cap was short, his face scrubbed and clean. "I seen your old horses, ma'am."

"You did—where are they?"

Pointing, the boy squinted. "I seen the buckskin, leastways. I thought of you, ma'am, when I saw him. I never forget a horse ... or a lady."

Dan grimaced. "Okay, youngster, enough of the butter. She's married now. To me."

"Did you at least give her the horse free and clear?" the boy asked defiantly. It was Dan's turn to look sheepish.

Meagan put her hand in her husband's and smiled at the young man. "How was the horse?"

"He looks good, ma'am. Fighting's not started, so we ain't been in anything yet. Had a cadet catch a squirrel pellet in his leg is all—"

"Can you take me to the buckskin?" she asked impulsively.

"*Sure* I can!" The enthusiastic boy started to detour toward the cavalry, but Dan caught her arm.

"Look over there, Meagan." He pointed to the opposite side of the pasture, where a glinting creek ran among a thin patch of trees. Soldiers in gray were entering the creek and filtering into the cover, calmly, steadily. "Rebs."

"We could find him quickly, before the fight. Red is a buckskin, Dan. He'll stand out." She tried to pull away. "Please, I just want him to know I'm here."

"Now damn it, Meagan, *think.* There's a battle coming, and this whole place is fixing to be a firing range. No Beardon has ever hit a woman, but I swear I'm getting you up to that tent conscious or not."

"That's okay, ma'am!" the boy called, backing away. "I'll do it. I can find him. He's near the front. I'll wave." With that, his oversized boots were running.

Dan shook his head. "You have to wonder about this war." He gripped Meagan's hand and led her behind the cavalry units and up the other side of the hill. They emerged to look out over the cleared area. Journalists jostled for places to sit. A few stationed themselves further down the hill.

"Can we go down there?" she asked, pointing to the journalists perched below on the hillside.

"You're bound and determined to get us killed, aren't you? This spot is supposed to be out of gunfire range, and I hate betting on that anyhow. We'll stay right here."

From the high vantage point, Meagan could see sprawling lines of soldiers behind the creek, facing across the field to woods filled with horses and blue uniforms. She scanned the edges of the forest for a glimpse of buckskin and caught her breath at one tan splash amidst the shades of brown and bay colors. A small figure waved, a boy, standing next to a buckskin that could easily have been Red. Meagan waved back—was it her imagination, or did the buckskin lift his head?

"Cappy Beardon! Well, I do say! How you been, boy?"

Meagan watched Dan turn and clasp hands with a whiskered man behind him.

"It's good to see you! How long's it been?"

"What, since that wild day at Spring Fair, the very least. What the hell you doing *here,* Cappy?"

"My wife's idea of a honeymoon."

A picture suddenly came into Meagan's mind, of a photograph she had seen under glass in Mrs. Bridgestone's den. It was of a leathery old cavalryman ... standing beside a decrepit horse named Pumpkin: the caretaker who supposedly taught Mrs. Bridgestone to ride. Cappy Beardon, whose letter from Chief Joseph spoke of the legend and led Mrs. Bridgestone to find the Great Horse.

Pricks of cold crawled up Meagan's back and raised the hair on her scalp. "Dan," she asked quietly after his acquaintance left, "why did he call you Cappy?"

"Cappy? That was my nickname at Transy. I used to wear a little red cap to the dances. Anything to stand out. There was another fellow wore a yel—"

A cannon fired below, a short boom and long whistle. The forest erupted in flashes and recoiling muzzles. Smoke drifted up in great sheets. Dan pulled her down and held her as she struggled to see over the ridge. "Let's go back a ways, Meggie."

"No, I have to make sure Red can see me. I want him to know where I am."

"Meggie, if he's—"

"Dan, do you remember the legend I told you about?"

"No."

"Dan, *please.*"

A raft of trees ignited into sparks over Foster's regiment as the Confederates returned fire. Flaming branches fell into infantry as more cannon roared.

"I'm taking you back!" Dan called above the chaos.

"No! You said we were safe here."

"I didn't think they'd start up yet. Hell, the Rebs must be crazy. They're not even in place!"

The forest was becoming a confusion of flame, horses and men. The Confederates were aiming for the timber with incendiary grapeshot. A bugle blew crazily as trees burst into red embers. Horses were sweeping out of the trees onto the field like edges of the fire out of control behind them.

"Meggie, you've got to listen, *please* move back! We'll look for Red when it's done. We'll find him."

They saw it together.

The rider at the head of the charge could have been on any horse, any lanky dark sorrel—any horse, except that this one ran with his head up like a deer. Both Dan and Meagan knew it was Blue. Gunshots exploded from the creek's side. Horses plunged into the earth, somersaulted, collapsed, slid onto their shoulders. Dan held Meagan tightly, tighter as Blue's front legs folded and his neck twisted under his body. The rider was flung into the air, coming down and rolling, up and running, leaving Blue kicking behind him in slowing spasms.

The Great Horse comes to men once more...

It was just like before ... time began to slow. The bugle went on and on, calling for more blood and effort and madness as horses continued to stream out of the trees, now leaping and stumbling over the fallen. Meagan pressed herself to Dan's chest, sobbing. Time was beginning to shudder.

The Great Horse takes a mighty leap...

"It's Red, Meggie. He's—" Dan's voice cracked as he held her head tightly. "Stay down."

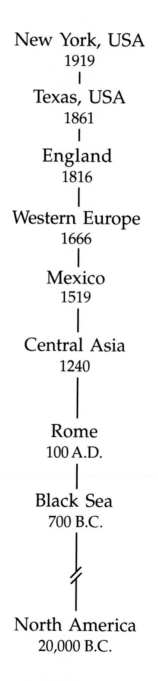

New York, USA
1919

Texas, USA
1861

England
1816

Western Europe
1666

Mexico
1519

Central Asia
1240

Rome
100 A.D.

Black Sea
700 B.C.

North America
20,000 B.C.

Birthright of Eagles

"YOU STOP SNORTING at that nice woman, Red! She ain't got time to be messing with your foolishness."

Red! Meagan opened her eyes to see an imposing chestnut horse standing before her, nostrils wide. The horse was a stallion, thick-boned and blocky.

"I'm sorry, ma'am. You have to excuse ol' Red. He don't mean nothing." A heavyset black man, well-dressed in a striped vest and suspenders, stood next to the strapping, ungainly horse. He gave the stallion's lead a mild tug. "Now see there, Red, you've gone and disturbed the nice lady."

Meagan felt her hair and smoothed her dress automatically, trying to become accustomed to the sudden quiet. She was sitting on a bench between long, neat stable rows. Tight-waisted racehorses were being led through the aisles with tense and ready steps. The smells were of popcorn, tar and hay. Not sweat. Not gun smoke.

"It's not like Red to warm up to folks like that, not like him at all." The man reached up and gave the horse an affectionate rub along his withers. "You doing all right, ma'am?" he asked gently.

Meagan wanted to reassure the groom that she was fine, but the words would not come. She bowed her head and closed her eyes again. She knew it would happen—she had been prepared. It was still a shock to lose him. And poor Red ... poor Blue. A quick, dark wish came to her that she had remained with Dan in Lexington and never pursued Red.

"I see we best leave you alone ... but, young lady, this ain't a good place, just now. People's coming from all around for the big race."

A loudspeaker blared incomprehensibly in the background. Meagan made herself look at the groom and the horse, trying to see them and not burning trees and smoke and dying men and horses.

Colorful in their silks, oblivious to her reality, jockeys strutted amongst the horses. She watched as if it were a costumed play, or something behind glass. It was, wasn't it? Cannons had shattered her world, and this was all ridiculous pantomime.

"*Where* is Loftus? I'd like that monkey to be on time for once." A man in a tan suit walked past, acknowledging neither horse nor human as he ranted. He fished in his coat pocket for a large gold watch and snapped it open. "It's not enough to keep me waiting, now he has the damn *stewards* waiting and you know how *they* are!"

"Ain't seen him, Mr. Riddle," said the groom holding the stallion.

"Yeah, I know you ain't. Never do. And here comes another reporter! We're sitting ducks, standing here waiting like this. Lord, I need a drink. Who the hell's idea was Prohibition anyway?"

"We argued about that didn't we, Mr. Riddle? 'Keeps the men out of the bottle and at work' is what *you* said."

"Yes, Will. I had forgotten since the last time you reminded me."

Meagan saw a thin-faced journalist approaching. He held a small notebook high. "Mr. Riddle, can I have a word?"

"Free country." Riddle absent-mindedly removed a comb from his pocket and ran it through his oiled hair. "Make it fast. We're about to go to the paddock."

"Still using Johnny Loftus? Even after the big story the *Post* ran?"

"Of course I am. He's a good jockey and he's done all right by me. It'll be the day you boys tell me how to race my own horse. Next question."

"Have you any fears about going a mile and a half? Your horse is only two."

"No, I haven't any fears. My colt is the best two-year-old in the country. Next question."

"Well, Mr. Riddle, some say Jim Rowe has the best crop of horses he's ever had, and your horse is just taking all the press."

"I prefer to let my horse do the talking. So I guess that means I've got nothing more to say. Thank you." Riddle motioned to the chestnut's groom to move the horse forward, and followed them down the stable row.

The crowd's buzz seeped around Meagan, insinuating itself into her consciousness. A new, once-familiar feeling came over Meagan: gray depression. Band music played in the distance. At the end of the stable aisle a slice of race track was visible: dark, smooth dirt below a white rail, and beyond was the infield's inviting green—but Meagan did not want the invitation. If she remained very still, perhaps she could go back, like when she sometimes awoke from a dream but held on to it, keeping the waking world at bay.

"Hey *tomato*, snap out of it. This here's a closed party!"

Meagan looked up to see a thick-necked man whose shirt-tail was untucked on one side, leaving one half to curtain his frayed and faded pants.

"You leave that woman be!" the chestnut stallion's groom called from the end of the row. "She ain't bothren you or nobody else."

The chestnut stallion was coming down the stable row again, circling. The regal animal seemed to be accompanied, not led. Handlers scurried around him, but the horse paid them no heed—when he stepped, they moved aside.

Then the stallion raised his head, and Meagan felt the horse's eyes upon her, soft and solemn. The eyes woke her into this world: into the fact that she was alone again, and there should be tears.

Meagan stood slowly. She walked toward the track, through the mass of people that cut in front of her and pressed past. She drifted behind the crowd at the rail, wanting to be away from noise and people. The crowds began thinning as she walked along the track railing. Coming halfway around, she saw a clump of officials and supporters surrounding the elastic web starting-gate. The grandstand stretched across her field of vision. The colorful background of crammed bleachers seemed to vibrate with tension.

The post parade was on the track. Entrants pranced in single file, trotting in jigging strides with heads bent toward their pony horses. The chestnut stallion called "Red" cantered slowly in the middle of the pack. While standing still the horse had seemed heavy and angular, but in motion he flowed.

The first horse at the web gate pressed hard against it. Another came against the strap, a lithe gray with black markings. The red chestnut stallion jogged up next.

The webbing bobbed as the horses chested it and backed up. One horse swung to the side and collided with the chestnut stallion, and his jockey fanned his stick close to the stallion's head. The horse laid his ears back and half-reared. The red stallion was in the center of wringing tails and flashing hooves.

They're doing it on purpose, Meagan realized numbly.

The start official was a bent, gray man—the jockeys ignored his shrill shouts to straighten their horses. The chestnut stallion was jostled from either side and another crop sliced the air near his head. His jockey tried to hold him straight but the horse reared again. Sweat was darkening his flanks. Coming down, the jockey slipped out of position just as the web sprung up and a ringing bell sounded. The field exploded from the gate in a pack, leaving the red stallion half-turned away.

The jockey reclaimed his seat and swung straight as the pack dashed down the track. Before the chestnut could reach his stride, two horses blundered into each other out of the start. Meagan could see the red stallion's jockey stand and haul on the reins to keep from plunging into the collision. The horse threw his head against the pull as he swerved from the lagging horses and went to the outside.

Meagan could see pumping hindquarters enter the turn, blurred by thrown dirt. The chestnut stallion moved up from behind and took the rail, but rival jockeys drifted hard over to prevent the horse from passing. Blocked for a second time, the stallion fought another tight pull, taking wild strides as his jockey drew him back to the outside.

Meagan was glad for the noise and confusion, and welcomed sound loud enough to block her emotions. The crowd's roar swelled as the two leaders, a bay and a gray, rounded the final turn into the homestretch. The chestnut stallion was at last in the open, but placed far behind the two leaders. The jockey opened his reins and let the horse run.

The red stallion's late bolt out of the turn hushed the crowd. As if a flame suddenly caught, the chestnut seemed to take two strides for each one of the leaders before him, gaining and gaining as the air started to shake with cheering.

The leaders were side by side as the chestnut stallion came on. The gray overtook and steadily passed his rival. The chestnut's jockey drove in behind, ready for the gray to gallop into the clear so he could breeze past. The gray jockey's helmet flickered as he looked behind him. The crowd's cheering dipped as those who understood fell silent.

The gray's stride shortened as his jockey reined him in, slowing to come even with the faltering bay. It seemed impossible, but the red horse was trapped yet again, running behind the two leaders, bottled in their flying dirt. The chestnut stallion's jockey pulled hard and this time the big horse ducked his head as he tried to escape, striking out in frustration at being thwarted once more. The jockey stood in the irons and fought to bring the stallion around the outside.

Just as he did, the gray's jockey raised his whip and drove his horse for the finish. There was no room left—the wire was coming directly ahead. The stallion closed to the gray's hindquarters. Another stride brought him to the gray's flank. A stride and the red horse's head was to the jockey's irons. The gray's shoulder. Neck. Bridle. The wire flashed above.

The red stallion was beaten by a nose.

Some of my best leading men have been dogs and horses.
- Elizabeth Taylor (1932-2011)

Open doors in the lobby allowed a breeze that gently rocked
the potted palms. The hotel was enormous, surrounding a
square on three sides. People were everywhere, talking in
groups, seated, standing. Reporters flowed between them.
Snippets of conversation about the race floated around her.
Hardly anyone seemed happy with the outcome.

Eighty-five dollars was in Meagan's new purse. It was what
the pawn brokers thought of a mint condition Civil War derringer and two gold "Eagle" coins, minus the cost of a
modern calf-length blue silk dress—which felt shockingly exposed after her well-wrapped experiences as a female in
history. She did not sell her wedding ring, of course, but
slipped the simple gold band off her finger and tucked it
safely away. She could not have the reminder, not yet.

"Can I help you, Miss?"

"I'm looking for a room for a few days. A single bed. Anything you have."

"Sorry, ma'am. Everything in this town is booked for tonight. Nothing until tomorrow. Want something for then?"

"Yes, please." Meagan paid the clerk and turned away. At
the end of the lobby were doors to a smoky, dimly lit cavern.
It seemed a safe retreat, so she entered. The crowded room
was lit by lamps above a wide mahogany-framed mirror. The
men were in suits; the few women were impeccable in long
skirts and thin, filmy tops. The dark room smelled of alcohol,
though it should not have—it was the era of Prohibition. Besides the day's race, it was the single most discussed, and
cussed, topic of conversation.

A worker stood industriously chopping on a sideboard beside the bar. Meagan requested orange juice and sat on a tall stool facing the mirror. She recoiled from her own dark, hunched form staring back.

"You can do better than juice, little lady."

Meagan looked at the patron sitting next to her—a nice looking fellow, young, her age or maybe less. Blondish. Blue eyes in the light, probably. Combed hair. Suit.

"Little lady?" she asked, sipping. "Is that really what you said?"

"Here, lean down your cup. I have some vodka."

Meagan smiled. She was almost tempted, she really was. "I'm fine, but thank you, anyway."

He ordered a tonic and, when it came, slipped out a flask and tipped it into his glass. "Are you sure?"

Meagan toasted the air with her juice. "I'm sure."

He poured for himself. "Did you see the race?"

"I did."

The young man took a long drink, watching her over the rim of his glass. "It sure seems strange the horse that finally beat him is named *Upset*. Don't you think so?"

"Yes, it is," agreed Meagan absently. "It is very strange to be beaten by a horse named *Upset*."

"I think people have been reading too much about old Red, anyway. He's a good horse, but *great*? People always want to find something to call great. What do you think?"

"I don't know. I'm trying not to."

"Come on, now. You can't be serious."

"Oh, but I am. I'm sorry, I'm not really up for conversation. Can you point out the little ladies' room for me?"

The young man—the boy, she thought—pointed to the darkest side of the lobby. Meagan excused herself. When she came to the restroom's tall glass doors, she hesitated at her reflection, half-seen in the dim light. Her face was solemn, her cheeks were hollow, and her tightly pulled-back hair was escaping into springy tufts. Half was all the reflection she wanted to see.

Meagan stepped off the empty subway, aimless and without lodging. The racetrack's train was running, so she went. It had been her first time to ride a subway; it seemed more civilized than the honking lines of belching traffic she remembered from home.

The rambling Saratoga racing grounds were dark and silent. She had always loved the final hours before dawn, when the world seemed crouched and ready. Tonight it just seemed ... over.

A light shone at the guard station. Other lights could be seen in the stables beyond, dull yellow centers of orbiting insects. A gray-haired gentleman waved her through and returned to his newspaper.

Following the racetrack's perimeter fence, Meagan walked the wide turn along the quiet, dark earth. The infield grass was cool and wet, and a misting fog blew lightly against her face. Clean air was mixed with scents of mown grass, horses and a trace of diesel. She came closer to the stables, disturbing a flock of birds that rose and wheeled overhead, alighting again to scour the track's dirt.

Horses were already walking the long rows with dungareed grooms, clopping, heads low. Grooms used scrapers to swipe water from the horses' gleaming coats, making long splats onto the ground. Steam rose from the drying horses. Scattered groups of owners and trainers talked to each other softly under the pools of yellow light.

Meagan walked along the stables, watching, soaking in the familiarity of the Thoroughbreds and the quiet labor of their care. These were long-legged runners, Meagan's long-favorite breed. On a Thoroughbred, you could win the Derby or jump to an Olympic gold medal—on the back of a Thoroughbred, anything was possible.

Her first time riding a Thoroughbred had been frightening, a little. The horse stood prancing and eager as she took the reins and tried not to look at the ground so far away. She remembered hinting to the horse that she was ready and the sudden jolt forward in response. She was riding quicksilver; such a horse demanded her utmost effort, skill and focus. She had to balance and reassure the animal; she had to both follow and lead. She had to remind herself to breathe.

Only once did she truly gallop on a Thoroughbred. Her mount had been a claim horse on a backwater racetrack, a "prospect" being bought by her trainer. She remembered letting the reins out a notch and standing in the stirrups, feeling the horse opening his stride. The chiseled head mouthed the bit and pushed into the bridle, bounding forward in fluid strides that spilled across the soft earth.

She had opened the reins and felt the horse leap into them. The wind rose above all sounds, narrowing the world to just hooves exploding along the ground—and then the horse uncoiled and lifted, and the gallop was not a gallop anymore but a bolt and she was shooting through a tunnel of wind leaving the world outside stopped and static, a frozen background to the thunder beneath her that pounded on and on.

———

Meagan began spending early mornings at the racetrack watching the honest, unadorned grace and power of the Thoroughbreds. Solitude was the only way she could manage her sorrow. Something new had entered Meagan's feelings: the seeds of bitterness. They were not yet planted, but had arrived. She was furious with the Great Horse for having snatched Dan and her life from her. *How could something as wonderful as love hurt so much?*

A group of racetrack "regulars" shared the quiet mornings. Railbirds, they were called. They were lean-faced men in windbreakers, lined along the racetrack railing like crows with stopwatches, intent on the horses galloping by in the light fog. Rhythmic hooves intermingled with chugging breaths as each horse approached and swept past.

Thumbs punched and faces studied timepieces. Notes were scribbled in margins of racing forms. "Nice colt," grunted one. "Newcastle, by Norbut." The railbirds took turns grumbling and spitting. The morning workouts were important, a glimpse of the form a horse might display in his next race. Hoof beats approached, and all eyes were on a dark form slipping along the racetrack rail.

"The Trout's coming. Supposed to breeze in quarters."

"Who's he by?"

"A stallion standing at Belmont. Out of Donnaco, I think."

The railbirds wrote quickly. At the far end of the track a new form entered, resolving itself into a horse and rider. Each rocked against the other, plunging and holding. Railbirds leaned, watches out.

"Good morning, gentlemen!" an approaching voice boomed inappropriately in the solemn early air. "My Red is sure glad you've come to see him." Meagan recognized the warm voice of the chestnut stallion's groom, Will Harbut, the black man who had been kind to her. Newsmen in long coats flanked the groom as he strode up to the rail.

The horse coming on the track was a blocky shadow in the early light. As the horse came closer and passed, Meagan could see it was the big stallion the groom called "Red." His jockey's face was tight with exertion. The horse's breath rose in vapory flames and evaporated into the lightening sky.

"Horse wants to run," a reporter commented, nodding.

"Well you can just write that down!" Harbut answered jovially. "Racehorse wants to run! *Evening Special.*"

A sharp intake from the railbirds caught Meagan's attention, followed by clicks from stopwatches. "He'll start at the quarter pole," advised one observer.

"Which is the quarter pole?" asked one of the reporters.

"What outfit you write for, *Ladies Home Journal?*" snapped the groom, Harbut. The railbirds chuckled.

"Who is the horse by?" asked another.

"Ol' Red's by *hisself!*" Harbut roared. "And that's how he's gonna *stay!*"

The chestnut stallion and his rider were now moving on the track's far side, ticking along the rail as if on wheels. A pole flashed past, watches clicked, and the stallion stretched lower as if he heard them, stretching until he was a gliding shape in the fog. The stallion's legs blurred in the mist as he swallowed the ground, soaring onto the homestretch—and then the jockey was standing up and bringing him back. The pair thundered by. The stallion bowed his head to his chest in frustration of being reined in. Stopwatches clicked, a tiny, tinny sound, sterile and small against the pounding of the turf.

Meagan felt a tap on her shoulder and turned to meet a wide grin. It was the blonde fellow from the night before.

"Good morning," he said cheerfully. "So you *do* think he's a great horse."

"Oh ... well, yes. *The* Great Horse, actually." She gave him a tight smile; it felt strange and awkward, and she turned back to the track.

"Are you handicapping?"

"Oh ... no. I'm sorry, how did you know I was going to be here?"

"I didn't. Did you know I would be?"

"No." Meagan relented. "As a matter of fact, I came on an impulse."

"It was a good one," the young man said agreeably.

"Yes, it was." She let go of the rail and stepped back. "Now I have another. It was nice seeing you again."

"I have a horse running in the Grand Union."

"Oh, how exciting, really it is. I wish you luck."

"I still don't know your name..."

Meagan walked away quickly, not looking back. This time, she wanted to stay alone and unknown.

Ducking into a deserted row along the stables' backside, she passed a waste can overflowing with trash. A folded newspaper lay on top. Picking it up gingerly, Meagan scanned the page looking for the date. Her eye stopped on the headline and she felt her heart skip. Across the top of the newspaper, in bold, the headline read: *Man O'War Loses to Upset!*

Meagan tried not to stare out the window of the subway car. It always led to the same thoughts. It was 1919, and somehow she had to realize that Dan—her husband, Cappy Beardon, the cavalryman who Mrs. Bridgestone once knew— was *gone*. Perhaps he was alive now, an old man; would he know her? When she left Dan, had she simply vanished from his arms? How had it been each time she left ... did she blink away, or was it like she had never been?

Meagan wanted to spent as much time as possible near Red—Man O'War—but security limited her chances; she felt resigned now to fate. She tried to concentrate on the people around her. They hunched over papers, or stood with an arm up to the handhold, staring straight forward. Their faces held exhaustion. They seemed hard-pressed, these people, and pressing back. It felt an odd time for Prohibition to be en- acted. If anything, it seemed everyone could use a sociable drink.

The Great War was over, the "war to end all wars." The conflict would not be called the First World War until the Second. Meagan had never seen war except on television: to her it was narrated and delivered in special, continuing coverage. But she could see in the eyes around her what mechanized war had cost. Prohibition was born of disillu- sionment: faith in one's fellow man had been replaced by an attitude Meagan recognized but had forgotten—*cynicism*.

Yet these same disillusioned people had crowded on a train to see a horse. Not for wagering, either, because the odds on Man O'War made winning money on him impossible. The people went to see an honest hero, an item in short supply.

The train slowed and Meagan stood, making her way out. She was glad for the long walk from the train stop back to the hotel: it gave her purpose and destination, if only for a few blocks.

The hotel was already filling again for another big race fea- turing Man O'War. The red stallion's defeat was the first in his career and the question was whether the horse could come back to win. Newspapers and the streets were alive with talk of it, but even those arguing against Man O'War seemed anxious to be proven wrong.

Meagan walked into the hotel lobby. It was loud and crowded, and after obtaining her key she hurried to the red-patterned stairs up to her room.

"Oh, Miss! Wait!" The blonde young man from the lounge and the racetrack pushed through the crowd to block her way. He pulled his hand from behind his back, bringing forth a spray of flowers.

Meagan stared. "Are they for me?" she asked, and then felt foolish.

He shrugged. "They came from a party. I was there, but suddenly couldn't think of why."

"So you came here with flowers? Look, I don't know your name—"

"Anthony Jones. What's yours?"

"Anthony, I don't know how to say this."

"Then don't."

"I can't take these. I'm sorry." Meagan pushed past him, brushing against the flowers he held and accidentally tearing one from his hand. It fell and lay bent on the tile floor. She walked back and slowly picked it up. Its stem was broken. The pale green stalk was darker where she had crushed it, and one of the petals was torn away. "They were lovely..." To Meagan the small ruin seemed strangely, inexpressibly sad. "I didn't mean that. You brought them to be nice, and I've been so—"

"It's okay, really it is. Please don't cry."

"How silly." Meagan sniffed and wiped her eyes quickly. "I didn't know I was." Young Anthony stood awkwardly holding out the remaining flowers. She took them. "Thank you. I could use them, really. Can we be friends, Anthony?"

"Of course. But I think that means you will have to tell me your name."

Meagan smiled; it felt good to smile. "Very well, *now* I'm getting what I deserve. My name is Meagan Roberts—*oh!* ... Beardon, rather."

"Meagan Roberts O'Beardon-Rather?"

"It's Irish."

"Are you going to be leaving suddenly again? I would like the chance to say goodbye properly at least once."

Meagan held out her hand. "You have been very nice, Anthony. I'm sorry I haven't been good company."

"You seem fine company to me."

"Thank you again. You are a gentleman. Now, shall we say goodbye?"

"I hate to, but okay."

She turned to the long stairs toward her room. The empty space waited with memories and recriminations. Pausing, she turned back. "Did you say you came from a party?"

"It's a polo match, really. My aunt holds it every year to celebrate her wedding anniversary. Everyone is nice but they're mostly older."

"Do you suppose we could go back? Suddenly a party sounds like a very good idea."

The entrance was exactly as she would have expected. Rolling, grassy hills parted for a long driveway lined with straight-rail fencing and shady oaks. Anthony drove the sweeping curve around the huge house and parked in a haphazard line of cars tucked at angles under the trees. A colorful quilt of people spread along the edges of the green swath that was the polo field.

"Anthony, you've returned!" An elderly woman sailed across the grass, glorious in a filmy turquoise dress clearly meant for nighttime wear. She held a cigarette holder straight out to the side, sweeping it in time with her creditable stride. Her other hand cupped a decanter. Pin feathers brushed her throat. "Dear, *dear* boy, you've come back to me!" The woman swept up to Anthony and pressed her cheek upon his.

"You've brought someone with you! Oh, *Anthony,* what a wonderful surprise!" She turned to Meagan, extending a hand. "How perfectly *marvelous* to meet you. I am Eleanor von Kane. My friends call me Candy."

"This is Meagan, Aunt."

"How awful of you to interrupt, Anthony." She pushed him lightly on his chest. "You must excuse my nephew. He has too much of his father in him."

"Is this your place, ma'am?" Meagan asked. "It is so lovely."

"*Candy,* dear—call me *Candy.* Yes, this is my place. Wendell and I bought in back in, well, I'm not going to tell, am I? I don't detect an accent ... are you from around here?"

Meagan shook her head. "I'm from California, where there isn't an accent."

"Then you must be here for the race! It is so *exciting,* isn't it? I simply love occasions." From across the lawn a woman dressed in black shrieked and started toward them. Mrs. von Kane met the woman cheek-first. "Of course you look stunning, Margaret darling, but are you in mourning?"

"Candy von Kane, you old shoe!" the woman fussed back. "Eve Timble told me you've been snooping around the Auxiliary without so much as a word to me!"

"I was on business, darling." Mrs. Kane took a draw from her cigarette and returned it to position at arm's length. "Now meet my nephew's lady friend! Her name is *Meagan,* she is visiting from California."

"Oh, how do you *do?*" The black-garbed Margaret greeted Meagan warmly. "I have always planned on a trip out West, but we spend so much time in Europe we never seem to."

"Don't bore, darling," Candy admonished. "Anthony, you are my dearest nephew but an incorrigible oaf. You should ask your lady friend what she wants to drink ... and incidentally have mine freshened." Meagan started to protest and Mrs. Kane dismissed her with a flick of her cigarette. "Nonsense, have a drink. It's become fashionable again."

Light clapping pattered through the crowd lining the polo field, and a loudspeaker buzzed an announcement. Riders trotted onto the smooth, manicured grass. Waiting for the start, the mounts jigged tight circles as if the ground were hot to touch.

"Do you enjoy polo?" asked Mrs. Kane. "It's my Wendell's great passion." The woman spread her arms to encompass the field. "And we both *love* the horses. What a glorious run we've had together!"

A swirling rush of players and horses tangled and broke down the field. Two riders galloped side-by-side, mallets high, with the entire field in pursuit. One rider leaned for a strike, and the tiny white ball darted away. Horses and riders turned, tearing divots, meeting in a pileup of missed swings and curses. The ball wandered out of the confusion as if escaping a fight and rolled to a lonely stop.

"She's not *really* my aunt," Anthony informed Meagan after Mrs. von Kane excused herself with a flourish. "She is my grandmother's friend and tells everyone I'm her nephew. But you will like her once you get to know her. Most people do."

"I think she is perfectly wonderful, Anthony."

"And you don't *have* to have a drink, of course."

"No, I think I do," Meagan took his arm. "Lead on."

The pastel-sporting crowd was well dressed, but the event's color was decidedly with the decorations. Low branches shaded an oak table covered with blazing yellow zinnias, silver platters, crystal decanters and red linen napkins folded into accordion fans. Bootlegging was not legal, but it was not striking a low profile. Black-liveried gentlemen bowed at her approach. "A drink, Miss?"

"Gin-and-Tonic please. Lime." Meagan ignored Anthony's stare. He moved gently to hold her hand. Just as gently, Meagan removed it. "Do you play polo, Anthony?"

"No, I'm not very good," he replied sheepishly.

"Is the trouble your riding or your hitting?"

"*Both*. I'm an embarrassment to the family."

Voices caused Meagan to turn. A group of girls approached the bar, hanging upon each another and tittering. A brunette with bobbed hair saw Meagan and smirked at the other girls.

"Oh, Delia, look, *do!* Your brother has brought us someone to *meet!*"

Anthony reddened. "Hello, Lisa. This is my friend, Meagan. She is from California, visiting."

"It's nice to meet you. I'm Meagan."

"Lisa. From Long Island." The brunette's accent was distinct and nasal. "Are you a polo fan, or an Anthony fan?"

The pounding swell of hooves thundered as the action approached. Meagan took her drink from the bartender. "I get so engrossed in the game," she said pleasantly between the players' shouted curses. "Don't you?"

"I wonder why you're *here*. We don't get many visitors from the outer provinces at the *Matches*." The girls behind Lisa giggled.

"Well, I travel quite a bit."

"Do they play polo out West? They must play on *sand*, from what *I've* heard."

Lisa's half-smirk was engendering in Meagan a feeling of positive dislike. "I don't play polo, though I do ride. I was hoping Anthony might be my guide."

"Oh, so you *ride* ... that means you have been on a Hunt, of course?" Sidelong glances passed among the girls.

"Do you mean a fox hunt?"

Meagan's question was answered by titters. "Yes, silly," Lisa sneered. "Of course *fox* hunting. Did you think we meant squirrels? Or do your people mostly hunt *b'ar*?"

"I wasn't sure which you meant," Meagan replied evenly. "My hunting rides were mostly for stag."

"*Stag?* What horrible thing is *that?*"

"A deer with antlers. The staghounds hunt by sight. Some prefer it to foxhunting, but that might be for its association with royalty."

"Oh. Do the royalty hunt stags?" Lisa's voice was smaller.

"I'm not sure anymore. The Louis's did. Do you enjoy dressage?"

"Anthony, dear Anthony! You are a sweet child, but no, I *can't* have another! I've already had my medicinal half-cocktail for the week!" Candy von Kane flowed across the grass with an entourage behind her. Women poured around the bar. Mrs. von Kane fluttered a hand against Anthony's cheek and held her glass out to the bartenders. "Perhaps freshen it a smidge. As they say in the South, it is *simply* sweltering. If I weren't a Yankee, I'd faint from the heat—bartender, would you keep the ice? There's a dear."

"How *are* you, Mrs. von Kane?" Lisa simpered.

"Lisa, dear, how is your mother?"

"Mother's fabulous as always. We have been staying on the Island all spring, but we *had* to get out once before summer, even if just to come *here*."

"Yes. Have you met Anthony's friend, Meagan?

"We've met," Meagan answered pleasantly.

"You know, Mrs. von Kane," Lisa prodded. "I've heard Mother say *so* many times that the von Kanes *haven't* visited in ever and ever. Do visit, *do*. It would make Mother so happy."

"We go for the horse shows, you precious thing, but my grandniece is on to boys and my youngest nephew isn't out of ponies yet. Perhaps next season." Mrs. von Kane leaned to Meagan. "I'm glad *someone* could get a drink here. Atrocious party, even if it *is* mine." She saw an older gentleman pressing up to the bar and patted his arm. "Chester McQuire! I hear you've been calling me an 'old war horse' behind my back— and don't you *dare* leave without looking at my new colt."

"Another polo pony, Candy?" he asked dubiously.

"Of course! You know the saying, 'polo is a disease for which poverty is the only cure.'"

"Well, as you know I'm trying to cut back. The world is changing, Eleanor."

"Oh, *Chester*, then rebel! If people are losing their horses to be modern, I'm acquiring more. We can't let all the magic out of the world ... whatever will the children do?" Mrs. von Kane accepted her refreshed cocktail and winked at Meagan. "Dear, you must think me a silly, fluttering old fool. You look just that perceptive."

"On the contrary, Mrs. von Kane."

The woman took Meagan's hand in her own soft, powdery clasp. "You seem such the practical, sturdy old soul. What you must think of all this!" Mrs. von Kane gestured to include the party and green field with its multi-colored players.

"I love it," Meagan assured her. "I'm just glad it didn't rain too much."

"Oh, but it did, child. It rained all night."

"That was a Presbyterian rain, though, don't you think? If it were a Baptist rain you would have had to cancel."

Mrs. von Kane's face lit with a mischievous smile. "Anthony, I *like* this girl! I am so glad you brought her!" She squeezed Meagan's hand. "My husband, Wendell, would love you, child."

"Is Mr. von Kane here?"

"No, child, not in the corporal sense. Wendell passed some years ago."

"Oh, I'm so sorry! I thought—"

"Don't say a word, not a word. Wendell still lives with me." She placed a pale hand over her heart. "In fact I am celebrating our anniversary. When else would I celebrate? He disliked Christmas and I abhor birthdays. No, we love the horses, and we love our friends." She held her hand up. The cigarette holder was woven among grandly withering fingers. A gem-encrusted band sparkled. "My wedding ring. Do you like it? It's quite the simplest thing I own, Wendell's taste was wonderfully pedestrian. He is with me always. Never forget—that's my motto! It keeps me sane, or within close approximation. We must be faithful to our memories."

The crowd noises and thunder of hoof beats receded as Meagan thought of her own wedding anniversary. Yes, it happened in the 1800's, but she would honor it always. *I will never forget you, Dan.* Meagan looked at the woman with glittering eyes. "Thank you, Mrs. von Kane."

"Oh, child, I've made you cry!" Mrs. von Kane tossed her caped arms around Meagan lightly and pressed her cheek close. "Dry quickly before Margaret sees and ruins my reputation! Imagine a hostess making her own guests cry."

"No, I'm fine." Meagan dabbed her eyes and smiled. Another tear streaked down and she quickly brushed it away. "Everything is fine. Really it is."

"What a lovely smile you have, dear! We shouldn't cry around horses. Do you ride?"

"Yes, my mother was a horsewoman."

"Your *mother*, even as the great noblewomen of old! Is she here, may I meet her?

"No, she isn't here. My family isn't ... here now."

"Oh. Yes, I see." Mrs. Von Kane nodded, pin feathers gently bobbing. "We are never alone, dear. And the horses need us too, the men are forgetting so quickly. Farmers ridding themselves of draft horses. Cavalrymen want machines. After all their centuries in the saddle, after all the..." The woman trailed off and for the first time fell silent.

"No, not everyone forgets." Meagan said impulsively. "The horses have more to give us. Please believe me. I ... just know."

The woman looked intently at Meagan for a moment, and then clapped her hands together and threw her head back in a brassy laugh that rolled across the gathering. A raucous, uncouth, joyous laugh not in defiance but transcendence—"You see it *too!* If I end up owning all Chester's mounts, I'll put them in riding schools so every child in New York has the chance to know horses. The children will know what to do!"

Meagan joined in laughing, more mildly, and smiled when the woman's eyes settled back on her with a gaze suddenly serious. "What is it you do, Meagan. Must you be in California?"

"I'm just visiting. I don't know how long I will stay."

"If you ever could, dear, I've lost my assistant stable master and have horses coming in every day. I need new stables, new people, new ideas—it's quite an emergency—could you stay?"

"I don't know, I never know."

"Find out! And then come here. Consider it. I have the room and the employment. Or is there a reason you can't ... a special someone?

Meagan nodded tightly. "He would be an old man now though. Even if I could find him."

"Oh *age*," Candy answered dismissively. "A state of mind and some inconveniences, dear, nothing more. It is the great secret we keep from youth. Is it your father ... your grandfather? Whoever it is, bring him too! There is so much to do."

Meagan swallowed. Even a short time, even a few years with Dan—a flash of hope lit her world. "Thank you, Mrs. Von Kane."

"*Candy*, dear. Candy. You're hesitating, that's good. I could make it happen, whatever you need. The only good use for money is helping others. Please agree."

"If I can ... it would be wonderful."

"We'll show the cavalry boys a thing or two about horses— oh *Anthony!* My sweet angel, how *could* you leave us without beverage?"

About the head of a truly great horse,
There is the air of freedom unconquerable.
The eyes seem to look on heights beyond our gaze.
It is the look of a spirit that can soar ... it is the birthright of eagles.
- John Taintor Foote (1881-1950)

MEAGAN WAS JOSTLED but kept her seat. She had come early and her view was good. The fog on the track had burned away hours before. She was invited to the Clubhouse as a guest of Anthony and the von Kanes, but Meagan had decided to watch the race with the crowd and go up to the Clubhouse afterwards.

She wore a new floral-print dress, and her wedding ring was on her finger. Putting the ring on had been difficult, but afterwards she felt clean and content. There was no time for regrets; for they would be infinite.

Meagan had decided to try to find Dan. If not already passed, he was an old man now; she didn't care. She only wanted to hear him laugh, to hear him call her "Meggie" one more time. With that hope, she felt herself returning to life.

Earlier, joining the railbirds at dawn to see Man O'War, Meagan had been stopped at the gate. The famous horse had been threatened anonymously, and the stables were now a cordoned area filled with police and reporters.

"Money talks louder than the Lord to *some* people!" Man O'War's loyal groom, Will Harbut, told a crowd of reporters.

"Do you think it's someone close to the horse?"

"I don't think nothing. I just watch. Most people is crooked *sometimes,* just gotta make sure they is straight with *you.* I slept with old Red last night—you believe someone calling Mr. Riddle and say he's gonna cut my Red's throat? Well I'm gonna be sleeping in Red's stall 'til that man calls and says he was just joking, and maybe after."

When Man O'War was led out past his crowd of well-wishers there was a stir of people straining to see. His burnished coat shone in the sun. Meagan smiled at the horse from within the crowd, and the stallion paused. He turned his head and seemed to deliberately look in her direction ... and then the horse allowed himself to be led forward.

The stands were filled with a well-dressed and poorly behaved crowd, loosened by liquor in omnipresent flasks. Tip sheets were touted in the plazas surrounding the bleachers, and flocks of boys perched on grandstand rails hurled insults through cupped hands.

The early races had been run. Following the gentle rhythm of a race day, Meagan had earlier visited the paddocks between the races, tip sheet in hand, studying each horse carefully to pick the best. She watched for sweat on the entries' necks, which horseman's lore claims is "scared sweat," a sign the animal may be exhausting himself though nervousness ... unless, of course, it isn't.

When Meagan saw a gray mare enter the paddock, she knew she had the winner. The mare's expression was sharp, and she had a good front end and was tightly coupled, which could mean power. The race was a sprinting distance, and power could mean early speed. Of course Meagan knew she was easily wrong, but in the sunshine it was better to believe her hunches and enjoy the magnificent animals.

Mixed scents of the racetrack infused the air. The track's breeze had traveled over mown grass and raked paddocks, through haynets and shavings, past liniment and turpentine and saddle-soaped leather; it flowed across the asphalt parking lot and through popcorn concession stands, floating between rows of flowers, hedges and freshly-painted benches before finally filtering through the grandstands laden and rich.

Meagan had spent the day drifting with the throngs of people. After placing each wager she had hurried to the homestretch fence and waited. She had watched each post parade and each lining up for the start. The bell came, the cheers rose, the blur of colors streaked over the course. As the field entered each final turn, coming at inhuman speed to the roar of the grandstand, the crowd's noise spoke in waves of emotion. The pounding bass of hooves formed within the deafening cheers, subsonic, felt as much as heard. The roar rose to climax and receded, spent.

Now excitement rippled through the bleachers. The crowd's expectancy was taking hold: the Grand Union Hotel Stakes were about to begin. Slowly the crowd rose to its feet, hushing each other and whispering. Heads turned and people pointed. Meagan craned her neck, trying to see over the spectators. Strained talk simmered around her: could Man O'War come back from his recent—his only—defeat to fulfill his promise; *could greatness remain in a disillusioned world?*

Man O'War stepped onto the track. Where the other horses in the parade looked like graceful, immense greyhounds, Man O'War was burly and solid. He started to jog in place, swinging occasionally against his old friend, a gelding named Mr. Treat, the only horse he would settle next to. Crowds pressed against the rail as they passed.

The parade strung along the track, coming around the far turn to the gate's webbing. Tiny in the distance, the horses danced in anticipation as men swarmed over them, straightening, holding. The crowd fell to a hush, watching anxiously for fouling. The horses were promptly lined up: no mistake would be made *this* time.

The elastic rose in a flick of motion. The horses paused for a split second, and then the field broke into an uneven charge. Leaders swept to the rail, others jostled for a berth—and one red streak surged from the line, ignoring the rail and running out ahead of the pack, pulling away even as he reached for his stride.

An awed chill formed along the back of Meagan's neck as Man O'War entered the turn alone and in front. All the other jockeys were going for their whips, fanning desperately as Man O'War's rider stood in his stirrups to hold his stallion back. The red stallion fought for his head, leaving the turn and entering a lonely homestretch as his jockey struggled to keep him "under wraps," pulling so tightly the horse's crested neck bowed.

Man O'War galloped before the grandstand as if borne on the rapturous waves of sound. The big horse plunged once and gained his head—in that instant Man O'War broke free and poured across the track, a living flame sending spectators into frenzy. In happy pandemonium the crowd flooded onto the course, filling behind the late-finishing horses and swamping the infield. Meagan rushed to join them.

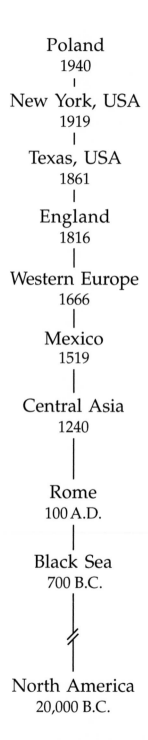

Poland
1940
|
New York, USA
1919
|
Texas, USA
1861
|
England
1816
|
Western Europe
1666
|
Mexico
1519
|
Central Asia
1240
|
Rome
100 A.D.
|
Black Sea
700 B.C.
|
⫽
|
North America
20,000 B.C.

A Pale Horse

T HE GROUND TWISTED and heaved. A swath of sand lifted and fell to earth in the near distance. Curtains of spray rose in lines from the earth. Aircraft seared the sky, flying low with black trails following, like the rising dust of other marauders from long ago.

In all directions Meagan saw multicolored forms, misshapen and sprawled, but her eyes would not focus, could not comprehend the thousand squirming remains of a massacre. Shapes of animals—both man and horse—lay crushed and struggling, or else staggered blindly across acres of death.

Screaming came from the sky and Meagan instinctively ducked lower as mechanical whines grew and planes dived, releasing packages to detonate in flashes and thunder around her. On the horizon, a line of gray tanks dipped and bobbed over uneven ground as they came. Her thoughts flashed to another battlefield, another time: the chariots were coming.

A twitching form stirred. Clotted mud moved, and a horse pulled itself from the earth, a vacant saddle on his back. The horse stood unsteadily on three legs. As she started to go to the animal, Meagan heard a tiny groan. A voice called her, a Polish voice, beckoning. Begging.

"*Prosze.*" Please.

The drone of aircraft changed pitch as dark slices began to climb against the sky. The voice was coming from a mound of bodies—she was not sure which until a wheezing gasp escaped from one, and a twisted whiteness rose in the form of a hand.

"I'm here," she said, taking the grasping hand.

There was no further sound for a moment, and then words: "*Prosze* ... please. Water. Canteen, horse."

Meagan looked at the line of machines streaking toward them, cold machinery bringing fire. She was in the middle of the dying, and there was no escape from this place. She could only watch the tanks come.

Crouching low, she went to the horse. Bewildered, shaking, the animal limped away from her in a lurching hop and stood, one mangled foreleg raised. Keeping her eyes away from the ruined limb, Meagan spoke to the horse as she walked to the saddle and detached its metal canteen. Stroking the horse softly, she saw familiar, intelligent compassion in the dark eyes. The faraway look of the Great Horse; frightened, confused ... yet still seeing beyond the battlefield.

She brought the canteen to the fallen soldier.

"*Prosze!*" he gasped. He spoke to Meagan, but for a moment all she could see was the man's leg sprawled across another's chest, propped companionably—had the chest been attached to anything resembling a man. Thin droning announced new lines of planes appearing dark and low. Sparks of fire erupted from tank guns. As technology advanced, each conflict was becoming more deadly than the last. A society forged through cooperation had founded a new world—and again gorged itself on conflict to founder upon the old.

The gasping soldier wanted Meagan to tie a rope to his horse's saddle. "Horse ... pull me to camp. Before. He save me."

She did not move. There was no rope. There was nothing. The horse lurched again, holding his shattered leg. The droning planes were louder, the tank fire was louder.

Time began to shudder and a rush of wind swept over her. Only the shrillest screams of horses spiked above the din of mankind's latest tools of war.

"*Prosze...*"

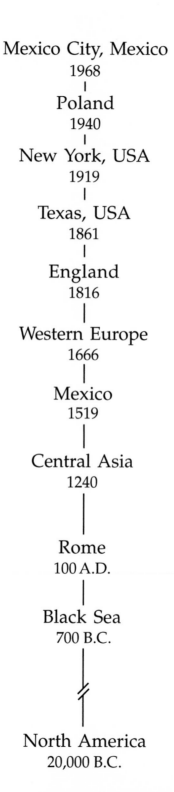

Mexico City, Mexico
1968

Poland
1940

New York, USA
1919

Texas, USA
1861

England
1816

Western Europe
1666

Mexico
1519

Central Asia
1240

Rome
100 A.D.

Black Sea
700 B.C.

North America
20,000 B.C.

To Fly Without Wings

THE SOUNDS CHANGED. Rumbling tension hummed around Meagan. She could see filled bleachers ringing the sky, and her first terrified thoughts were of Rome's arena—until she saw international flags fluttering overhead. One displayed the rings of the Olympic symbol, and below in bold letters: *Mexico 1968.*

The sound of planes still droned in her head; Meagan flinched at a loudspeaker's crackling and fearfully checked the sky. Her reflex came with the reminder of past horrors—Mongolian rampages, Conquistadors' carnage, the bloody acts of Rome—what were the human effects from the violent traumas of history?

Meagan took her eyes from the sky and almost cried out with relief. Before her was a stadium with spectators packed high on all sides, a vast bowl of color above green turf dotted with flower banks and brightly colored obstacles. The stadium floor was strewn with brush, water, gates, and walls.

Sunshine smells of popcorn and horses mixed with heavy damp odors of mud and grass. A horse's sculpted head appeared above the crowd. A path was cleared and the horse and rider walked forward; the Italian flag was emblazoned on the saddle pad. The horse was a gelding, and every inch of his gray coat was smooth, clean and white. Tight braids decorated his long neck, crowning the crest. The animal's glossy coat stretched tight over muscle and veins. His hooves were slick and black.

The horse stepped in springy steps and broke into a jog as he passed, holding his head high in anticipation. The pair trotted through the corridor of spectators onto the field as the in-gate closed behind them; people surged forward into the empty space. Meagan was pushed into bright sunlight. She stood with a standing crowd behind the in-gate, looking over the field's wall.

The horse and rider circled among the jumps as people crowded around Meagan, pressing along the closed entry gate. The rider opened his reins as they sped into the first fence. They suspended over it as the crowd gasped, and then were moving across the turf to another jump.

A flood of memories warmed Meagan as she watched the familiar exchanges between horse and rider. When the gray horse jumped, he flipped his French-braided tail so artfully it disguised the sheer physicality of his feat—catapulting a man over a fence higher than himself. This was the brave new sport of show jumping, a challenge of skill and daring which provided a supreme—and humane—test of a rider's partnership with the horse.

Circling on the bit, the rider imperceptibly adjusted his horse's stride as they cantered toward the next obstacle. The horse has an odd visual handicap: the equine eye is crafted for a wide arc of vision and lacks the depth perception of human sight. A horse can see an obstacle's distance only in the last stride—time enough to make a jump, but not to correct deficiencies in balance, approach or stride. That is the duty of the rider.

The horse tossed his head once before he thumped off the ground, launching and folding in midair. The rider released the reins to let the horse's neck stretch, taking back again as he opened into the landing. The horse's legs missed the rails by a well-timed fraction.

Cantering to the next, the rider took back on the reins to meet the obstacle in stride. The horse tucked his forelegs and then hind; the jump's pole rocked but stayed in place. The next was the closely-set Double. The horse jumped from a good "spot" but the rider rose late. A foreleg caught the top rail and knocked it out in front; the horse tucked his back legs tightly to avoid the falling pole.

The simple object of show jumping is to keep the obstacles intact, and so retain a zero "fault" score. There are no points for style. Now carrying four faults—the penalty for a knock-down—the pair rounded the far turn. The rider's head bobbed among the jumps; television cameras pivoted. The Water loomed, sixteen feet across, followed immediately by another set of jumps. The horse struck the ground with both hind legs and popped into the air. The water flashed beneath them and they were back to earth; the rider pulled and gathered, and they were in the air over the next. Spontaneous clapping burst out and quickly silenced as the rider threaded past obstacles toward a narrow gate. The horse curled over the top but left it standing.

A hush settled across the stadium as the horse and rider glided past the in-gate, fixed in concentration. The rider straightened to the Triple combination—a wall followed by two spread fences, with space for only one stride between each.

The rider sat still, gauging the take-off. The gray flicked his ears to listen as his rider adjusted ... and lifted into the air, spraying divots of wet turf as he arced over the wall. A stride later the horse and rider bounced back into the air, but flattened low and knocked the rail. The pair landed and took a stride to the last element, hitting that too and having it down.

The horse shook his head in dismay: he did not like to touch fences. The last obstacle came quickly, a wide hedge. A cheer rose as the gray made an enormous effort and left daylight between his legs and the brush. The round ended to echoing applause. The final score for three fences down: twelve faults. A middling score usually, but over this demanding course it was excellent.

Meagan felt better as she watched. Horse jumping is one of the most inclusive sports because the horse is the common denominator. Men and women may compete equally, for what matters is the equine partnership.

Officials came forward to push the crowd from the gate as shrill whistles filled the air. Meagan was still in her 1919 floral-print race dress, not too inappropriate for the occasion. She and the people around her complied with the officials' request and moved back.

Next to Meagan a young girl sat on her father's shoulders, enthusiastically flailing his shoulders with a program. "Excuse me, could I see your program?" Meagan politely asked.

"Give it to the lady, Kathleen," the man said, patting his daughter's leg. The girl held it out shyly.

Meagan thanked him. "I'll give it right back." Unrolling the program, she flipped through the pages with an electric thrill in her stomach. Here were the sport's legendary horses and riders she had read about, horses and riders from history. An insert fell out and she picked it up quickly. *"Individual Champions!"* declared a headline over a striking photograph of the American rider, William Steinkraus, stretched over a fence with his brilliant partner Snowbound. Meagan studied the picture. It showed a perfectly balanced Steinkraus stretched over a fence, his grim expression matching his horse's concentration—pure athleticism, pure partnership. Underneath was a photo of a young lady standing with her arms around a dark pony. The caption read: *British Pair Win Silver!*

Meagan looked for the man who had lent the program, and found him talking to a woman leaning over the bleacher railing. The first child was off his shoulders and an even younger girl was perched happily in her place; the youngster had waited eagerly for her turn to see the horses up close. The man took the program from Meagan with a friendly nod. His second daughter watched everything with big eyes from her high station.

"De Australia, John Fahey y Bonvale." The Spanish introduction issued from wide, black speaker horns above. Translations in English and French followed.

A new competitor sporting the flag of Australia emerged from the corridor into the stadium. The horse was a tall, wiry chestnut. His diminutive rider rode with short stirrups, rising high as he trotted between the jumps and halted. The rider doffed his hat in the steward's direction and waited for the bell. Loud partisan cheering rose from a section of the stands.

The sound to go was given. The rider picked up a canter, circling to the first obstacle. The Australian pair were experienced campaigners and crowd favorites. Though a clear round was not expected, they could be trusted to put up a serviceable score for their team.

The pair was smooth to the first, over and clear. On to the second, they tapped the top rail for an unlucky knock-down. Clean to the water, the horse jumped it with authority, knees snapping up and neck forward, pulling through the air and looking for the ground. The horse felt his way over the next two fences, rapping each but taking nothing down.

The crowd hummed with excitement as the Australian rider tried to settle his mount for the difficult gate. The horse slipped on the wet turf and flattened in the air, pulling it down for four more faults.

Flowers and paint could not hide the truth of the Olympic course. The sport was still very young—less than a century—and the mechanics of proper footing were not well understood. Wet from heavy rain, the Main Stadium's newly laid turf was coming up in strips to reveal slick, suctioning mud underneath. Hooves were chopping the footing into sticky mire.

The chestnut came into the Triple fast and slipped as he started to lift into the air. Horse and rider came down on the top of the wall, collapsing it down. The rider closed his leg and sent the horse on, and the chestnut waded through the second part of the combination, landing just clear of falling rails and scrambling to the last element. More wooden poles clattered to the ground.

The Australian pair's five knock-downs scored twenty faults. The rider threw his hat up for his standing fans. Whistles pierced the air as loudspeakers blared to life and the stadium gates swung open for the chestnut and his rider to exit. The Australians trotted out.

Time was moving quickly now; the tempo of history had increased. Now even her small hope of seeing Dan again was gone—everything had been snatched away again. Meagan could not think of it. She would only wait and pretend she was home again.

This was made easier by the spectacle before her: for the first time she heartily agreed with the location chosen by the Great Horse. The event was a horseman's celebration and a showcase for mankind's ancient partnership. Equestrian sports preserve the knowledge and benefits of horsemanship and include eventing, endurance riding, driving, cutting, steeplechase, reining, gymkhana games, polo, modern jousting, rodeo events, vaulting—and of course, flat racing and show jumping.

Surprisingly, the horse's extreme jumping ability was not fully known until the 18th century. At that time, fox hunting was considered doomed by England's Enclosure Acts, which required farmers to fence their property. It was the end of galloping sport, or so it was thought, until daredevils found that horses would—with trust in the rider—clear obstacles they could not see over. Riding to hounds gained new thrill and became more popular than ever before.

This novel challenge in riding was soon contested over farmers' stone walls, with loose stones placed along the top. "Faults" were scored for the number of stones dislodged in a leap. Horse jumping soon became an international cavalry demonstration, evolving into a military contest of martial skill.

After World War II and the disbanding of the cavalry teams, show jumping began to emerge as a popular civilian sport. Since that time, jumping sport has come to emphasize the horse's welfare as the paramount concern, with 'zero tolerance' for drugs or the slightest indication of unsoundness. The vibrant new sport arrived on the eve of the horse's predicted obsolescence—before motors replaced actual horsepower—and thrives today as an exciting, humane sport.

When God created the horse, He said to His new creation:
'Oh, Horse, I have made thee as no other.
Thou shalt fly without wings and conquer without swords.'
- attributed to the Koran

EXCITEMENT RIPPLED THROUGH the in-gate. Every head was turned to the entry corridor, watching a young woman in a black hunt cap. Her small, pale face could barely be seen over the spectators. As she glided forward, her horse's tiny dark ears became visible. Meagan, standing beside the in-gate, saw the girl was not riding a horse at all, but a pony. The saddle pad bore the flag of Great Britain. These were the Individual Show Jumping Silver medalists.

"*De Gran Bretaña, Marion Coakes y—Stroller!*"

Meagan knew of this pony, a famous jumper of the twentieth century. He was Marion Coakes' childhood mount, a pony talented enough to outjump every full-sized horse in the world on one occasion or another. Something else Meagan remembered: Stroller's tail had been in constant danger of being plucked bare by souvenir seekers.

Equestrian sports were a special symbol of hope for Great Britain. In the 1952 Helsinki Olympics, during a time when that nation still struggled in the aftermath of World War II, Great Britain had been without a single Gold medal up to the final day and the final event, the Team Jumping. That competition was covered by radio, and a war-shattered nation thrilled to victory with the announcer's words, "Foxhunter coming to the last..." Show jumping burst onto British television in the 1950's as the first major televised sport to catch the public's eye, and it heralded a new era by proving the potential popularity of sports on television.

The program which Meagan had borrowed contained a report of controversy about sending the tiny British pair to the Olympic Games. There was doubt the brave pony could handle the huge fences, but Marion and Stroller were simply too popular with the public to leave off the Jumping team for Great Britain.

Proving doubts wrong, the pair had won the Silver medal, putting in one of only two clean rounds of the entire competition. This insured a spot in the British line-up for the final event of the 1968 Games now in progress: the Team Jumping.

The stadium erupted in cheers when the pony trotted out before the crowd. Programs fluttered onto the arena floor as the crowd's appreciation drowned the loudspeakers' sound. The pony looked around the filled stadium, seeming not to understand what all the fuss was about. Perhaps his eye stopped on Meagan before he walked on; perhaps it was only her imagination. Not since her Mongolian mount Targa had she known a Great Pony. "Good luck," she whispered.

Sounds of crying caused her to turn. It was the little girl in the stands with her mother, the one left behind while her older sister took her turn at the front. She was pointing to Stroller, tears streaming. "Pony!" the girl said around her fist jammed in her mouth. "See, momma! Pony!"

"We'll watch from here, Lisette. It's not your turn." The woman held the girl back from the railing.

"Ma'am!" Meagan called as the lady turned toward her seats. "I can hold her if you like. I'll be right here, next to your husband."

The woman hesitated, looking at Meagan worriedly before deciding. She gave a tight nod and whispered to the child, "Lisette, this nice lady will take you closer to see the pony. What do you say, Lisette?"

The girl looked up at Meagan with wide eyes, suddenly unsure. "Thank you," she answered shyly.

The woman brought the child to the bleacher's rail and held her down to Meagan. "Thank you *so* much. She's always talking about ponies, you just don't know."

"I think I might. Come on, little one. Your name is Lisette? Well, Lisette, we're going to have a wonderful time watching the pony." Meagan pushed through the crowd lining the in-gate and found a space as the start bell sounded. The girl called to her father, waving. He waved back and gave Meagan a silent, "thank you."

Meagan adjusted Lisette's light weight around her shoulders. Spectators bent over the stadium walls waving and tossing flowers. The jump crew circled with rakes, taking up anything thrown too far inside. Marion saluted and started Stroller, circling wide to give her pony a chance to settle. Stroller's ears flicked back and forth, listening for the plan.

There were practical reasons for Stroller's phenomenal success. He was well matched to his rider in size and attitude, he had been well-trained and his jumping style was impeccable: the pony used his neck, rounded his back, and folded his legs tightly and square. Years of smaller fences had given the pair experience together. Yet if there was a secret to Stroller's success in the ring, it was his great "heart."

When Stroller turned to the towering first fence, Meagan gripped the arena gate and heard the involuntary gasp of a nervous spectator beside her. Stroller picked up speed before the fence, ears set forward. Three strides out, the pony raised his head and charged. Stroller seemed to skip off the ground, carrying his little girl up and over, his hind hooves giving the back rail inches as flashbulbs and cameras snapped. The pony had no idea he should not be able to jump such huge fences.

They came on to the second jump at the same pace, and Stroller set himself high in the air the same way, up and over. Both the rider and the pony disappeared from Meagan's view then popped out the other side, cantering away lightly, rails intact. The crowd applauded spontaneously, and thousands of voices hushed them as Marion pulled Stroller back, adjusting to the third fence on the line. The pony's ears were taut as he sped to the fence, launching into the air and gliding back to earth.

The rider barely checked as they galloped away and turned to another big spread fence. Stroller soared, a flitting shadow that stretched over the span of poles, tucking his legs to avoid rapping the rail.

"Pony," Lisette said in a whisper, mesmerized.

The Double combination loomed, and from where Meagan stood it seemed to be set directly in a corridor of mud. Marion went deep into the corner and swung out, letting Stroller see the fences ahead. The dark pony opened his stride, gathering for the leap and launching into the air.

Stroller pulled his legs high and skimmed over the parallel rails, his belly grazing the tops of the poles as he tucked his hindquarters up. A soft cry came from the in-gate as the pony disappeared behind the first element of the combination, and then they were back, visible in the air. Stroller jumped high out of the suctioning mud, twisting in the air. The stadium gasped as Stroller hit a pole and it tumbled down.

Four faults.

It was plain to Meagan the ground was troubling Stroller, who required all his ability to clear international-sized fences under ideal conditions. The unforeseen mud was taking more of a toll on the pony than on the full-sized mounts.

Looking small and insignificant as they turned to the water, Marion let Stroller take the reins and stretch in his canter. They launched high into the air to land clear. Marion held her pony straight across the slick ground, coming close to the next obstacle to increase their security in the holding mud. Stroller rapped the back rail and nearly pulled it, then tossed his head going to the next fence and exploded up, clearing it by fractions.

Marion let Stroller break into a trot to settle, and then started a canter to the gate. She picked her spot and rode gently, letting her pony find his way. Stroller vaulted over.

The crowd buzzed as Marion settled her mount and came around. Heads and cameras followed. The rails and flowers of the bogey Triple waited ominously in the scored, soggy ground. The British medalists still had only four faults...

Stroller was too short to see over the wall that made up the first part of the Triple. He galloped down into the mud and leaped, folding his legs tightly and clearing it well, but took a surprised, short stride when he saw the second fence—and slid to a stop.

A great shocked gasp went up from the crowd, and then stunned silence fell as Marion pulled Stroller out of the Triple. Unknown to most, this was the first refusal by the gifted pony in major competition; it was also not widely known the diminutive champion was suffering from an infected tooth, which may have contributed to the unusual stop.

The refusal was only three faults, according to the rules of the day; not disastrous if Marion could finish the course, but the British team required her score to avoid elimination.

Lisette squirmed silently on Meagan's shoulders as Marion brought her pony to a trot and made a long circle; the stadium was as quiet as if the horse and rider were alone.

Horses do not see the jumping course before a competition—only the riders may walk it. Yet now the pony knew something lay in the slippery ground beyond the high wall. Marion lifted the reins and sent Stroller on. Around they came at a canter. Cameras followed silently. It was not hard to imagine the pair as colorful jousting knights, cantering solo past pennants hung over the stadium walls like the Circus banners of Rome, or to recall the ominous grandeur of Berber stallions galloping Conquistadors to conquest, or the ages of cavalry reflected in the pony's disciplined dressage. But it was also a nervous young woman on her discouraged pony, alone before the eyes of the world.

Marion closed her leg and took Stroller back to the Triple. The pony tossed his head once and started his run. Determined, he leaped into the air over the wall, vaulting it, landing and starting a long stride to the second element.

As in a nightmare, Meagan and the world watched Stroller slide into the second element and fall against the heavy wing holding up the poles. The pony and Marion disappeared under crashing timber. Marion rolled away but Stroller was trapped, thrashing the muddy ground but unable to rise. Deadly silence fell as Marion stood and ran to Stroller, trying to help her pony to his feet.

No, Meagan thought, gripping Lisette tightly. This could not be happening. Stroller kicked against the rails, struggling under the jump's wreckage. Stewards, cameramen and jump crew ran onto the field as Marion hovered, desperate. Her pony could not rise.

"Why did the pony fall down?" Lisette sniffed. Meagan could hear the girl starting to cry.

"Here, Lisette," Meagan said, bending down to let the child slide off. "Let's go find your mother."

The father came and took the child's hand, but she struggled: "No! Pony!" A scene suddenly flashed in Meagan's mind. Maybe it was like Targa—the pony was lying on the reins and could not move his head to stand up! *"The reins!"* Meagan shouted into the hushed stadium, ignoring the stares. *"Check his reins!"*

Whether the steward heard her call Meagan was not sure, but the man was running across the turf, shouting to the young rider. Marion bent down and pulled the leather reins free. Stroller lifted his head and kicked again, thrusting his forelegs under him and rising from the mass of timber. The crowd clapped in happy relief, and real cheering erupted as Marion led Stroller away from the fence and carefully checked over him.

Mud greased one entire side of Stroller, and Marion's white breeches were splotched dark. The steward assisted Marion in remounting, but the rider moved slowly, as if in a daze. The crowd applauded support as the sodden pair began their jog from the arena, retiring. As they trotted away, shouts began in pockets around the stands.

The fence was being rebuilt, and the clock was still running. Marion and Stroller had against them a refusal, a knockdown and a fall, but due to the course's difficulty Great Britain was still in contention for a medal—*if* they could finish. The treacherous Triple combination had to be attempted again, and completed. A third refusal would be elimination for both Marion and Stroller—and for the entire British team.

Marion's face was white and frozen as she rode toward the in-gate. Shouts behind her grew, but she did not seem to hear. It was not until a rider in British livery pushed through the in-gate, waving her back, that the situation became clear to her. Marion pulled up and looked back at the course. In determination, she turned Stroller back onto the field.

Meagan felt a coldness in her stomach as Stroller started to canter. A hush fell as the crowd realized what the girl and her pony were attempting: to face down one of the bravest challenges in sport. The tiny pair circled, straightened, and began the improbable run.

Splashing strides in the muck sounded across the silent stadium. Stroller saw the Triple coming again and lifted his head—higher this time—his ears flicking tensely back and forth. Marion found the distance and the courageous pony did not hesitate but dug into the turf and bounded in, reaching off the ground and sailing over the fateful wall to vanish on the other side.

Marion stayed forward and slipped the reins; Stroller landed and scrambled through the slick turf, grabbing for footing to launch over the second element, stretching over the wide fence and floating over. Touching down, one fence to go, Stroller brought his hindquarters under him and set his back hooves into the muck. Marion clung to the pony's neck as he stretched over the third fence, soaring across the poles as the Olympic stadium leaped to its feet.

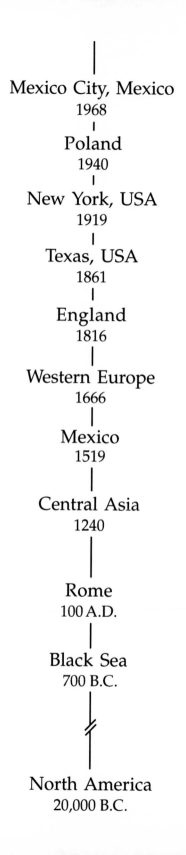

Mexico City, Mexico
1968

Poland
1940

New York, USA
1919

Texas, USA
1861

England
1816

Western Europe
1666

Mexico
1519

Central Asia
1240

Rome
100 A.D.

Black Sea
700 B.C.

North America
20,000 B.C.

A | P | A | R | T

LIKE A FILM splotching and burning on a projection screen, Olympic uniforms and spectators' clothes melted into patched, dingy overcoats. Banners faded to garish signs waving and bobbing around her. Arena music and cheering were lost in discordant chants, and instead of a popcorn-filled grandstand floor there was cold, grimy concrete.

Where the judges' stand had been, Meagan's eyes were drawn to a huge, freestanding board highlit with beams of intense light that shimmered and changed as she watched— *billboard advertising!*

She was finally home ... *HOME!*

Meagan was hit from the side as the crowd shifted like a tide going out. She moved with them to stay on her feet. A tall, pale girl in an orange overcoat carried a sign with bold red words: "Free Nature, Free Man!" A horse's stick figure bobbed over the chaotic scene.

The crowd surged away, pulling Meagan along. Soft bodies and pallid skin streamed by. The tide of people carried her across broken signs and refuse, rushing her into a dark corridor.

The air changed to oily coolness. The ground here was smooth and dry, with the slickness of polished concrete. A column of cool air flowed from a space beside her, and Meagan ducked into it, out of the milling torrent of people. She flattened against a hard wall, watching the stream of bodies passing in the dim light.

She waited, frozen, until the crowd began to slow and move steadily, driven numbly forward. Then she moved to follow the flow, keeping close to the wall. Smooth, chilled metal passed beneath her hand. A section gave way as she passed it; she pushed it open and slipped into a lightless alcove.

Alone now, in darkness, hints of odors swirled around her—scents too weak to identify, as if the air were too thin to hold them. She struggled against her growing feeling of being buried alive. In the dark she hit a concrete step and fell forward. She stood, brushing dirt off her hands.

A glow shone against a far wall, and Meagan moved towards it carefully. She was entering a large cavernous space. Then she heard in the sterile gloom—muffled but unmistakable—a horse's whinny.

Meagan felt her heart's strong beat as she peered into the shadows, making out black squares as large as horse stalls. A dull, rhythmic kick came from one of the square-shaped shadows. When Meagan moved to investigate the sound, a shiny gleam caught her attention: the white of an eye. Startled, she jumped and stifled a cry, but the eye was not looking at her, or at anything. The glitter was the glass eye of an imitation 'fox' perched on a simulated wood-rail fence.

She crept closer. The fox was appealingly fashioned as a caricature: the face was full and round, with a plush coat and polite teeth. The fluffy tail lifted high as if wagging. It was precious and adorable, and unlike any animal that had ever existed.

The muffled sound of kicking started again. Meagan walked past the box structures to find the source, and stopped at the spot the sound was loudest. Meagan stepped closer, running her hand along the cold sides. The smooth metal did not even tremble under the blows.

Further down the aisle, Meagan noticed that one of the box structures was open. She walked to the opening and carefully stepped inside.

The crackling of a loudspeaker came from the darkness: "WELCOME TO THE DATAPLEX NORTH CONVENTION CENTER. PLEASE LISTEN TO THE ENTIRE MESSAGE, AS OUR OPTIONS HAVE RECENTLY CHANGED. FOR QUALITY PURPOSES AND TO BETTER SERVE YOU, YOUR ACTIVITIES MAY BE MONITORED AND RECORDED."

Meagan flattened against the black metal structure ... *was this something she had done?* The unseen loudspeaker paused, and low overhead lights clicked on.

"FOR YOUR SAFETY AND TO BETTER SERVE YOU, PLEASE REMAIN STATIONARY UNTIL YOUR STATUS HAS BEEN REVIEWED. WE DO APOLOGIZE FOR ANY INCONVENIENCE. WAIT TIME IS ESTIMATED AT ... THREE MINUTES."

She could explain herself to the authorities. Wherever she was, she told herself, at least she was no longer lost in history. All that mattered was finally going *home!*

"SECURITY VERIFICATION IS EXPERIENCING HIGH VOLUME AND OUR OPERATORS ARE BUSY WITH OTHER CUSTOMERS. WE DO REQUEST YOUR COOPERATION AT THIS TIME. ESTIMATED WAIT TIME ... TWO MINUTES."

The dim overhead lights brought a dusky gloom to the space. Meagan crouched down and hugged her knees as the smooth voice intoned:

"WE ARE EXPERIENCING HIGH VOLUME AT THIS TIME, AND YOU MAY EXPERIENCE DELAYS. PLEASE REMAIN STATIONARY AND YOUR STATUS WILL BE REVIEWED BY THE NEXT AVAILABLE SECURITY TECHNICIAN. ESTIMATED WAIT TIME ... CONTACT NOW." Floodlight beams criss-crossed the air. Meagan turned, holding her arm up, squinting to see what was beyond the beams.

"Speak your name, last name first."

Meagan swallowed and gave her maiden name. "Roberts, Meagan."

"Speak your eNet at the beep." A low tone sounded on the other side of the lights.

The sound repeated, and she backed a step. "I don't know what you mean..."

A figure moved forward between the lights. "Be advised that your confirmation number is R34XC003. Company policy requires detention of unrecorded personnel. You are hereby advised of your currently applicable rights under Universal Commerce Law which may be waived subject to independent verification under Commercial Code 212 for Class C Corporate entities. Please step forward."

Sirens howled distantly above as Meagan stepped out to meet people whose faces she could not see. She was escorted from the cavernous area and down a corridor lit only by flashlight beams. "Please, there has been some mistake." She tried to stop but was forcibly directed ahead. "I was trying to get away from that crowd of people. I'm just trying to get home."

Doors opened to a warehouse-sized space below florescent lights. A sallow-faced official approached. "Disorderlies are to go to Rose Room South. Third corridor, second on the left."

"Wait, this isn't right!" Meagan pleaded as she was urged forward. "I wasn't being disorderly—I am just *lost*. If you show me the way out or let me use a phone ... please, I only need a minute!"

The horses of Achilles stood apart from the battle weeping...
When Zeus saw how they grieved, he took pity on them:
"Poor creatures, why did I give you to mortals destined to die?
You, who are immortal."

- Homer (c. 9th century B.C.) The Illiad

"Your name, please: last, first, and eNet." The female clerk looked expectantly at Meagan.

"Ma'am, I've told six people my name already."

"We require verification for our records. Last name first."

"Roberts, Meagan." She had decided to use her family's name so public records would match: she wanted no delays in returning home. The woman typed importantly, frowning at the screen.

Meagan was in the Daffodil Room North because she had forgotten her confirmation number. The off-white walls were bare except for a dismal painting of a window, complete with curtains. "Why do they call this the Daffodil room? It's not even yellow."

The clerk ignored the question. "Roberts ... Complaint R34XC003. What is your eNet?"

Meagan shook her head, sending the clerk into a clatter of keystrokes. "I have a phone number though, if I could just borrow a phone. See, I've been lost and I would like to call home. Please?"

The clerk continued to stare at the screen and type. Meagan surveyed the room. Televisions were mounted on the walls: everyone not staring at a computer monitor was watching the screens absently. "Would it be possible to use a restroom?"

"Facilities on this floor are reserved for eNet active customers." The woman looked coolly at Meagan, and handed her a form. "Please sign in the designated space."

Meagan looked at the closely-typed printout. "What is this?"

"An Indemnification Order. Please sign in the designated space."

Meagan bent to read the words. Small print jumbled into illegible words of indecipherable sentences. She looked up. "What is an indemnification order?"

"Please sign in the designated space."

"Is there an attorney I could consult? Am I being charged with anything?"

"It is company policy," intoned the clerk in a bored monotone. "All personnel must have a valid Indemnification Order on file while on corporate property."

"Well that's easy then," Meagan said, holding the woman's gaze and lifting the printout. "Since I have no desire to *be* on corporate property, we won't need *this*." She slowly tore the sheet in half. "Now, where is the exit?"

"Excuse me, is there a problem?"

Meagan turned to an elderly man's bland, lined face. His eyes were sunken deep in their sockets; his oversized jacket bore a strange corporate logo.

"Yes, I'm trying to get out of here and go home. If you could let me borrow a phone—"

"She won't sign the Indemnification Order," the clerk broke in. "And she's an Offnet."

The official's bland expression hardened. "Our policy is to obtain signatures of all unregistered personnel before further processing. I am afraid I will have to refer you to someone else." He lifted his small cell phone and began pushing buttons. "Where was she found?"

"In the Lower Containment section L."

"Even better. She isn't our problem. I will contact Event Security."

The clerk nodded and smiled dismissively at Meagan. "Next," she said, and called another name.

The official talked into the phone as he stepped away from Meagan. "She was trespassing in your section. We believe she was part of the protest and got lost. She has no reported eNet and there's no record of her in Central."

With a desperate lunge, Meagan grabbed the man's cell phone and ran to the entry doors. No bystanders tried to stop her; only a few even looked away from the video screens. Meagan reached the doors—they had no handle. When she pushed they would not open. As several personnel came toward her, she quickly moved to dial her home phone number ... and stood staring in confusion. The numbers on the phone were missing, replaced by a panel display with smooth buttons encircling a logo.

A security guard took the device from Meagan's stunned grasp. She watched the guard hand the device back to its owner.

"That will be enough to move the intruder into General Security's jurisdiction," sniffed the elderly official. He made an empty smile. "Take her to Lower Detention. She isn't eNet compliant, so enter her alphanumerically."

———

The gray cinderblock walls were scarcely relieved by the three misbegotten paintings of a drably outfitted ballerina in various poses. Meagan paced the room nervously. Something was wrong, very wrong. She told herself to calm down. *I only thought it was a phone ... it was just a palm computer or something. A security walky-talky.* She pushed away the fear growing in her mind.

A red light blinked over the door frame as a short beep sounded. The door opened to the dark jackets of security employees, each emblazoned with identical company logos. An older gentleman was escorted inside, and then the two guards waited by the entrance.

The gentleman came to stand directly before Meagan. Another dark jacket was folded over his arm. He stared at her for an uncomfortably long moment and finally put out his hand in greeting. Meagan shook it, and felt the man's fingers clasp longer than necessary. "I've arranged for your release, Miss Roberts." His voice carried a slight British accent. "I'm very sorry, I came as soon as I heard."

"Oh, thank you ... and you are?"

"My name is Dean Harbinger, Vice President of APART-Australia." Well into middle age, the man's graying hair was neatly cut and combed. His nondescript suit was well-fitted. Deep rings cut under his dark eyes ... but he was smiling. "You are very pretty, Miss Roberts."

Meagan held her irritation at the unbidden comment. "That's fine, Mr. Harbinger. What is *Apart Australia*?"

"The Association for Prevention of Animal Rights Trespass, Australian chapter." The man's tone was apologetic. "You were arrested during an unofficially sanctioned protest."

"I'm sorry, did you say Australia?"

"Yes, ma'am. Darwin, Australia, in Yarrawonga Area Precinct No. 17. The year is 2063, just as you said it would be."

"As I..." It took a moment to hear it, a moment before Meagan felt for the wall and slumped to the floor. Blood seemed to rush from her head. "No, it can't be." She hugged her knees as the room closed in. "I thought I was going home."

"Miss Roberts, please." Mr. Harbinger leaned over her. "Don't be upset."

"Please leave me alone. Just..." Meagan closed her eyes, pressing out tears. *No—this is impossible.* "Please. I need time."

"I know how upset you must be, but everything will be fine. It will, I ... *promise*."

"No, I don't think so." Meagan concentrated on breathing calmly. There had to be a mistake. She was coming closer to her own—she looked up at the man. "What do you mean, 'as I said it would be'?"

"Oh. I see. Then you must not have." He stammered in confusion. "I must be mistaken."

"Why did you tell me what year it was?"

"I was only ..." Mr. Harbinger recovered his congenial manner. "I was only answering your question, Miss Roberts."

"I asked about being in Australia. You told me what year it was."

His smile remained fixed. "So many personnel lose their bearings, being on the road for long periods."

"They don't know what *year* it is?"

A slight twinkle entered the man's eye. "You have me there, Miss Roberts. I suppose they usually know the year." He held out the spare jacket. "Come, please stand up and put this on. And this wristband. It will make things much easier."

Meagan took the coat silently. It bore the same logo as the others, a word symbol—A | P | A | R | T—superimposed over a globe of the world. The wristband had no latch but snapped on easily.

"Excellent, Miss Roberts, we are free to go." The odd man seemed in a hurry. "I have so much to show you."

Meagan decided not to argue. Dumbly she rose and followed the man, entering the outside corridor lined with off-white linoleum. The glare from overhead fluorescent bulbs flickered as they walked into an open area with desk grids of workers.

A man lay stretched out along the wall, dressed in the same clothing as the other workers. No one seemed to notice the stricken figure, who stared quietly blinking at the ceiling. "Mr. Harbinger!" Meagan took her guide's arm and pointed.

"Oh, yes, a *laydown*," he answered discretely, courteously moving her hand back to her side. "Pointing is considered impolite. Sometimes people simply stop nowadays. They are healthy by current standards and it's not despair exactly, it's just a ... separation. A broken connection. Extreme passivity. It doesn't seem painful, but they have slipped from our reality and they don't return. Afflicted persons are removed at the end of each day."

"Oh." Meagan didn't ask what 'removal' entailed, trying not to stare at the motionless figure while Dean Harbinger strode purposefully to a worker's desk and presented a small card.

"Release for APART-Australia. One of our employees."

The clerk was male, but otherwise similar to the previous clerk. "What is the ID number and eNet?"

"Miss Roberts has no eNet, but this *is* the Offnet processing center, isn't it? The company ID is 5B."

"'D' as in dog?" The clerk squinted at the computer screen and absently hit the keyboard. "We don't have record of her."

"If you will process Miss Roberts under APART-Australia," Harbinger repeated patiently as he held out his wrist. "Put her on our account, thank you." He turned to Meagan. "We can go now."

"Where ... and why did you say I was an employee?"

"Miss Roberts, I can explain," he said evenly. "We are going to my office so I can show you."

"I really have no choice, do I?"

"Not really, no."

Take most people, they're crazy about cars.
I'd rather have a goddam horse.
A horse is at least human, for godsake.
- J. D. Salinger (1919-2010), Catcher in the Rye

HARBINGER LED MEAGAN through the building and outside. The air was heavy and humid as from a recent rain. Gasoline fumes and the metallic scent of rust burned her nose.

A long beetle-like vehicle and its driver advanced to meet them. The mirrored exterior was painted solid with advertising images. "What is *that?*"

"You would call it a car, Miss Roberts." Harbinger answered as if he did not think the question strange. "We are going to my office." They slid inside, and the driver joined the sparse vehicle traffic grinding past in either direction along a patched and rutted expressway. "As you can see, the roads aren't kept up anymore," Harbinger said conversationally. "There are only these private caravans, the people have no real transportation. And the Humane Edicts prevent them from having horses or mules. It was accomplished by animal welfare groups. Funny, don't you think?" The expression in the man's eyes was not amusement. "Enforced primitive conditions—no, excuse me, the primitives had horses. We are something less. We're safe, though. Under lock and key."

Meagan looked out, away. "This organization, APART-Australia, what do they do?"

"We protect animals from abuse. It sounds wonderful, doesn't it? The slogan polls very well."

"Do you always visit prisoners personally?"

"You were not a prisoner, Miss Roberts. I apologize for the mistake."

Meagan stared out the vehicle's window. They passed battered buildings covered in a kaleidoscope of luminous signs and garish lights competing for attention to product. She thought about her countryside ride with Danvers. How far those green hills and clear spaces were from this boxed concrete and steel.

Harbinger looked out his own side. "We're all here now, the last of humanity together, tightly bound. Actually there are colonies, but ... you look flushed, Miss Roberts. Are you all right?"

Chaotic images flowed past her window. "Not really." *It would look better dark.* "What was that crowd about? You said they were protesting."

"As it happens, they were protesting a horse exhibition." He cleared his throat softly. "Our organization helped end the archaic practice of horseback riding over thirty years ago. Officially, we consider it horse slavery."

Only dimly did Meagan feel her hand clench around the armrest: a short time ago she thought this was home.

"*Un*officially, you and I share a love for horses, Miss Roberts. I had the advantage of a great patroness who taught me." The man's tone was extremely cordial. "Would you like me to put up the screens? Our caravans are licensed for them."

Meagan sat back. "Please."

Mr. Harbinger stabbed an access code into the door's panel, and solid plates slid over the windows, blocking the ugliness. "The people must look at it, of course. It is the law. Commercial Right of Access."

Meagan watched the man. His gaze kept flickering to her even when he was supposedly looking away.

Harbinger reached out. "Show me the underside of your forearm. Please, Miss Roberts? I won't hurt you."

Meagan extended her arm, rotating it so the pale underside showed in the dim light. Harbinger gently rubbed his finger across her wrist.

"Smooth," he remarked, pulling back the sleeve of his own jacket to reveal a rectangular, ridged scar just below the wrist tendons. "You don't have an implant for an eNet address, which makes you a non-compliant, subject to processing in a substation for Offnets. Most unpleasant."

Meagan was repulsed by the precision symmetry of the raised scar. "Can't I just get an eNet address and not have one of those things?"

"You don't *have* an eNet address, Miss Roberts, you *are* the address. Oh, there is something I want you to see." The opaque shield over Meagan's window lowered. Harbinger nodded at the emerging view. "We are just passing our zoo."

Meagan squinted, seeing people filing among clustered buildings like ants traveling the mortar between bricks. "I don't see any animals."

"We don't keep as many as the old zoo did. APART won the facility in a humane suit against the zoo. As animals die we simply don't replace them. We've found people don't really notice things if done slowly over time."

The car maneuvered into a circular drive and stopped. The doors automatically unlocked and opened, and Harbinger stepped out. "Home, sweet home," he said, looking up at the enormous block building. Not a feature upon it stood out except the name, $A|P|A|R|T$, and the address spelled in blazing red neon. "Twenty stories up, six stories down, paid for with tax-deductible contributions. A monument to human compassion for animals, made of concrete."

Meagan gave Harbinger a tight smile. She let him escort her through glass entry doors into a crowded lobby.

"*Mr. Harbinger!*" barked a summoning voice. Meagan followed her escort closely as he pushed his way through the pressing crowd. They were ushered into an office and a door closed behind them. "Hurry-durry time, Dean!" The speaker was a portly middle-aged man standing in front of an uncluttered desk. He wore a black suit with the company logo of a broken-up world. He spoke in a strangely garbled manner. "The nets want a quote about the APART horse protest and national sent a crew. Telex-WorldCom is waiting outside. I said-and-said *no media!*"

"I don't understand, Mr. Bromfield. We requested conditioned treatment from Central."

"Well, Central didn't pick it up," the man snapped. "I'm with enough trouble on this damned ReElection Act—can you believe people's still pushing *that* gobble? What, so any lazy-laze can waste all my efforts with a flip of a switch?"

"It might be best if you gave a statement," Harbinger gently suggested. "It may defuse the matter. You know how these things can get out of hand."

"Never heard that-*not.*" The man glanced at Meagan. "Is this the horse rider?"

"Yes, sir. I'm taking her to see the horse now."

"Capital good." The man strode forward and extended a hand to Meagan. "Pleased to meet you, missum. Chester Bromfield, Counselor Region 9."

"Meagan Roberts." She clasped his thick fingers in greeting.

"Alright, Harbinger. Have Security come down. I'll tell a short statement." The man hitched his pants decisively and walked to the door. He exited and moved through the crowd outside.

Harbinger and Meagan followed, joining the head-craning assembly. Glistening banks of digital eyes focused on Counselor Bromfield as he stepped to a wall under the APART logo. He put his hands behind his back and waited for questions.

"Mr. Bromfield, is it true that APART sponsored protests against the horse demonstration? Is APART taking responsibility for the injuries to the targeted groups?"

"No, no, no. APART cannot assume liability for our protesters," the man answered officiously. "That said, APART feels that, just as peoples are entitled to the fruits of technological progress, so too are the correct animals. We are determined to extend human progress to all. Not including accepted food species, of course."

Another reporter interrupted. "Do you agree with the recent upholding of St. Bernard dogs as a food species?"

"My agreement is no matter. I am a mere humbly-humble public servant." Mr. Bromfield cleared his throat and repeated a sing-song slogan: "*APART* assures the moral community that authorities have complied with the research requirements to ensure St. Bernards are not a legitimate sentient organism, and exist explicitly as a protein source for higher mammals."

Behind Meagan's fear, she was very much repulsed by the proceedings—at least, that which she could understand. Grammar was not evenly distributed among the speakers, and though some conversation was clear and formal, much was muddled or incomprehensible.

"APART will issue a statement to assure all supporters of our commitment to animal protection. Now if I may, I would like and wish to discuss my own interpretations on moreother legislation coming before the Council..."

"We should go," Harbinger whispered, and nodded to men in Security uniforms. He took Meagan's hand as they pushed through the clog of people and left the commotion behind.

Thick glass and steel had to be opened with an access card at every junction. Finally they came to a large opaque door that looked like frosted plexiglass; Harbinger slid his card into a slot and the door clicked open. Ahead was a dark, simulated-wood hallway with recessed lights. "One moment, Miss Roberts, and I can show you everything."

"Could you tell me, please? Not to be rude, but if it is like the rest I've seen, I would prefer to get it over with."

"Soon you will understand," Mr. Harbinger said confidently, and ushered her along. The hallway opened to a room with dark hardwood floors, dominated by a long, glossy black conference table in its center. Chairs and consoles were spaced around the table's rim. The smooth walls were tinted an odd, hazy gray and were without feature or ornament.

A colorful antique globe sat on a wood pedestal at one end of the room, encased in glass. Meagan stared at it a moment, thinking it looked strangely familiar. She walked slowly around the windowless room. "Nice view," she said dourly.

"I can fix that." Harbinger walked quickly to a table console and began typing into a keyboard. The four walls glowed and came to life, each with a separate nature scene: a blazing sunset, mountain peaks, an ocean's waves, trees in a forest.

Meagan traced a line across the forest as she walked past. "I prefer the original." She caught a smirk from the man, and walked over to his console. "Is that a map?"

"It's the Pacific region. Here, I'll expand it."

She leaned closer to the display. "What are the red places?"

"We call them 'wipeouts.' Mostly caused by biological weapons. No people are allowed in the red zones. Some are actually livable spaces set aside to maintain the remaining ecosystem, but the public is told the spaces are radioactive or poisoned. Central Australia is one example." He looked up and grinned. "Virtually all remaining human population is now here in Northern Australia. Things worked out a bit differently than anticipated."

She shuddered and straightened. "It doesn't make sense."

"No, it doesn't. Even so, we gave the reins to commerce and it led us back into the dark."

"You don't seem to mind, Mr. Harbinger."

"I'm taking it well?" The man seemed strangely well-humored. "These times bring many emotions, Miss Roberts. There is good news happening too." He pointed to the antique globe behind glass. "Do you like the globe? I had it brought in especially for you."

Meagan stared at the man. The implication of his words remained in the air. "For ... me?"

He pressed a switch and leaned forward. "Systems? Request by HD514, Conference Room 9. Install *Bridgestone Collection*. Confidential mode. Thank you." The wall flickered. Hanging artwork materialized on the walls where the nature scenes had been.

A series of virtual framed paintings hung along one wall. Meagan walked down the row slowly, examining the artwork. "It's ... all horses." The first image was a Roman-nosed horse carrying a rider who held his sword high. "I remember this painting, it's Bucephalus and Alexander!"

"APART attained copyright. I thought you'd like to see them."

Meagan stopped in surprise. The next painting in the series was of a horse herd being driven off a cliff.

"They were commissioned long ago, Miss Roberts."

The third painting was a Scythian horse in gold regalia, followed by a view of an oncoming chariot. The next painting was a dusty-colored Mongolian war pony, and then a tournament Knight. Meagan walked slowly past them.

"I especially like that one, Miss Roberts. Cortés' horse."

"El Morzillo," she said softly, and walked to the next painting. The image was a bay horse performing the leaping *Capriole.* Further portraits were of steeplechasing, fox-hunting ... a cattle drive.

"Mr. Harbinger, these are about me. Places I went."

"Yes, it was a commemorative set."

Meagan stared at the soaring portrait of Marion Coakes and Stroller. She hugged herself as she studied the dark pony, his forelegs tightly folded in flight. She felt exposed and vulnerable. *This strange place knew her.*

Harbinger peered at his monitor. "Did you know large durable goods mimic the life cycle of a horse? A horse's prime was four to six years long, so old-style automobiles were manufactured to the same cycle. Every year, instead of a new crop of foals, came the introduction of new models."

"Are you mocking me, Mr. Harbinger?"

"Why," Harbinger looked up from the screen, the shine of excitement fading from his expression. "No, Miss Roberts. I am repeating arguments made by horse preservation organizations in years past. The subject is becoming public again, and I enjoy the discussion."

"I don't think I do."

"But they were—they *are*—so wonderful! Like the inspirational *Appeal to Empathy* issued by the International Equestrian Federation." Harbinger leaned to study the keyboard. "It's about the horse's new roles to heal, to inspire..." The screen flipped to darkness; he sighed and straightened. "I can paraphrase. The Appeal was a plea that horses be preserved to 'sustain a standard of natural beauty, owned and patented by no one, uncorrupted.' The statement was released after fox hunting was banned worldwide."

Meagan watched Mr. Harbinger carefully, trying to avoid reacting to his words. She thought about something she once heard, that insanity may be a sane response to an insane world.

The man came around his desk and walked toward the Bridgestone globe. "Did you know writing and horsemanship developed in the same time and place in ancient Mesopotamia? Equestrian nations led the world since the earliest civilizations found a way to harness a chariot to a horse. From Hittites to Greeks to Asians to Europeans to Americans—East and West—whether charioteers or knights or cowboys or jockeys. Virtually all successful cultures have a rich horsemanship tradition. Horses are part of human consciousness.

"It took only one generation to forget." Harbinger stopped before the antique globe, hands behind his back. "I've often wished I could turn this globe, to touch it. The procurators assure me it wouldn't last a month in the open air."

"You said I'd understand everything, Mr. Harbinger. I'm sorry, but I still don't."

"It wasn't meant to go so far, Miss Roberts. APART was begun for good purposes. Certainly our donors were well-intentioned. There was a backlash against wealth after the finance disasters, and horses were one of its most ancient symbols. It could have been greed itself, or certain investments or beach homes or designer shoes. It just happened, tragically, to be horses." The man was trembling slightly. "It was the money. Donations kept coming and APART kept going. We accused the horse community of cruelty and waste in more and more activities. Instead of policing slaughter-houses, we lobbied for them ... and picketed stables."

"I thought you were about *saving* horses?"

"The worst abuses of history have come from those claiming to 'save' things, Miss Roberts. Save the Republic, save traditional values ... it is an easy way to put on 'hero's clothing.' Who doesn't want to be a hero?

"Events took on a life of their own. Industry wanted to render horses for profit, and hired APART to help them find a way. It worked, too well. APART turned its attack on the very idea of humane horsemanship, and provided cover for the liquidation of the horse population behind the scenes." He faltered when he saw Meagan's expression.

"You did *what?*"

"It was over thirty years ago. Let's not dwell on—"

"I didn't hear correctly. I know I didn't." Meagan wanted a window to look through; some escape. "We were going to a good future enjoying horses. Taking care of them."

Harbinger looked at Meagan with stricken eyes. "We have been without horses for so long, some denial organizations claim they never existed, any more than sea serpents or polar bears."

"But ... polar bears *do* exist, or did."

"Not officially. This is not a subject for today, please."

Meagan turned back to the series of paintings, trying not to cry, or scream. Vivid impressions passed through her mind ... dewy grass in spring and graceful necks reaching to graze. Quiet hours of grooming and horse chores, the smells of saddle soap, hay and shavings. Cold frost crunching underneath hooves. Steamy breath against icy landscapes, hot days of flies and swishing tails. The wind of a gallop, feeling a horse stretch his reins and blow softly at the end of a workout, the glow of a good ride, the quiet communion. A thousand scents, ten thousand moments—banished, not only from her life, but from those who would never know them. The ultimate cannibalization is to steal from the unborn.

Her eyes stopped on the final oil portrait in the series. The painting was of a middle-aged woman. Her graying hair was pulled back severely; her face was set in a stern expression. Meagan felt Harbinger's eyes watching her.

"Do you like it, Miss Roberts?"

Meagan swallowed. The pictured woman had strong features. She was handsome and ... striking. Imposing, even. "My first thought was how much she looks like Mrs. Bridgestone."

"I agree it is a very good likeness."

Meagan stared at the image, fighting tears. "It's ... me."

God forbid I should go to a Heaven where there are no horses.
- R.B. Cunningham-Graham (1852-1936)

"I'M SORRY, MISS ROBERTS. I didn't mean to upset you." Harbinger's smile was kind. "I just wanted you to believe me. I know about the Great Horse and how you can go home."

Meagan had never quite realized the reason for sitting down before receiving news. She numbly maneuvered to a conference chair and focused on settling into it, feeling the slick plastic, the smooth surfaces. "Who are you, really?"

"Dean Harbinger is my name, and as I said I'm a company man. At the present moment, my supervisors believe you are advising us on the display we will be using for our new equine campaign."

"Is that why I am your employee?"

"Yes, exactly."

Meagan hesitated. "What do you know about the Great Horse?"

"Well, I know that one such specimen departed from your backyard in North America on June 21st, 2004 at approximately 5:50 a.m. And I know you joined that departure, and have traveled through over a hundred centuries of history. Do I have the correct person?"

Meagan stared. She had dreamed of a day of recognition and it was becoming a nightmare.

"I was contacted by *The Bridgestone Foundation* many years ago, and entrusted with passing this information on to you. You see, Miss Roberts, I once had a Great Horse of my own. His name was Mister."

"You had a Great Horse?" Meagan repeated the strange words. "What was he like?"

The man smiled. "You ask the important questions first. My Mister was gentle and patient, Miss Roberts. So patient. He never returned the bad treatment he'd received. He became a therapy horse, helping the handicapped as part of a new world of horsemanship that was opening up to heal mankind..." Harbinger closed his eyes briefly before continuing.

"Miss Roberts, you know humanity has endured dark ages in the past, when literacy died and civilization stopped. Ours is stopping. Society is crumbling around us. There is almost no creativity in the population. No empathy or curiosity or attention span. After gaining final, ruthless control of the population, now those in charge are desperately trying to relight the spark.

"About a year ago people began having dreams about a galloping horse. Horse figures began to appear on walls and gates. Then a recording was made of a horse's whinny echoing across the Australian Alps, from one of the immobilization zones. Researchers from APART were sent out, and it was found from his droppings that there truly was a wild stallion. It seems horses may be out there, perhaps descendants of the old feral *brumby* population that escaped the last roundups."

"You think this stallion is the new Great Horse?"

"I think so, but no one else accepts the legend. What everyone *can* see is that the horse has brought excitement. People are eager to share stories about the stallion. There is new energy and hope. Ironically, APART was asked to capture and care for the horse. I lead the project." Harbinger moved to a display console and placed his hand over a sensor. A wall section resolved to a screen with rows of familiar black boxes. "You've seen our Animal Containment Units, or what you'd call 'stalls.'

Meagan moved closer to the wall screen and stared at the monolithic, sterile structures. "The poor animals."

Harbinger tapped the screen and the display changed to a camera's view of a gray horse. Thumbnail images filled the wall screen at angles taken from the side, front and above. A handsome, chiseled horse head showed in close-up. "This is the subject of our discussion. Our organization lists him as Equus Prime, but I call him Raphael—or Rafi. The Great Horse."

"Hello, Rafi." Meagan walked closer to the images. "He's cute. How did you capture him?"

"Let's just say that carrots work better than loud explosions. That was an actual discussion, too. He's surely one of the brumbies, but Rafi seems to be a throwback with all the speed, endurance, soundness and spirit of a Bedouin founding sire. An original Arabian."

Meagan looked quizzically around the glossy room filled with images of her own journey. "Is *this* what the Great Horse wanted to show me, to frighten me with a future without horses?"

"Well ... not exactly." Rafi's image shifted on the wall screen as the gray horse moved. "The Bridgestone Foundation made several discoveries. Archeology is a fascinating science with lots of little keys, if you know the right lock. Your legend was not a prophecy of doom. Chief Joseph's poem was to indicate that the horse's abilities were potentially dangerous. It was a warning."

Meagan frowned. "So *that's* why I was stranded for months at a time, dropped in deserts and ships and stalls and every other random place. I was punished because I didn't listen to the warning?"

"No, not at all. I'm sorry to say Promise has been a rather bad girl. She ran off and left you several times."

"Why do you say Promise was being a 'bad girl'?"

"She didn't mean it, Miss Roberts. Promise was so young and inexperienced. I am sure it was confusing to you both. The situation was not obvious."

"I'm afraid I am *still* confused, Mr. Harbinger."

"Imagine the reaction of a high-spirited Thoroughbred of your time, a young horse like Promise, to a frightening experience. Such as Promise's experience with the two thieves."

"You mean the two men in my backyard?"

Harbinger nodded. "Exactly. Any horse would be likely to run off in similar circumstances. You know the equine creed: *He who quickly runs away, lives to run another day.* If the frightened horse were a Pegasus, he might bolt across the sky. And if the horse could travel in time?"

Meagan thought back to the beginning. "The men—Promise *was* scared. Then we jumped the pasture fence..."

"She understood you wanted to escape and so she did. Her way. Promise bolted through time."

"She *bolted* with me—like running away?"

Harbinger was compassionate. "It seems to be what happened, Miss Roberts. And though Promise can travel time, she can do so only through lives of other Great Horses. She comes to hover close, Angel style, you might say."

"I thought it was a planned journey, with the Great Horse guiding me." Her voice became a whisper. "It wasn't only about me."

"Promise ran more than ten thousand years away, by the *Foundation's* estimate. The Great Horse doesn't think like a human. No horse does."

Meagan nodded, head bowed. "The gypsy-woman told me the Great Horse wasn't a human angel. I didn't know she meant Promise was a *horse* angel."

"The woman sounds perceptive. It is unfortunate we discarded our old wisdom. We mistook our technology for superiority, not sequence." He hesitated. "I'm glad you came now ... I was worried Promise might not return."

She looked up. "Has Promise has been here before?"

"A few times. Promise is running loose in time ... did you understand that part?"

"Well I—*no,* I didn't understand that part!"

"Promise never stays long. This future is uncertain to her, as it is for you. It's not inevitable from your point of view."

Meagan felt she could not quite grasp the words. "Why does Promise come *here?*"

"She is curious, like all horses, and Rafi is here. Promise gallops across time, visiting other Great Horses. Sometimes she picks you up and moves you along, but she doesn't understand your distress. Of course, horses don't always come when you call."

"All that time I was stranded, Promise was off *visiting?*"

Harbinger chuckled, rather inappropriately in Meagan's view. "Loose horses are a problem. Always have been. No one wants the horse let out of the barn. Though I will say in Promise's defense, she was gradually bringing you closer to home."

"Very gradually, I would say," Meagan replied stiffly. Promise was supposed to be a benevolent, all-seeing deity—not an uncorraled horse on the lam. "How did you get her to come?"

"We feed watermelon rind to Rafi. It's Promise's favorite."

"*Watermelon* rind? *That's* how I could have gone home?"

"Maybe I shouldn't tell you now."

Megan took a long breath and let it out. "No, I'm glad to know, thank you. Is there any way I can go home?"

"Actually there is, Miss Roberts." Harbinger swiped his hand over a sensor. The display screens dimmed to black. He moved to a wood-paneled wall section. "Do you remember the story of Pegasus and Bellerophon?"

Meagan nodded. "The winged horse and his rider. They killed a monster, I believe."

"The Chimera." Harbinger inserted his security card into a slot and a panel sprung open to reveal a locker. "The important part is *how* Bellerophon tamed Pegasus." He reached inside and retrieved a black satchel with a long strap. "With a Golden Bridle."

She took the satchel and was surprised at its weight. "Can I look inside?"

"Please do."

Meagan found the clasp and opened it. She walked to the table and pulled out a folded mangle of leather and yellow metal, and set the satchel aside.

"It's made to resemble the Golden Bridle of Pegasus, Miss Roberts. I know it seems strange—"

"No it doesn't." She was far from a cynic in these matters. "Mrs. Bridgestone said something about it. How does it work?"

Mr. Harbinger smiled. "In myth, the Golden Bridle tames the *Pegasii*. I had a model made up to give you a way to control Promise. Rafi has been getting used to it, so it's been adjusted to him."

Meagan unfolded the bridle. The headstall and reins were tanned leather, but the mouthpiece was jointed in the center and made of smooth, hammered gold. It shone with a faint glow. "The whole bridle isn't gold?"

"No, only the mouthpiece. Of course it's only a replica, and I don't know if the gold really matters. The idea is to focus your attention on guiding Promise, not letting the reins go ... as you have been doing." The words hung in the air.

"I thought Promise was taking me on a journey," Meagan said defensively. "I didn't know she was running away!"

"It's understandable. Misinterpreting equine behavior is an ancient trait of humans, Miss Roberts. However, if you hold the reins, you can better control where Promise takes you."

"I can even go ... see someone I knew in the past?"

Harbinger nodded. "Yes. You only need to locate a living Great Horse first, so Promise can find you."

"Oh, is that all."

"This brings me to the final point. You're to be the rider for our new horse exhibition next week. It will be the perfect excuse to be near Rafi and wait for Promise."

"You want *me* to ride your wild horse?"

"Our wild and untamed horse, yes. Stallion, actually."

"The legend says only the *owner* can ride a Great Horse."

"No one owns our Great Horse, Miss Roberts. APART has custody, but that isn't a real person. Legally, yes, but sophistry fools humans, not horses."

"Why me?"

"Because no one knows how anymore. After the horse ban and the rider roundups, people stopped admitting they ever knew. We have no riders left."

Meagan clutched the bridle tightly. "And once I try to ride your Great wild Horse there might not be me, either."

"Unless Promise comes."

Meagan blinked. "Will that happen?"

"It should. Promise brought you here, so the good news is she is close by. Unfortunately she doesn't like to stay long, so the bad news is that we have to hurry. There is a fresh watermelon slice in the handbag. My advice is to feed it to Rafi first, and then bridle him so when Promise arrives you can mount and go home."

"Okay, it's the mounting up on a wild stallion part I'm unclear about."

"I don't have another idea, Miss Roberts, but I do have reason to believe Promise will come and take you home. There is a legend of a Great Horse in our time. It's not as long as Chief Joseph's poem."

"It's so strange to hear you talk about this, Mr. Harbinger."

"As I mentioned before, I had the benefit of a great patroness. Our own legend is simple: '*A rider will come to renew the world.*' I believe that is you, Miss Roberts."

"You think *I'm* part of the legend? Does that mean you and this time will disappear?"

"Not disappear, I don't think, but this future was a mistake. You must feel that." Mr. Harbinger's voice was solemn. "Now things will be set right. We should go meet Rafi before they take him."

"Where are they taking him?"

"I'd rather not say, Ms. Roberts. He will not be injured, I will say that. Not intentionally. Is there anything else you wanted to see here?"

"No." Meagan scanned the sterile room. "If you've seen one executive meeting room, you've seen them all. Cathedrals and castles were better, I think. This tends a bit Roman."

Mr. Harbinger smiled. "Shall we?" The man opened his coat and removed a small object, putting it to his ear. "Building Security? There will be one visitor with me."

The room seemed to brighten. *I might be really going home,* Meagan thought nervously, repacking the bridle and slinging the satchel's strap over her shoulder. Her stomach was knotted. It was strange how close the feeling of excitement was to that of sheer terror.

Horses and children, I often think,
have a lot of the good sense there is in the world.
- Josephine Demott Robinson (1868-1948), Circus star

HARBINGER TOOK MEAGAN gently by the elbow and guided her toward a side door. He swiped his card—it clicked open—and they moved through several corridors before coming to a service area. An elevator groaned as it approached. Steel doors squealed open. Meagan and Harbinger stepped inside.

Meagan watched the man carefully. His neatly combed hair had become unruly and his shirt ballooned around his waist, becoming untucked. Yet Harbinger seemed in a buoyant mood, excited, smiling to himself.

"I don't know how to thank you," she said sincerely, meeting the man's eyes; he looked away as if embarrassed.

"Quite unnecessary, Miss Roberts. It has been wonderful to see you again."

"See me *again?*"

"No, no ... I meant, meet in person."

Doors opened to a cement-floored corridor. Uniformed men guarded the entrance to an open warehouse space. Inside, rows of shed-sized black metal "stalls" lined each cinderblock wall. Long yellow slashes of paint marred the side of one in dripping letters that declared: "USE = ABUSE."

Harbinger proudly strode to one and patted the metal sides. "You saw these before. They are self-contained, fully automatic, climate-controlled, detonation-resistant Animal Containment Units. You can see the name there—*The Trojan Project.* A little joke no one understands anymore."

Meagan looked down the aisle of black structures. She remembered hearing kicking the first time she had seen one of these machine-stalls. A living horse was entombed inside one of the sterile cold shells. "Which is Rafi's?"

Harbinger led Meagan to one of the units. "He gets led around the warehouse twice a day. I watch him on the internal video. He gets bored in there, just circling. Sometimes he dunks his hay in his water to make it taste better. He's quite a character."

A pair of women in lab coats entered. Harbinger glanced at his security device and whispered to Meagan: "The attendants should have finished an hour ago." He seemed impatient. "We'll wait. After they've gone, we'll bring out Rafi so you can bridle him."

Meagan nodded.

"If Promise comes you can mount up—this time *hold on* to the reins and focus on your old backyard at home."

"What happens then?"

"Promise should take you back home. From my point of view, you will dissolve and hopefully everything will get better." He gave her a genuine smile. "It does in my dreams."

The two uniformed attendants approached Rafi's metal stall. One worker consulted a clipboard before reaching to enter a code on the stall's side. Tones issued from a metal panel as it slid away.

Rafi's velvet nose appeared in the opening, sniffing the air. Holding a flake of hay at arm's length, the second worker poked a handful toward the hole. Most drifted to the cement floor. "Stop playing games!" the woman with the clipboard demanded, but the horse pushed his nose still further out into space, blocking the opening. Exasperated, the attendant lowered the slot's door; the horse withdrew reluctantly. "He must learn to behave."

Meagan was surprised by the action. "Excuse me," she asked politely, "can I help?"

The clipboard-wielding attendant looked at her irritably. "The horse won't move so we can put the hay inside. I'm too tired to play games."

"The horse is not playing games. He just wants his hay." Harbinger quietly interrupted. "Miss Roberts, please..."

"Yes, but the horse doesn't understand, Mr. Harbinger. Don't people know that horses are not like humans?" Meagan felt helpless at the attendants' smirks.

"What I *know* is that I am a dangerous predator and represent danger to the horse," the clipboard woman lectured. "'Horse*man*ship' is about cruelty and domination, and I refuse to learn about such atrocities. Now, if you don't mind, I have my schedule to finish."

Harbinger leaned to Meagan, speaking softly. "She is repeating APART's rhetoric. These two are the best we have—most riding protesters won't go near the horse."

"Poor Rafi."

The two attendants in white coats were making another attempt to feed the stallion. The first worker entered a code and the feeding slot slid open. The second stepped up with the hay; the occupant's nose appeared, stretching for an early bite as before. The surprised worker dropped the hay.

"Oh, for Heaven's *sake*." Meagan stepped forward and scooped the hay from the ground. She reached inside and pushed the horse's nose away, tucking the hay into the slot.

"*No*, Miss Roberts!"

Red overhead lights blinked on. An alarm started low and began to climb. The workers backed away, smug expressions on their faces.

Meagan turned unhappily to Harbinger. "Is this going to be a problem?"

"UNAUTHORIZED ACCESS. PLEASE WAIT FOR THE SAFETY PROFESSIONAL NEAREST YOU. BE ADVISED WE RESERVE THE RIGHT TO DETAIN ALL INDIVIDUALS SUSPECTED OF TAMPERING WITH CORPORATE PROPERTY. YOUR WAITING TIME IS... ONE MINUTE."

"I'm so sorry, Miss Roberts, I should have warned you the stalls are monitored." Harbinger's face was tight. "This is unexpected. Don't worry. I will find a way to have you released."

Light flooded the hall. Meagan looked at Harbinger. "Released from what?"

"You will be fine, Miss Roberts. It was so good to meet you. I want you to know I have always—*will* always—remember you."

"Thank you, Mr. Harbinger ... *Dean*." Meagan reached out her hand.

He returned her grasp. "We can never know all the good we do, Miss Roberts." The man struggled to say more.

"UNAUTHORIZED ACCESS. PLEASE WAIT FOR THE SAFETY PROFESSIONAL NEAREST YOU. YOUR WAITING TIME IS ... NINE SECONDS."

Men were entering the hallway: efficient, emotionless men in black uniforms. Floodlights swept the floor and found Meagan, blinding her. The last words she heard from Mr. Harbinger were to the security personnel: "Miss Roberts is not to be harmed. All property she carries is corporate property. You are not to confiscate *anything!*"

And I saw heaven opened, and behold a white horse;
and he that sat upon him was called Faithful and True.

- Holy Bible, Revelation 19:11

The PLASTIC-COATED CHAIR reclined comfortably, conveniently allowing Meagan to watch the video monitor. Almost lost amongst headlines, tag lines and logos, the picture on the screen was a burning building—perhaps several—with hysterical victims in close-up. A digital anchorperson's head bobbed among the scenes of disaster.

Banal paintings of still-life fruit baskets on red-checkered tablecloths hung on otherwise blank walls. Besides that, Meagan thought the people and facilities quite nice for a place called "lockdown." The satchel with the watermelon slice and bridle was tucked safely beneath her reclining chair. The threat of corporate lawyers had worked like a magic spell.

Before Meagan could be tried for "trespassing" she was forced to receive an eNet implant—only eNet active citizens had the legal rights afforded to corporations. As she awaited this peculiar doom, she stewed about recent revelations.

Promise was only running away. Meagan was upset with herself for not realizing this before. She *knew* horses lived in world of different perceptions: perhaps she might have offered up watermelon rind to the Great Horse if she, Meagan, had not been so self-centered. Her complete summation of possible reasons for the journey had been—herself.

In the meantime, the hospitality was weak but not entirely missing. Meagan contemplated a thin, soft sandwich still in its plastic wrap, now with one bite out of it. It had tasted like styrofoam gel. *Probably very efficient,* she thought, *in every way except as food.*

The door clicked and opened. A woman with a pleasant face entered. "Good afternoon," she said, smiling, her temperament well-matched by her aggressively-cheery yellow apron over a white dress uniform.

"Good afternoon." Meagan had decided to be as polite as possible. "They said I was going to see a counselor, but they didn't say why."

The woman bustled over and pushed the lunch tray away. "I'm here to explain the process of receiving your own eNet address, and help you decide on the best program for *you.*"

"If you mean that implant thing in your wrist, I'd rather not."

The lady seemed mildly taken aback. "But the FirstTime-Online program is corporate sponsored, so you have Nothing to Pay for 40 Days!"

"It does sound generous, but I hate the way they look. Thank you, though."

"Oh, but you haven't seen the newest designs! I agree the old ones were ugly, but have you seen the latest hologram styles? I just had a new one put in." The woman flashed the underside of her wrist, moving it back and forth so a silvery pattern shifted.

Meagan shuddered inwardly. "That's very nice, but no, thank you."

"Some people are putting them on their ankles, but I'm more traditional."

"Me, too. So thank you anyway, but I'd rather not."

"Once you are a member of the eNet community, you can take the T-band off your wrist." The woman's slightly scented hand delicately indicated the bracelet Meagan had been given to wear. "Won't that be nice, to be part of the community? You may speak with a Customer Care Professional about specifics, once you have decided on a basic plan."

"Did you hear me?" Meagan asked. "Or are you saying I don't have a choice?"

"Oh, no, no. We are here to serve the client and provide him or her with every individual choice. Look here, you have twelve options under the Omni-Plan, plus any—"

"I choose the *No-Plan-At-All* option," Meagan replied firmly.

"You just haven't seen the brochures," the woman said, helpfully producing several. "Even the basic plan includes fourteen-hundred channels and free hookup to CyB-World and DotNet. With the minimum upgrade we include AutoAlert, Location-Mapping and digital wireless voice-activated roaming TeleWonder messaging. For an additional fee you can get audio connection, and with AdvancePay drafts you get a limited time offer of ten hours of SensoryIM, free and Tvision-enabled!"

"It sounds very nice, but I don't really watch that much television."

The woman looked as if Meagan had just spoken against breathing air.

"I was kidding," Meagan said quickly, remembering to co-operate. "Which plan do *you* have?"

"Well, I like the SecurityOne NoThought Plus. It gives me streamlined checking-in at all sanctioned facilities and RiteTime Escort service, with weekend minutes included."

"Perfect. I want that one."

"But I haven't shown you the other FirstTime-Online offers! We have a lovely video explaining the many improvements and future upgrades."

"That's okay, your plan sounds perfect. Just knowing I have fourteen-hundred channels makes me happy."

At last hearing sense, the woman beamed and shuffled to a cabinet, laying out a folder and making notes. "I'll have an Installation Specialist along shortly. We're experiencing high customer volume right now, you will be implanted in the order you were received." The woman began opening cabinet doors. "I know the SR-620's are in here somewhere..." In one cabinet a set of shiny metal implements gleamed. Racks of long needles glistened. The woman perkily attached a printed form to a folder and slipped it into a rack on the door. "A technician will be with you shortly."

"Oh." Meagan eyed the gleaming metal. "Excuse me, ma'am—maybe I *should* see the video. Like you said, I should take my time deciding."

"Very well," the woman agreed, pleased with her own salesmanship.

Meagan toyed with her thin wristband as she watched the woman program the video and prepare to depart. *Could it be so simple?* She sat up. "Ma'am, before you leave ... I'm sorry to be so much trouble, but is there a restroom I could use while I wait?"

"Yes, certainly. I will get a custodian."

"I hate to be a bother ... could you show me? I want to hurry back and get started." Meagan stood and gave her an ingratiating smile. "Thank you *so* much for your help. Is there anything else I should know? I'm just so excited."

"It will all be explained," the woman said confidently, pleased to have turned around another hard case. "After installation, there will be a Scheduling Professional to arrange your training."

"Great. Sign me up." Meagan quietly retrieved her satchel "purse" and followed the woman out of the room. Together they entered a filled waiting area. The woman punched a short code into a panel by the restroom door. The door's lock clicked open.

"Don't be too long, if you miss the appointment we will have to reschedule. You might miss some good discounts."

"I'll hurry, thank you!" Meagan said brightly. She entered the restroom and closed the door behind her, and hurried to the wash area. *Why not?* she thought. *I can always plead ignorance.* She looped the band around the faucet spigot and pulled back hard, using both hands and all her weight. The band stretched before popping open and falling into the sink.

No alarms, no lights. No guards or loudspeakers. Meagan tossed the band into the trash canister and rearranged her satchel's strap. She returned to the restroom door, composed

herself, gently turned the handle and stepped into the waiting room. Instead of walking back to the entrance doorway,
Meagan went the other way. A few sitting people watched
her escape, too broken by the system to ever defend it.

The corridor was sterile, a clean passage sparsely popu-
lated with efficient workers gliding in soft steps. Meagan
traveled the crisscrossing halls, tending toward the darker
and less peopled areas. She came to a door marked *Employees
Only* and tried it. The door opened. The stairwell was lit by
exit signs. She took the steps down, two at a time. The stairs
ended with a door bearing a warning that an alarm would
activate if it were opened. Meagan hesitated. With any luck,
the tracking wristband would place her in the restroom
wastebasket. She pushed the door open.

A small LED switched red above the door. Meagan hurried
into the dark corridor passage. Overhead, aged cylindrical
pipes passed between conduits and corroded cables. Listening a moment and hearing nothing except the humming
sounds of machinery, she began jogging down the corridor,
holding the satchel.

She fought a rising panic, imagining security personnel
flooding into the waiting room, calling backup, notifying
higher-ups. A stairway offered a detour, which she accepted.
The stairs opened to an intersection with more subterranean
paths. A yellow-and-black sign indicated directions: an arrow
labeled "Zoo Facility" pointed down a florescent tunnel.

A plan. It would be like this: Meagan would emerge into
sunlight, where crowds of insistent children would be pulling
parents among the zoo's attractions. Smiling and calm, she
would walk with her fashionable satchel, asking directions
until she found a way to contact Harbinger. She jogged faster,
imagining swarms of black uniforms finding the band and
widening the search. She ran until the signs indicated she was
below the zoo complex. The first stairway up was locked, as
was the second. Finally she saw a beautiful sight—a stairwell
door propped open by a trash can.

The stairs were dark, but Meagan held to the guide rail. She came to a landing below a window gridded with reinforced wire, and moved cautiously to the landing's metal door. She took the cold, round ball of the handle and pushed the door open. Before her was a lobby, air-conditioned and quiet. People meandered in clusters around the polished floor. Crowd noises murmured in the distance.

It was all too easy. Meagan had to suppose people never tried to escape. She thought about the wrist band and implants: the system did not account for simple disregard of norms. She walked across the lobby, forcing herself to move casually. The few people present were drifting toward a roped off area, from where Meagan could hear the hum of a crowd. She approached an exit. She had her hand on the door. Sunlight beckoned...

And there were security guards.

Meagan pulled the door closed and reversed herself. *How stupid of me*, she thought irritably. *That was suspicious. Why didn't I just walk through?*

A guard entered from outside. She walked back the other way, toward the crowd and away from the attended entry doors. Moving past rope barricades, Meagan saw she was in a wide hall with exhibits on one side, each set behind glass. A sizeable group milled at the end of the hall. She walked with hurried nonchalance toward the assembled people, hoping to be lost within the crowd.

She slowed before an exhibit in surprise. A skeleton the size of a small dog was pegged before a prehistoric diorama with ferns and red-trunked forest trees. The display sign read, "The Dawn Horse."

Walking on, Meagan glanced at the exhibitions as she continued toward the crowd. She passed a replica of a racing chariot. *Shoddy construction*, Meagan thought, noticing the poorly joined wheel yokes. The contraption wouldn't have survived through a single racing turn.

There was a knight in rusting armor, sitting upon an Appaloosa horse that would have fallen to its knees under the weight. A dressage rider rode in a late twentieth-century western saddle, upon a high-stepping Tennessee Walker. Other exhibits lined the side of the hall.

Behind her, Meagan saw a cluster of guards forming. She pressed into the crowd and pushed her way through, slipping past people to seek the safety of numbers. She was struck by the blank, sallow faces and how familiar they seemed: like the waiting room patients, or the harassed crowd in APART's office—all seemed to be dull staring echoes of actual people. Only the children seemed normal and alive.

"Look, Mommie, look!"

"Be careful, don't touch the glass. You'll make it charge."

Meagan ignored the babbling speech around her, moving through the disheveled crowd. She was pushed against a railing set before a six-foot plexiglass wall and looked up in stunned amazement. Standing behind the plexiglass—on a slightly-raised platform of artificial turf—was a living horse.

"Look!" hooted a spectator. "How would you like to clean up after *that*, honey?"

"I want to pet the horse, Mom!"

"No dear. It's cruel to them."

The manure had not been cleaned from underneath the horse, and there were no water buckets or haynets visible. The animal's smooth gray coat had lumps of scurf from poor grooming and his halter was fitted too tight. Meagan recognized the horse's Arabian breed by the dished profile of his diamond head and the long tail which draped from his level croup. The animal's muzzle narrowed to a mouth that could almost "fit in a teacup." Dark, expressive eyes turned their faraway gaze to Meagan. The Great Horse, Rafi.

The gray stallion was held between handlers in upbeat yellow shirts, standing before a small crowd of helpers wearing matching green *Animal Hero* t-shirts. Meagan found herself growing angry; no one seemed to know how to care for the animal properly. She wanted to brush the horse's unkempt coat, to oil his cracked hooves. Her eyes fell to a plaque. It was a metal sign with raised letters, fixed to a podium before the plexiglass stage:

Animals of Our World™
Horses® *Horses*® *Horses*® *Horses*®
Horses!®

Exhibit donated to The Public© by
Telex-WorldCom™ *and* **DotNet**™
in cooperation with the
National Animal Registry®
& *thanks to generous endowment of the*
Association for Prevention of Animal Rights Trespass™
A | P | A | R | T™

The Horse® (*equus caballus*) avg. ht. 62" to shoulder, length various, weight 1500 lbs.

Four-footed mammal with single horned toe, short-haired coat and long mane and tail. The horse originated in North America and migrated to Asia Minor, distributing itself through Europe and Central Asia. Indigenous to grasslands and prairies, the horse is a vegetarian sustaining itself on forage and grains. The practice of riding and driving horses thrived from antiquity to the last modern age, until social and economic pressures curtailed its use.

This unique exhibition can be seen at zoo and museum tours exclusively with TicketWorld™ *and A | P | A | R | T*™

For more information and dates/times for viewing, check our eNet: I-L I K E -H O R S E S©

A spotlessly-clean woman in a white lab coat paced in front of the horse's platform, speaking to the crowd. She sporadically lashed the air with a classroom pointer as she spoke, causing Rafi to jerk in alarm. Meagan waved at the horse, trying to attract the animal's attention.

"Yes?" the lecturer asked, stopping to look at Meagan.

"Oh, I'm sorry. I was saying hello to ... never mind."

The lecturer responded by swinging her pointer with special authority. Another hand from the audience went up; Meagan was grateful for the distraction.

"Does the horse get to exercise very much?" asked a young woman in a nervous voice.

"Excuse me, what is the point of your question?" Apparently the quota for audience participation had been exceeded.

The speaker's hand lowered. "I just wondered when the horse goes outside. Horses like to run, don't they?"

"I don't know, do you think they talk to us in private?" Titters ran through the crowd.

"I'm sorry, I didn't mean to ask the wrong thing."

Meagan pitied the poor questioner; her apologetic words were an incitement to the lecturer: "Perhaps you know better how to manage a horse. Would you like to show us?"

Actually... The exchange gave Meagan an idea. She felt the bulk of the bridle folded within her satchel. *Come on, Promise.* She began to move sideways through the crowd, pushing towards an opening beyond the plexi-glass wall, behind a separating chain.

Rafi was fidgeting nervously on the artificial turf, ears swiveling tautly as he watched the crowd and the pointer-swinging lecture. The horse was restrained by leadropes attached to the halter's side rings, held tightly by three yellow-shirted handlers on each side, presumably to increase anchor weight.

"Stop, Miss! You can't come back here."

Meagan's winning smile was lost on the heavyset gentleman wearing a 'Security' vest. He held a riot baton. "I'm here for the horse exhibit ... the demonstration?" She opened her satchel and let the guard peer inside at the jumble of metal and leather. A little embellishment of facts seemed excusable: "I need to put this on the horse before he realizes he isn't under control. Everyone knows what a loose horse can do, yes? We don't have much time."

The man grunted and let her pass; leather bonds and clinking metal proclaimed authority in his view. She walked to the crowded platform, coming close enough to see the stallions' untrimmed fetlock hairs.

She looked up at Rafi: the stallion seemed increasingly unsettled. The horse shifted and gave a short, concerned whinny. He scanned the crowd with flared nostrils, veins standing on his thin coat. *He looks so much like Saxon,* she thought, recalling the Emperor's flighty chariot horse from Rome.

No one else had noticed her yet. Meagan moved to an uncrowded spot at the rear of the platform and stepped up. From the platform she could see beyond Rafi to the bland faces of the crowd filling this end of the hall.

The lab coat-wearing lecturer was still pacing and swinging her pointer. Meagan called politely: "Should I start now? It's quite late."

The lecturer turned. One eyebrow was raised archly; her gaze narrowed when she saw Meagan.

Meagan excused her way to the front of the platform to be near Rafi. The crowd milled below, instantly restless. "I'm sorry I was delayed. We should get started with the demonstration."

"Who are *you?*" The woman gathered herself as if to pounce; Meagan sensed that if the woman had a tail it would be twitching.

"A representative of APART," Meagan said in her most officiously disinterested voice. "Are you current with correspondence?" The woman's stricken expression told Meagan she had hit on the right path to disarmament. "The demonstration was to begin ten minutes ago and you haven't introduced me yet." Meagan paused. "I see you didn't read that memo either, so let's skip ahead to the bridling." She slid the satchel's strap off her shoulder to retrieve the bridle, and held the golden-bitted headstall high for the audience to see. A few members of the audience gasped.

Rafi was growing more agitated, his head high and ears forward. Two additional handlers were added to the stallion's leadropes for security. The horse's prominent dark eyes watched Meagan's cautious approach.

"Easy boy." Talking softly and steadily, Meagan reached to stroke the stallion's neck. He accepted her touch. She ran her hand to the horse's withers, scratching in a friendly gesture. Removing the watermelon pieces from the satchel, she let Rafi sniff and take the offering. "Does anyone have more treats?" She looked around at the blank-faced lecturer and well-armed handlers. Clubs and weapons, yes ... simple treats, no. The basic misunderstanding had returned. Dark Age thinking.

Continuing the demonstration, Meagan showed Rafi the bridle and held it up for the audience in another flourish of showmanship. "It doesn't hurt him, see, it's not harsh." The crowd was rapt, as if watching a snake charmer and a cobra.

Meagan quickly unclipped the farthest leadrope from the halter—surprising the handlers—and unbuckled the halter's top strap to secure around the horse's neck. She cupped the gold mouthpiece to present to Rafi, who lipped it before opening his mouth, and slipped the headstall over his ears.

Rafi bowed his neck, mouthing the bit in agitation. The stallion made a sudden trumpeting call that rang through the hall.

The crowd drew back amid the handlers' spontaneous decision to drop their grips and abandon stations. The platform was a scene of pandemonium as the attendants fled, colliding with each other to escape.

"It's loose! It's free!" The lab coated-lecturer scrambled madly against the plexiglass wall and departed as the stallion raised another piercing, brassy call. The audience fled as if under fire; the platform was deserted before the last high strains of the stallion's neigh had faded.

"No philosophers so thoroughly comprehend us as horses"
- Hermann Melville (1819-91)

"Oh my *goodness*, Rafi," Meagan said, watching the rout. "One whinny and everyone freaks out." The crowd that had jammed this end of the hall to see Rafi's exhibit was fleeing to jam the other side in escape.

She released the halter, staying close to the horse's shoulder as he shifted and eyed the plexiglass wall. "No you don't," she said firmly, holding the bridle's reins tighter in case the stallion had wild ideas. The flooring was as slick and solid as polished marble.

This was the daring part and where her great journey might end. "I hope it's okay if I ride you, Rafi?" she asked the fidgeting stallion. "You don't have an owner yet, and it would be a *huge* favor."

The milling crowd was pushing to exit the narrow egress doors. That direction was closed, but wide service doors beside the platform were still open to the outside air...

The decision was made for her, as Rafi began making clear his intentions to be elsewhere. "Easy boy," she urged, putting the reins over the stallion's head as Rafi pressed against Meagan and began to move past; she put her arm over his back and hopped up.

The stallion ignored her weight and moved quickly to the back of the platform. She held onto Rafi's long mane as he lowered himself gracefully onto the slick, hard flooring behind the exhibit.

With Meagan as passenger, Rafi clopped through the backstage clutter of chairs and equipment. The stallion emerged back in the main hall through a side access door, and moved in clipped steps across the rock-hard surface. She attempted to guide the horse toward the open service doors, heading outside, but the stallion resisted, tossing his head and trotting in the direction of the crowd.

The clear melody of hoofbeats struck loudly against the cavernous hall's flooring. People stopped to listen. The staccato rhythm which had punctuated human experience now brought the crowd to silent attention.

Rafi halted and trumpeted again: a resonant, high-pitched cry of warning; a primordial call to gather. The large hall was hushed now, the people frozen in place, hearing sounds of forgotten memories. Meagan remained motionless as the stallion's call rang through the hall and echoed into silence.

The crowd parted as Rafi walked forward, dividing into lines of people watching the gray horse and his bareback rider pass solemnly between them. As the stallion moved deliberately toward the exhibition displays, the crowd receded, leaving two figures alone in the empty space.

Rafi walked towards them, slowing as he went. Meagan saw a young man trying to move the second figure, a young woman, from the horse's path ... but the woman resisted, calmly watching the stallion's approach. She was perhaps in her 20's; her thin hair was tousled and her ill-fitting maroon sweater was torn. The young man, a teenager, turned and saw the horse.

Rafi stopped and watched him, ears forward. "Leave her alone," the teenager said loudly, his voice shaking. "She didn't do anything wrong."

The young woman walked forward and looked up at Meagan with eyes shining in wonder: the wonder of seeing dreams made manifest. She held out her palm to show an aged silver broach-pin, a horseshoe. Knitted threads hanging from the broach matched the torn place on her sweater.

"They tried to take it!" the teenager said defiantly. "We just came to see, that's all. Nothing wrong!"

"Who says it is wrong?" Meagan asked.

"My brother is afraid." The young woman spoke softly. "Our grandfather was a horse-trainer. Before."

Rafi nickered softly. The horse's nostrils quivered as he stretched and set his chin on the teen's shoulder. The young man did not flinch, his wide eyes indicating perhaps he was afraid to move.

The owner is chosen, Meagan thought suddenly.

The stallion shifted and delicately smelled the woman's hair, nostrils trembling. He nickered again, chortling softly.

"I think I should tell you, this is a very special horse." Meagan hesitated. *Which one was the owner?*

"I know he is special. I have dreams with him. He runs and the wind comes to chase him."

Meagan smiled at the young man. *Very well, we have our believer.* "The horse's name is Raphael, or Rafi for short. He is the Great Horse—"

Suddenly the two siblings were talking over each other in excitement. "I have dreams with him too!"

"He runs after the other horses!"

"He always likes to jump and play."

Rafi turned around toward Meagan's leg and nudged. Her ride was ending, it was another's turn.

A slight rumbling began as an underground vibration, until a new sound temporarily overpowered the rumble: security alarms climbing to higher decibel. Searchlights circled over the crowd. The alarm peaked and held, but the distant vibrations could still be heard approaching, increasing.

Meagan was sure the alarms were for her. She looked up and firmly told the empty air: "Promise, *please* come. I'm not upset ... but come *now*." *Please girl.*

The crowd milled in confusion as the security alarms receded to make way for a synthetic voice—*for your safety and to better serve you*—but the roaring vibration was still expanding, widening in scope. Searchlights found Rafi and centered, flooding a circle around Meagan and the stallion with blinding light. The stallion gave another shrill trumpeting blast ... one answered this time by a distant whinny.

The announcement's drone was washed away in the rolling thunder of hoofbeats. A lean bay mare entered the hall's open service doors, followed closely by a band of horses. The stampede sound of hooves filled the air. People shrank against the walls of the exhibit hall and looked wildly around to see the new equines.

For a moment the two species contemplated each other, a respectful stillness between them. People began to edge closer. The stallion laid his head close to the woman's shoulder in the floodlight's glare, and then bumped the young man playfully.

The hall's clamor shifted, seeming to stutter to the rhythm of unseen hoofbeats. Meagan felt a familiar slowing and stretching of time. Rafi tensed beneath her ... a bright haze ghosted the stallion's neck.

"Talk to a man named Dean Harbinger!" she called urgently. Wide wings rose around her in the floodlight; her mount's mane and coat burst into shining white. "Tell him you met Meagan!"

A sharp whinny from the lead mare pierced the air. Meagan was wrenched upward as Rafi spun away beneath her. She held the reins tightly as she looked back to see Rafi following the mares. The stallion's neck snaked low to herd his band from the hall, leaving the honored siblings in the spotlight.

Meagan and winged Promise rose together. Dust-trailed specks were soon all that could be seen of the horses below, as the stallion drove his mares into the Outback ... to start again.

The wind rose around them, clean and cool, her mount's strong muscles straining as they soared higher, climbing to reach the clouds. Together they swept into the veil of sticky mist from below. As they rose, the mist became brighter until Meagan's eyes hurt from the bright glare...

California, USA
2004 A.D.

Home Again

"SHE'S AWAKE, TOM!"
Meagan heard voices and squinted into the light; then someone moved the light away. She awoke in a bed, a hand held by each of her parents. They were crying, her mother in long streaks and her father in heavy drops through red eyes. *She was back home—with her parents!* To them, she had been no further than the hospital bed, where she had lain unconscious for many days. One leg was severely broken.

"Mom, Dad?" Meagan murmured groggily.

The answering voices were as from Heaven. "We're here, we're *here*, dear. Hush, don't talk now. Tom, call the doctor."

They did not tell her everything at first.

"How is Promise?"

"Rest now, Meagan," her mother said, stroking her hand. "There will be time to hear everything later."

"Did you find her? What about the men with the gun?"

"Yes, we found them. Neighbors saw the—" Jennifer hesitated and looked at Tom.

"They saw you and Promise and alerted the authorities," her father finished briskly. "The thieves were picked up driving a stolen trailer. The report said they were seeking a reward."

"It was something about a horse legend," Jennifer said gently.

"Was Promise wearing the Golden Bridle?" Meagan asked, disoriented.

"A golden bridle?" Tom smiled at his daughter. "The doctors said you might have some strange dreams, tiger."

Meagan sat up on her elbows. "Wasn't she?"

"Please lay down, sweetheart." Jennifer looked concerned as she eased Meagan back. "Quiet now, don't get excited."

Meagan lay back on the pillow. "Is Promise okay?"

"Now honey, you need some time to recover. We will tell you everything very soon."

"Did something happen? Please tell me. I would rather know."

"Hush now, trooper," Tom insisted. "We'll all be back home soon enough."

Meagan knew before either of her parents would admit it, knew from the furtive glances at each other and their small, distressed motions when she brought it up. Promise was gone. That first night, Meagan finally accepted it and cried herself to sleep.

The next morning, she asked her parents to tell her about Promise. At first they both tried to change the subject, but she asked quietly, dry-eyed, "Did she suffer?"

Jennifer looked at Tom. "No, Meagan, we don't think *that*. Not at all."

"The horse is just missing," Tom assured her. "We let the authorities know and filed reports. They will find her."

"What about Mrs. Bridgestone? She would know!"

"Honey, your mother tried."

"I did call," Jennifer assured her. "Mrs. Bridgestone has sold her property. She didn't leave a number or way to reach her. Now please lay back and try to be calm."

"And we will find Promise," Tom said confidently. "We will."

Her Great Horse was gone.

Meagan's recovery was much delayed by medical advice, in her own opinion. The doctors all had thoughts about her condition, but none could account for Meagan's remarkably quick recovery from what was assumed to be major brain trauma. Though older than when she left home with Promise, changes in her appearance were attributed to the accident and hospital stay. She was expected to carry a slight limp from her broken leg, but otherwise seemed to have no further effects.

When Meagan was well enough to leave the hospital, Jennifer held out a small, dirt-encrusted object. "Do you know what this is, sweetie? It was on your hand after the accident."

Meagan swallowed. "It looks like a ring."

"Yes, I can see that. I just wondered where it came from." Jennifer held the simple object up and studied it. "It needs a good cleaning to really see it." She looked at her daughter. "Is this something you want?"

"Yes, please." It was her wedding ring.

Jennifer handed it to Meagan, watching her daughter closely. "You gave me and your father quite a scare, little girl." Jennifer's tears started again. She reached to brush Meagan's cheek. "You seem so quiet and grown up. It frightens me."

Meagan almost told her mother everything then—started to—but turned the dirty ring over in her hand and said nothing. No one would believe her anyway; she would only be given more medical tests. There would be time enough to tell.

For now there were tears, wishing for Dan, wishing for Promise.

Not all her tears were unhappy ... *for she truly was home at last.* Arriving at her house on crutches, Meagan stood in the front doorway and ran a hand lightly over the smooth, painted surfaces. So modest and well-ordered, so comfortable, so clean.

"Are you all right, Meagan?" Jennifer hurried to her in concern. "Let me help you inside."

"No, Mom, I'm fine. It's just so nice to be home." And it was. Home had waited for her, unchanged—it was she who was different.

For the first weeks back home, during what would normally be her summer vacation, Meagan had to contend with being homebound. It was sheer bliss. To their mutually pleasant surprise, fights with her parents not only ceased, but became unthinkable.

Meagan spent her convalescence investigating the times she had visited and finding intriguing notes in the pages of the past. She was amused to discover that her one-time nemesis, Françoise, the Madame de Montespan, had indeed become a mistress of King Louis and bore him numerous children before her predictable retirement to a convent. Meagan eagerly read with fresh perspective the exploits of Conquistadors and nomads and knights.

The history she most lingered over, however, was Dan's Civil War Kentucky. As wonderful as it was to be home, she still mourned her lost love. The heartache was pain beyond imagining; it was humbling. Like layers, she reminded herself: *solve one thing and something else was right behind it, making you just as miserable as before.* Yet, this time she knew she would endure.

Inevitably, lawsuits had followed the accident. The neighbors first sued for damages, but the fact soon emerged that the Cromwells had refused to allow the pasture fence to be raised to a safe height. The tone of the exchange changed;

changed so much, in fact, that talk of a settlement to pay for Meagan's rehabilitation began.

The horse thieves were also dealt with: Fred Jeffries was said to have been a welcome, if reluctant, addition to the prison mess hall; and Randy Wells was reportedly engaged in a long letter campaign to convince his wife he was not guilty, or at least, not very.

———

Once she was considered well enough to visit, Meagan's first non-medical appointment was a ride to see 156 Haversham Avenue. The stone walls remained, and Meagan hobbled on crutches to the closed gate. Beyond, through the side gap in the fence, she could see bulldozers and construction flags in place of the wide lawns.

The Bridgestone mansion was still there, but darkened and draped with tarps. The roof of the silent stables beyond could be seen in the distance. The eccentric woman who told her about the strange legend of a Great Horse ... was utterly gone.

———

Meagan's return to school for the new year was both easier and more difficult than she had expected. Friends welcomed her back, but noticed the changes in her. It was fun to astonish the school's French and Latin teachers with her vast improvement over the summer—she gave the credit to rigorous self-study—yet she felt like a woman in teenager's clothes, playing a part. She had not only grown outwardly older, she was older within.

Now Meagan looked with fresh eyes at the rituals of schooling, and put out of her mind its resemblances to herding cattle. It felt very strange to carry books wherever she went, and she felt ridiculous sitting in a roomful of children. Unfortunately she had two more years of high school remaining. *Two years!*

Clearly she would have to compromise if she wanted to fit in. She tried to contribute to discussions about her new science teacher, but in the end she decided an air of polite tranquility would be her goal and withdrew from the debate.

She trudged home that afternoon, thinking it might be best to concentrate on college. Though she cherished being back home, she felt like an outsider. It was hard to listen to tales of aggression as glory and hear prejudices she knew flowered into oppression. She assumed less, appreciated more, and carried an earned skepticism: she was changed, while others were not.

She missed her departed Thoroughbred with stubborn sadness. The dreams of the flying horse had stopped. *Where was Promise—just wandering through time?* Meagan sometimes wondered if she felt her presence, but dismissed it as imagination ... though, isn't that where the Great Horses live?

The loss of Promise was not the only disturbing aspect about coming home: she also considered herself married to a man who had passed away a least a half century ago. Did this mean she was crazy? *It's certainly a start,* she thought dolefully.

Meagan walked up her driveway and entered the backyard patio. The pasture seemed smaller than before her journey, which was ridiculous since she herself had hardly grown. The space was thick now with grass, and ironically looked more like a picture-perfect paddock than when it held hungry horses.

Entering the kitchen through the back door, it seemed strange to set her books on the counter and open the refrigerator, as if nothing had ever been different. She held the door open and saw, on the second shelf, a wide slice of watermelon. It gave her a quick stab to see the prized horse-treat. Memories of Promise were like a wounded place that touched everything.

Meagan started to close the refrigerator door and hesitated. What might happen, she wondered, if she placed her old bridle in Promise's manger with the watermelon rind? *It wouldn't work,* she told herself—*it couldn't work.* Meagan reassured herself with this disclaimer as she left her books on the counter and took out the watermelon slice. *It would not hurt to try...*

Walking outside and crossing the paddock, Meagan noticed the small backyard stables seemed to be converting itself back to a garage through neglect. She stepped into the cobwebbed shadows of the single aisle. The empty air seemed haunted with the ghosts of horses past. Meagan entered the vacant stall that had once belonged to Moose, and recalled the day she had found her beloved mare thrashing in the bedding. Tears came to her eyes as she remembered, and she bowed her head to let the sorrow finish.

Meagan walked back out into the musty barn aisle. She unlocked the small combined tack room and feed storage, kicking the doorjamb lightly to unstick the frame. Stale air exhaled over her, smelling of mold and dust.

She pulled the bare light fixture's chain: its dim yellow light seemed to highlight the gloom. Reaching to the rack where Moose's old bridle was hung, she turned it over her hands, discouraged at the dilapidated appearance. The mouthpiece was plain metal; the headstall was cracked and scored and seemed quite shabby. She walked with it to Promise's former stall, and with a pang of guilt noticed the old feed trough had become a spider's enclave. The place needed a good cleaning, and with a few repairs it would be serviceable again. It would never be Mrs. Bridgestone's fantastic horse-palace with rubber mats, fans, brass fixtures, and automated fly spray, but she would surrender all such luxuries for a chance to ride Promise again.

And the *first* place she would go would be to Civil War Kentucky to see Dan.

Meagan carefully placed the bridle in the trough, and folded the reins and headstall tidily into place. She put the cut watermelon on top of the mouthpiece—and stood back.

Nothing happened.

Meagan frowned, feeling foolish. She would not linger; it was time to move on. She pulled the bridle out of the trough, but left the watermelon rind. *Something for the mice,* she thought bitterly, and bit her lip to stop more such thoughts. Her horse was gone and wasn't coming back. Her memories were as empty as this once-beloved space. Like the journey through history, it seemed only dust remained.

Meagan retired to sit on the patio with these dismal thoughts. She daydreamed about her travels, searching for a summation as she held the old bridle tightly. Her parents came home and friends called, yet Meagan stayed to watch the warm sunshine fade across the backyard pasture. Long shadows grew into dusk. She knew she must look ridiculous sitting alone outside the paddock, clutching—it may as well be admitted—an old, disintegrating bridle. But she had thinking to do.

She didn't cry. She had done all that before. For Dan, for Promise, for Moose and so many others. The only way she could see to honor her losses was to remember, as the horse-loving socialite Mrs. von Kane had insisted. And she would. The next step was ... unclear.

She recalled her memories of Rome's fearsome chariot horse Cerberus and his only accepted partner, Helios—a gentleman before his time. Knight Henryk and Chouchou walk-charged through her thoughts; she missed Targa, too, her Great Pony. In her heart, Danvers and Molly restored their English farm to its height of glory. She remembered her special underdog, Nero, thrilling audiences, and Man O'War and Stroller captivating crowds in ways of their own. She smiled sadly to think about her competent horse professional, Red, and Dan's loyal partner, Blue.

Though the Great Horses of the past were mostly forgotten, Meagan knew the fates of Man O'War and Stroller, for they were contemporary sports stars. The famed British jumper Stroller lived to the ripe old age of 36 in happy retirement filled with well-wishers. He passed in 1986 and was mourned by horse-lovers young and old. America's own Man O'War ended his days in prolific retirement, living until age

30 and passing in 1947 only a month after his longtime groom, Will Harbut. His burial had been broadcast nationally, when hundreds of mourners filed past his specially-made casket, according to a newspaper of the day, "patting him gently in death as they had in life."

What about the other, long-passed horses of her travels? She fondly recalled the little gray horse from the ancient watering-hole, exactly the kind of dependable school pony who won the hearts of her pupils. She remembered the timid El Morzillo (when he wasn't being ridden) who became a symbol of Spanish spiritual and military might. And there were the horses she never knew: the sacrificed horse in the Scythian tomb, and the silently suffering horse on the World War II battlefield.

Yet now it seemed as if her travels had never been. Was it *possible* she had fallen on a chance ring, one lying in the dirt beside the pasture fence, and perhaps clutched it in the accident, dreaming the rest?

Meagan finally surrendered her paddock watch as darkness fell. She would try the bridle again tomorrow—maybe with crushed rind this time. *I made it back home and I'll find a way to see Dan again.*

That night Meagan retired early. She lay under the covers wondering how she would ever find the next Great Horse—it was her duty to tell the new owner, after all. She felt trapped now by time, being moved inexorably forward without chance of reprieve.

Do we greet our memories on the "other side?" If so, she thought sleepily, it was a happy universe, because the good memories remain...

A familiar nicker woke Meagan. The last rumbles of the friendly horse greeting faded as she opened her eyes, ending in the front doorbell's lingering chime.

Through the fog of sleep, Meagan heard conversation below end with the shutting of a door. She yawned and stretched. A knock sounded at her bedroom door, and her mother's voice came from the other side. "Meagan, there's a package for you."

"Thanks, Mom," Meagan called groggily, sitting up. Dim light outlined the window blinds; birds chirped in the early morning. Still yawning, she swung her legs out of bed, pulling on her robe as she went to open the door.

Jennifer was still in her morning bathrobe, holding a medium-sized package. "Sorry to wake you, hon, but the man said it was important. Are you expecting anything?"

"No. That's strange. Thank you though, I'll open it now." Meagan took the plain box from Jennifer and retreated to her bed, letting her door close as she set the package on the crumpled covers. There was no return address.

Meagan retrieved scissors from her desk and carefully opened the box. She cut the tape and lifted the flaps and pulled away packing tissue: an envelope fell out as she glimpsed a tangle of new-looking, well-oiled leather straps— and a sudden flash of gold! Her heart beat faster as she quickly lifted out a jumble of reins and a folded bridle—*a golden bridle!*

Meagan rummaged in the box to pull out the last packing materials. There was nothing else inside; she checked again before picking up the small envelope, blank except for the name: "Meagan." Inside was a brief handwritten note:

Dear Old Friend,

I am so happy to know you are back from your travels ... and so sorry we can't meet again in person. Our first meeting was always to be our last, young Meagan.

Please forgive my deception. You were simply told what I remembered from my own youth. I tried to make everything the same as I remembered, even this note, as I didn't want to further alter the course of time. Someday you will understand, if you do not already.

I wouldn't worry too much about the future you saw. There are many paths and we have the lessons of history to guide us. People just need some good horse-sense. Help them keep it, dear.

– Eleanor M. Bridgestone

PS. I was able to recover our Great Horse.
Please tell her hello for me.

Meagan stared at the note for a moment and then ran to her bedroom window to look excitedly down from her bedroom window to ... the empty patio. The garage-converted stables were dark and silent.

Then she saw something that made her heart jump—a tramped path led through the backyard's long grass from the barn's opening to the fence! A carefully arranged halter was hanging from the patio gate—

Meagan bolted for her bedroom door and threw it open, retying her robe as she ran for the stairs, "Mom, Dad! Hurry and come see! Promise is back! *Promise is back!*"

California, USA
2012

Somewhere, somewhere, in time's own space,
I know there's some sweet pastured place.
Where creeks sing on and tall trees grow,
some paradise where horses go.
For by the love that guides my pen,
I know great horses live again.
- Stanley Harrison (1889-1979)

Epilogue

"Someone is arriving, ma'am."

Meagan awoke from her reverie. "Oh. Yes. Thank you, Nelson."

"These may be the adoption clients." The uniformed chauffeur watched the lone elderly woman through the rearview mirror. The dark limousine was parked in a cul-de-sac beside a vacant sandy lot. Though now empty, on weekends the old neighborhood riding arena was the centerpiece of a crowd of horses, parents and excited children.

A faded silver car slowly rattled toward them down the street. "Yes, this must be the Hancocks." Meagan shifted on the backseat. Her leg had been troubling her lately. Age. Nothing to be done. "I'm excited about this adoption, Nelson. Do you remember the horse?"

"I believe so, ma'am. He was in poor condition if I remember." Years of living in California had left no influence on the French chauffeur's accent.

"*Such* a sweet horse though. He's a perfect gentleman in the lead line program."

"He seems wonderfully patient, ma'am." The horse in question was a partially crippled gray gelding named Mister, who had been part of a horse-abuse scandal involving a facility breeding horses for slaughter. The emaciated victims had made media headlines and sparked cries for national reform. Mister was one of the worst cases; he had been taken in by the Bridgestone shelter last year.

In addition to the shelter, Meagan had founded *The Bridgestone Foundation* to research the Great Horse legend. Unfortunately, the organization had not been able to locate a single new Great Horse. Records were searched, but not all horse births were recorded and there was no poem from Chief Joseph to indicate the whereabouts of the next incarnation.

Then, after years of absence, Meagan's horse dreams had started again, as vivid as those that once heralded Promise in years past. The horse of the new dreams was a small gray gelding—exactly the description given in a real-life adoption call for the "little white horse named *Mister*."

"He's going to a good home, Nelson." *I hope*, Meagan added silently. She did not often meet with adopting owners, but this time was different. Today she hoped to fulfill an old duty.

The approaching silver vehicle drifted to a stop. The car's front door squealed as it opened. Its driver emerged, a woman dressed simply in pants and long untucked shirt. Her red-dyed hair was tucked in a loose scarf. Lifting her sunglasses to survey the scene, she waved at the dark-windowed limousine before moving to the passenger door of her vehicle and leaning down. A small boy sat inside.

"Want to come with me, honey?" The boy gave no answer. His arms were crossed as he stared stonily ahead. Concerned, the woman opened the door and rolled down the car window. "Here, sweetie, this way you can have some air." When she reached to smooth his collar, the boy flinched away. She closed the door softly.

Meagan lowered her window as the woman approached. "Good morning, you must be Mrs. Hancock!"

"Yes, *hi!* Are you the horse adoption people?"

"I help sponsor the Rescue shelter. I asked you to meet here, thank you so much for coming."

"No, thank *you!* Please, call me Georgina."

"Pleased to meet you, Georgina. I'm Mrs. Bridgestone." Meagan indicated the seated passenger in the silver car. "He must be your boy?" The child remained staring blankly ahead.

"Yes, that's Dean." Lowering her voice to a whisper, the woman leaned closer to Meagan's window. "He's my sister's son. She and his father were ki—they passed away in an accident three weeks ago."

"Oh, my *dear!* That's too terrible." Meagan reached through the lowered window to take the woman's hand. "I knew from the adoption report there had been loss, but nothing specific. The poor boy."

Georgina held the frail grasp and nodded silently, looking back at Dean. "He hardly speaks, he won't do *anything.* We had the funeral last week and I've been closing things up here. He's coming to live in Phoenix with me and my husband."

"How old is Dean?"

"He's just turned seven."

"I am so sorry." Meagan could see the woman was distressed. Hair was wisping from her scarf and strands stuck to her forehead.

"I don't *know* if we're doing the right thing. Peggy said— Peggy, that's my sister—she said a horse is all the boy talked about. She used to take him to volunteer at your shelter, and when he showed us a picture of that poor abused horse ... well it's the first words he said since the accident. We have a little land behind the house, and I thought it might be nice to make the boy feel at home. We couldn't afford to buy a real horse."

Meagan patted the woman's arm. "I think a horse is a wonderful idea, dear, and he's *quite* real enough."

Another vehicle creaked down the street, pulling behind it a dilapidated horse trailer. "I'm just not sure," Georgina fretted, watching the noisy rig approach. "Dean won't even get out of the car. Maybe this is too much right now. Oh, *no* one knows what to do."

"Nelson," Meagan urged the driver. "If you don't mind?" The chauffeur exited his seat and moved to open the passenger door. Georgina stood back as Nelson waited for the emerging cane and helped Meagan from the car.

"Are you feeling well enough, ma'am?"

"Quite well, Nelson, thank you." Meagan stood shakily and put her hand on the driver's sleeve as he assisted her forward.

The ancient rig passed them slowly and staggered to a stop ahead of the limousine, adding to the line of vehicles. Lettering along the truck's side had faded beyond recognition, and was overlaid with a vinyl "Horse Rescue" sign. A bearded, heavyset man jumped from the truck's cab. "Are you the Hancocks?" he called.

"I'm Mrs. Hancock!" the scarved woman called back. "I was afraid we'd missed you."

"Me too! I know this old place is a bit tricky to find."

Mrs. Hancock walked back to her car and squatted beside the boy's open window. "Honey, your pony is here. Do you want to come see him?" The boy looked down at his hands and shrugged, saying nothing.

Meagan's voice wavered as she raised it so the boy could hear: "Well, *I* would like to see the new horse!" She took Nelson's help down the broken sidewalk, along the trailer's side. A furry muzzle pressed between the metal slats. Meagan stopped to stroke the velvet nose. "Hello there, Mister."

The bearded driver opened the back of the livestock trailer and stepped inside. "Come on back, little fellow."

Sounds of hoofs started in the trailer. Meagan winced as the driver led the animal out. The horse's neck and flanks were still sunken and his coat was rough. Barely short enough to be a *bona fide* pony, his shrunken frame made Mister seem quite small. He carried a slight limp from rope burn scars on both hind legs.

A car door opened. Meagan purposely did not turn around but stepped to the horse and stroked his neck and withers.

Mrs. Hancock approached quietly. In front of her, eyes downcast, was the boy, Dean. "The horse is so thin," Georgina said in a small voice.

"Well, ma'am," explained the bearded driver. "It's like, once a horse gets too far down, sometimes they never come back all the way. He is healthy, though. Nice as they come."

The boy took a tentative step forward and reached out his hand. The horse pricked his ears and reached cautiously to sniff—the boy snatched it back.

"He's saying hello, young man." Meagan patted the horse. "He wonders if you have a treat?"

"I didn't think to bring anything," Mrs. Hancock said nervously.

"You can borrow mine, dear. I have a selection of carrots, apples and watermelon rind. We can see which is his favorite. Here, why don't we pet him first?" Meagan stroked the gelding gently on the shoulder. "Go in the direction of the hair, like this."

The boy lifted his eyes shyly to the horse and took a step forward.

"That's right," Meagan encouraged him. "Move slowly so he knows everything is fine." The boy stepped closer. Meagan took Dean's hand and guided it to the white-gray coat, showing him how to slide down the hair. "Mister likes you to talk to him, Dean. Voices are important to horses ... maybe you can introduce yourself?"

Dean stepped back from the horse and stood silently, eyes down. He shrugged, and frowned deeply. He shrugged again. "No." His voice was ghostlike.

Meagan continued to stroke the rough coat. "See, he's a good boy."

Mister politely sniffed Meagan, who produced the plastic bag of chopped treats. The gelding smelled the watermelon, nostrils flared, and tentatively lipped it before gently taking it between his flat front teeth and crunching.

"Hello, Mister," Dean said quietly.

Meagan motioned to the driver. "The horse is very quiet on the lead. Would you take Dean in a circle?"

"Be happy to, ma'am. I'll walk them around the arena."

Meagan looked at Mrs. Hancock. "Can we let the boy ride Mister on the lead?"

"Is it safe? He's only been on carnival ponies."

"I could do it," the boy said suddenly, his voice stronger.

"Dean!" said a shocked Georgina.

"I'm sure it will be fine, dear," Meagan said gently. "Dean has the makings of an *excellent* horseman."

Georgina gave a quick, worried nod. "Yes. Maybe he should."

"Nelson, could you help the boy, please?" Meagan watched as the men took their places in front of and beside the horse. "Now Dean, stand close."

The chauffeur, well-versed in horses, hoisted the boy up and held him as the driver waited to lead Mister forward.

"Take the reins, dear," Meagan urged the boy gently, "and grab his mane tight. It won't hurt him a bit." The boy knotted his brow in concentration as he clasped the mane. "Now put your legs back and sit up straight." The bearded driver gave the horse a tiny tug, and the gelding swayed forward as a look of wonder filled Dean's expression.

Leaning on her cane, watching the men start the circle, Meagan felt memories and emotions swirling around her. She took out a pendant holding the old restored photograph of Dan and his cavalry horse, Pumpkin. Over the years she had watched her own photographs grow older, and now their images side by side were of a happy old couple. After a moment's silent communion she closed the pendant. *Soon, dear.*

After losing his wife and horses, Dan had joined Union cavalry out West. Tragically, Promise would never bring Meagan back to the horrific Civil War era, and would go no closer than the era of Prohibition. After several failed attempts Meagan returned to the 1920's to search for Dan...

———

Meagan remembered seeing her husband again, every detail. Promise finally brought her to a paddock of a small racing farm near Saratoga, New York. The paddock contained a friendly aged gelding who turned out to be Dan's former cavalry mount, Pumpkin. Dan was living alone in a ramshackle shed behind the property.

He didn't answer the door immediately; she knocked three times before hearing a gravelly voice telling her to go away.

"Dan!" she had called, knocking again. After several moments and more knocking, the latch on the door finally jingled and the door swung slowly open. She had tried to prepare herself for what age might have done, to not react, to pretend if necessary ... yet everything was the same. Well, not exactly the same—her young love was leathery and grey-haired—yet it was Dan. *It was Dan.* And her feelings were exactly the same.

"Yes?" His eyes were bloodshot and watery as he looked at her, confused. "Afraid you passed the big house, Miss. It's up on the road yonder. Might get a pair of spectacles next time you're in town."

She had planned what to say and forgot it all. "Dan, it's Meagan."

To her surprise, Dan only grunted. "So that's how it is." He turned and shuffled toward a pile of crumpled blankets that apparently represented his bed.

"I can explain." She hadn't expected that particular response. Dan reached the blankets and turned to her as he half-crouched and slowly tumbled back. "I can explain too," he said groggily, half-slurring, "and that'll be the last time I send *that* boy to fetch the hooch."

She had stepped inside then, and had avoided looking around the dingy interior. Dan's now-bushy eyebrows had lifted. "Well now, that's stepping it up. Never seen a haint knock to come inside."

"It's *me*. Meagan."

"'Course it is." He lay watching her, bleary eyed.

"I'm serious, Dan," she had insisted. "It's Meagan."

"Says you." Then he had lain back, closing his eyes. "But go on. Maybe I should ease up on the boy, he done fine. I might lay in a store of it."

"Oh, *Dan*."

"See, that's good. You got the tone about right."

"I'm your *wife*. Meagan." She sighed and said it: "Meggie."

Dan's eyes opened. He focused for the first time.

She nodded and held out her hand, showing her wedding ring. "I came to find you. I can explain."

He stared for a long moment. "You went away ... where did ..." He glanced around the dismal shack. Then he looked at her again: "Is it really you, Meggie?" It was the only time she ever saw Dan cry, his slow tears wer—

———

"Mrs. Bridgestone, are you okay?" asked a worried Mrs. Hancock.

"Oh." Meagan sniffed, returning to the present. *Dan hardly cried and I make up for it.* "Excuse me, Georgina. I do drift sometimes. I'm quite fine."

Despite the age difference, she and Dan had spent their remaining years—her very happiest—together caring for the horses and polo ponies owned by the flamboyant woman who became Meagan's benefactor, Mrs. Wendell "Candy" von Kane. After the too-short years she and Dan were together again, Promise had passed and she had no way to return to her old life back home. Meagan eventually married a wealthy cousin of the von Kanes and took his last name: *Bridgestone*.

She never forgot the dark future she had escaped. Hearing reports of the US cavalry being disbanded in the 1930's and the growing public opinion that horses were "obsolete" and outdated, Meagan became involved, living the remainder of the 20th Century helping to preserve a future for horses. She worked in a changing industry transitioning from employing horses for farm work, transportation and military uses to equestrian sports, recreation and therapy. The period was a transformative, pivotal time for horsemanship, and bequeathed the legacy of horses to new generations.

It was time to pass the torch to others.

Eventually she had caught up with her own life. She contacted her parents after young Meagan returned to find Dan and told them everything—another tearful reunion. She cared for Promise until her beloved filly finally flew away to return in another form. She had been tempted to contact young Meagan again, to share knowledge that would be so life-changing; though it could never happen: not with the lines of time already swaying in the thunder of celestial hooves.

When Mister completed his circle, Meagan hobbled to the horse's head and peered into the dark, patient eyes. "Hello, my friend," she said softly, smoothing the cheek below the familiar gaze that watched her with a faraway expression. "I've missed you so."

The horse was, as always, just a horse. Mister gave no special sign of recognition, made no gesture out of the ordinary. As Meagan stroked the rough coat, the horse placed his head solemnly against her shoulder in shared companionship. As always, it was enough.

Meagan stumped briskly to where Dean sat proudly on his prized horse. The boy's eyes had come to life. "Mister is smoking!" Dean said, patting his horse on the shoulder to raise a dust cloud.

"No, dear," Meagan said, smiling. "It's *dust.*"

Mrs. Hancock came to stand beside Meagan. "You look good up there, Dean!" The boy dropped his head, his shyness returning.

"I think the boy and I could become good friends, Georgina."

"Oh I *hope* so!"

"I saw you on the teevee before," Dean informed Mister seriously as the horse's ears swiveled to listen. "Your last name is 'Ed.' Your other last name is Harbinger now, like mine."

Meagan patted the boy's leg. "It is wonderful to see you again, Dean Harbinger."

"See me *again?*"

"No, no ... I meant, meet in person."

"Mister could run *fast* if he wasn't hurt before."

"Why yes, Dean, I'm sure he could! He's a *very* special horse. I'll tell you all about him."

Georgia Hancock smiled through her tears, listening to Mrs. Bridgestone's fading words as she followed the boy on another circle:

"I once had a horse like Mister, dear. Her name was *Promise* and she was born down the street, yes Dean, this very one. Her mother was named *Bright Lights* but everyone called her Moose—oh, you would have *loved* them! Promise was born a golden palomino, something very uncommon in Thorough-breds ... but the strange part wasn't that..."

THE END

A Note on Historical Representations from
The Legend of the Great Horse trilogy

The basis for the legend of a Great Horse is derived from ancient myths and religious beliefs of antiquity. The poems and writings from Mrs. Bridgestone's library are fictionalized, including the letter of Chief Joseph. With the exceptions noted below, characters are fictional representations of people of their time.

One historical alteration made in the story concerns the cattle drive era, which developed most fully after the Civil War.

The intention of **The Legend of the Great Horse** trilogy is to present a backdrop of accurate history. Historical corrections are appreciated and will be acknowledged in future editions.

Actual Historical Figures from the trilogy

Book I: *Eclipsed by Shadow*

Cornelius Tacitus, foremost historian of ancient Imperial Rome
Emperor Trajan, Roman emperor from 98-117 AD
Incitatus, chariot racehorse owned by Emperor Caligula

Book II: *The Golden Spark*

Françoise Athénaïs de Rochechouart de Mortemart, famous "chief mistress" of King Louis XIV of France
Hernán Cortés de Monroy y Pizarro, Spanish Conquistador
El Morzillo, favorite mount of Hernán Cortés

Book III: *Into the Dark*

Samuel D. Riddle, owner of Man O'War
Will Harbut, Man O'War's groom
Man O'War, legendary American racehorse
Stroller, British international show jumping pony

GLOSSARY OF TERMS

APART Acronym for the *'Association for the Prevention of Animal Rights Trespass,'* a fictional animal welfare organization.

Arapaho American Indian tribe that was forced West by European settlers; adopting the horse, they became nomads following the massive buffalo herds of the time. The remaining Arapaho people are divided between a Northern reservation in Wyoming and a Southern reservation in Oklahoma.

bay common equine hair color; reddish brown with a black mane, tail, and lower legs.

Bellerophon mortal hero of Greek myth. Bellerophon tamed *Pegasus* with a Golden Bridle, and rode the winged mount to pursue and destroy the *Chimera*. He offended the gods by attempting to ride Pegasus up to Mount Olympus, home of the gods—Zeus sent a gadfly to sting Pegasus, who threw Bellerophon to the ground.

bedding wood shavings, straw, sand, peat or other material used to line the floor of a stall.

Berber ancestral peoples of North Africa and homeland of the Barb horse, a light riding horse bred for desert travel which possesses great hardiness and endurance. The Barb horse influenced the Andalusian and Lusitano breeds.

bit mouthpiece of bridle.

breeze a sprint around a racetrack for exercise and conditioning.

bridle horse's headgear which carries a *bit* and *reins* for guidance by rider.

brumby unbroken, free-roaming feral horses of Australia.

buck natural movement in which a horse lowers his head and raises his hindquarters into the air. A natural equine defense that may become a vice.

buckskin equine hair color that resembles tanned deerskin. Buckskin shades vary from dark gold to yellow; the mane, tail and legs may be dark brown or black.

Butterfield Express An overland mail and passenger stagecoach service that operated from 1858-1861. Organized by John Butterfield (1801–1869), who was forced out by the Wells-Fargo partnership, founders of the express mail line, American Express.

cannon bone bone of the horse's lower leg between the knee or *hock* and the *fetlock*.

canter natural, controlled three-beat gait of horses, slower than a *gallop* but faster than a *trot*. The speed of the average canter varies between 10-20 mph.

cantle the raised rear part of a *saddle*.

cat-hammed poor muscling in thigh and *gaskin* of horses. *Conformation* defect indicating weakness in hindquarters that limits power and speed.

cavalry military force of mounted horsemen; derived from *cheval*, the French word for horse.

Charon The ferryman of Greek mythology who transported newly-deceased shades (souls) across the river that divided the world of the living from the world of the dead. Charon demanded payment, so a coin was traditionally placed in a corpse's mouth at burial.

chestnut common hair coat color of horses with a wide variety of shades from reddish to brown coat. The tail and mane are same or lighter in color than the coat, and no black hairs are present.

Cheyenne one of the major American Indian tribes that acquired horses and adopted a nomadic lifestyle of hunting buffalo on the *Great Plains*. Developed an oral culture and a ritualistic, centralized system of governance. One of the last Indian tribes to be forced to live on a designated reservation.

Chimera monster of Greek myth with the head and body of a lion, and tail ending in a serpent's head with a goat's head sprouting from its back. Terrorized the people of Lycia before being killed by *Bellerophon* riding the winged horse, *Pegasus*.

colic a general term indicating abdominal pain. The major cause of death in equines.

collar (horse) Part of *harness* fitting over a horse's neck and shoulders which allows the animal to exert its full strength. The horse collar improved previous harness methods which pressed against the horse's windpipe, and came into general use in Europe during the Middle Ages; earliest evidence of development was in China from the 2nd Century BC.

The horse collar dramatically increased the common usage of horses for plowing, as the horse's greater speed and endurance could provide more productive work than an ox. With the horse collar and improvements in the plow, farming peasants could produce a surplus from their efforts, an important factor in ending the feudal system of Europe.

collection *dressage* term for the process or state of 'gathering' the horse to increase energy and carry more weight on the hindquarters.

conformation structure and general physical make-up of a horse.

Conquistadors Spanish military leaders who explored and conquered native populations in North and South America, especially Mexico and Peru in the 1500's.

coronet band growth line at the top of a horse's *hoof*.

corset human garment worn to shape the torso into a specific shape; for either aesthetic or medical reasons.

cow-hocked equine *conformation* defect in which the hind legs deviate from parallel; the *hocks* point inward and the hooves point outward. Can be a debilitating weakness if severe.

crest top of a horse's neck between the *poll* and *withers*.

crop short riding whip with a loop rather than a lash. Properly used as an extension of "driving aids" to signal a horse to move forward.

croup the top of the horse's hindquarters.

crow-hop action by horse of jumping slightly off the ground with all four feet.

curb type of bit used for riding horses that uses lever action; typically more severe than the *snaffle*.

daguerreotype first commercially successful photographic process, announced by the French Academy of Sciences in 1839. A daguerreotype's exposure surface is extremely fragile: photographs were sealed at the time of framing to prevent oxidation.

dam mother of a horse.

Dawn Horse Translation of *Eohippus*; considered the earliest direct ancestor of the horse, which lived some 50 million years ago. (see *Hyracotherium*; *Eohippus*)

Double combination obstacle in equestrian jumping competition that has two obstacles placed in a row with no more than two strides between. If the obstacle must be retaken, the whole combination must be jumped. (see *Triple combination*)

dressage French term meaning "schooling." Ancient military cavalry training. Dressage is a humane system of developing a horse's balance, gymnastic ability, natural expression, and communication with the rider.

dun horse coat color in varying shades of gray-gold, tan or reddish brown. Characterized by a dark stripe down the middle of the horse's back, with a tail and mane darker than the body coat.

Eagle coin American gold coinage that represented 10 dollars; issued from late 1700's until termination in 1933.

Enclosure Acts Enclosure (*archaic*: 'inclosure') was a type of law passed to consolidate smaller plots of land, with the intended effect of redistributing land and wealth from common laborers to 'landed' classes. Limited Enclosure laws began as early as the 12th century, but the majority were passed in the 16th to 18th centuries. As a result of Enclosure Acts, masses of dispossessed rural workers moved into cities.

Eohippus (*Dawn Horse*) original name for the small extinct primitive horses which lived 55—45 million years ago) having 4-toed forefeet and 3-toed hind feet. (see *Dawn Horse, Hyracotherium*)

equestrian of or relating to horses or horseback riding.

equine a horse, or related to horses.

equitation the practice of horse riding or horsemanship. Equitation competition refers to the rider's position and skill.

ewe-necked "upside-down" thin horse's neck that bends upward into a concave arch; considered a *conformation* defect.

farrier person trained to tend to a horse's hooves, including the making/adjusting of horseshoes and the shoeing of horses. The modern equivalent of blacksmiths.

fault penalty points in jumping competition. Faults are scored for altering the height or width of an obstacle, exceeding a time limit, or a fall or *refusal*.

fence alternate name for an obstacle in equestrian sport.

fetlock lowest joint in a horses leg; the ankle.

filly female horse less than four years old.

foal young horse up to the age of 12 months.

forging action of horse's hind hoof striking a fore *hoof*.

Fort Laramie Located on the Oregon Trail where the North Platte and Laramie rivers meet, Fort Laramie protected settlers and provided supplies for settlers. A link in the Pony Express and Overland Stage routes, as well as a base for the early telegraph systems. The fort also served as an outpost for the Indian wars of the 1800's.

frog rubbery, wedge-shaped projection at bottom of horse's *hoof*.

gadjo term used by Romani people (gypsies) to denote non-Romani people; usually pejorative. Other spellings include *gadzé, gadje* and *gaje*.

gait pattern of footfalls of a horse in motion. The natural gaits are: *walk, trot, canter* and *gallop*.

gallop fastest gait of a horse, averaging between 24 to 45 miles per hour. An extended version of the *canter* with four-beat footfalls.

Galvanized Yankee American Civil War term for Confederate soldiers or prisoners of war who swore loyalty to the Union and joined the Union Army.

gaskin well-muscled portion of a horse's hind leg between the *stifle* and the *hock*.

gelding castrated male horse.

girth a strap, usually of leather, that encircles a horse to secure a saddle on its back.

Golden Bridle special bridle used by *Bellerophon* to tame the winged horse, *Pegasus*.

goose-rump *conformation* trait in horses of a sloping rump with high croup and low tail placement. Such angled hindquarters result in a shorter stride, a limitation for endurance and speed but potentially desirable for agility, jumping or weight-pulling power.

gray color that ranges from white to dark gray, including dapples.

Great Plains flat lands in America between the Mississippi River and east of the Rocky Mountains.

groom person who looks after horses; a stable-hand. Also the term for brushing and/or cleaning a horse.

grooming the care and maintenance of a horse's coat. Includes washing, brushing, trimming, and the treatment of hooves, mane and tail.

hackamore bridle without a mouthpiece.

haint Southern colloquial term for ghost or spirit; variation of 'haunt.'

half-halt signal from a rider to increase the horse's attention and balance, usually before the execution of a movement or transition. Given through coordinated action of the hands, legs and seat of the rider; ideally subtle and hardly visible.

halter headpiece harness that fits over a horse's head, used in leading or securing a horse.

hand unit of measurement equal to four inches, originally derived from the average width of a man's hand. A horse's height is measured in hands from the *withers* to the ground.

harness *tack* that allows a horse to pull a variety of conveyances or tools such as a plow, carriage or wagon.

headstall part of *bridle* that holds the mouthpiece.

heaves chronic condition resulting from allergic reactions, most commonly to hay or straw. The condition worsens with exertion. Acute treatments exist, but there is no cure; alleviation of environmental triggers can lessen or resolve the condition.

hock the center joint or "knee" of the hind legs.

hoof horny sheath covering the toe or lower part of the horse's foot.

horn hard, insensitive outer part of *hoof*.

horseshoes Iron or alloy material fixed directly to the dead horn of a horse's *hoof* by *farriers*. The horseshoe equips the horse to handle different types of terrain, as the human shoe does for humans.

hot-blooded typically high-spirited horses with ancestors from hot climates in the Middle East.

Hyracotherium Current scientific classification name for the earliest known horse, replacing the name *Eohippus* (*"Dawn Horse"*); confusion resulted as the first-discovered specimen was named a member of the 'hyrax' family in error.

Indemnification act of securing agreement to not hold a party liable for future legal action or fines.

knacker a person who slaughters or purchases carcasses of unwanted livestock, especially old or unfit horses, to process into meat or other products (not for human consumption).

lame disabled in the feet or legs; term used to describe a horse which is limping or has difficulty moving properly.

lead term to designate which foreleg "leads" or advances further in a gallop or canter.

lead rope rope or strap used to lead a horse while wearing a halter.

livery stables a stable where owners pay a fee to keep their horses.

manège area for training horses, may be rectangular or circular.

longe/lunge exercise in a horse's various paces on a circle using a longe or 'lunge' rein, with the horse circling the trainer.

lope relaxed, slow and uncollected canter.

maiden horse that has not yet won a race or other competitive event; also a race or event limited to maiden horses.

Man O'War (1917-1947) called the "mostest hoss that ever was" by his longtime groom, Will Harbut, Man O'War is considered one of the greatest racehorses in history. Owned by Samuel D. Riddle, the stallion won 20 of 21 races entered; the single loss was at the Sanford Memorial Stakes in 1919, in which Man O'War came in behind Upset by a half-length after a poor start and positioning.

mane hair growing down a horse's neck and on top of the head.

manger trough to hold feed or hay.

mare adult female horse; commonly defined as over three years of age.

mount a horse, or the action of placing oneself on a horse. A rider may mount from the ground or a mounting block, or by receiving a "leg-up" or assistance from another person on the ground.

mucking out removal of soiled bedding and replacement with clean bedding.

Muses goddesses of ancient Greek mythology that provide inspiration in literature, science and the arts. The Muses are the Keepers of *Pegasus*; some myths claim the Muses were born from sacred springs that opened when the winged horse Pegasus struck the ground on Mt. Helicon in Greece.

nag a horse of low quality.

nappy uncooperative behavior in which the horse refuses to go in the direction the rider indicates, by either stopping, running backwards, rearing or spinning around.

nicker common 'friendly' sound a horse makes, usually low and welcoming.

oxer a type of horse jump built with two rails to create a wide or 'spread' obstacle.

paddock enclosed area used for pasturing or exercising animals.

palomino a gold colored horse with blond or white *mane* and tail.

pastern the area on a horse's leg between the *hoof* and *fetlock* joint.

pedigree list of a horse's ancestors.

Pegasii race of immortal winged horses of Greek mythology.

Pegasus the immortal winged horse of Greek mythology that was cared for by the *Muses*; a symbol for the arts, especially poetry. Commonly portrayed as white, but has also been described as black, 'red as the sunrise,' or as having wings of another shade or color.

phaeton a sporty open carriage drawn by a single horse or a pair of horses; usually with four over-sized wheels and a minimal body.

picket tethering horses with a rope line.

pigeon-toed condition in which the horse's front hooves turn in; severe cases may limit athletic ability and/or cause lamenesses.

pinto *equine* hair color pattern of large white patches and any other color.

poll area between the horse's ears.

Polo equestrian team competition with origins from about the 5th century BC. Traditional polo is played with two teams of four mounted riders on a large field of 300 x 150 yards, the approximate size of nine American football fields. Arena polo is contested in a much smaller area with three horses and riders per team.

pommel the upper front part of a *saddle*.

pony horse under 14 *hands*.

Pony Express high-speed transcontinental mail service that opened just before the American Civil War. Relays of riders with saddlebags of mail galloped 2000 miles across the nation between the East and West. Some of the terrain was treacherous, but only one mail delivery was lost. The Pony Express's first riders departed with mail on April 3, 1860, and operations continued until October 24, 1861, when the first telegraph by the newly-completed Pacific Telegraph line was sent, making the Pony Express instantly obsolete.

pony(ing) to lead a horse from another horse or vehicle.

post the word as related to mail is named for the traditional system of horses and riders 'posted' at intervals to carry the mail in relays.

poultice Moist, soft mass applied to a cloth to treat injuries or inflammation, often used with heat or medication. Commonly used beneath leg bandages on horses to prevent or treat inflammation. Poultices are also used to treat abscess wounds or swollen glands.

Prohibition era that culminated with a national ban on alcohol production, sale or transport in America. Enacted by the 18th Amendment on January 17, 1920, the ban failed comprehensively while increasing the activity of organized crime, was repealed in 1933 by ratification of the Twenty-first Amendment.

proud flesh 'exuberant granulation tissue,' which is prone to occur in a *equine* wound, especially near a joint, due to the overproduction of scar tissue.

Quarter Horse muscular American horse breed of calm temperament, named for its exceptional speed over a quarter-mile distance.

rack fast man-made gait in which only one *hoof* strikes the ground at a time. Some horses perform the gait naturally; many other breeds can be trained to rack. Also called a 'single-foot.'

refusal the failure of a horse to jump a fence to which he was presented, by stopping or running to one side of the obstacle. In show jumping competition a refusal is penalized with four faults.

registry breed organization which maintains a horse's registration papers and ancestry.

rein(s) part of a *bridle* consisting of a pair of long straps attached to the *bit*, used to direct and control the horse.

Reining judged event in which a horse and rider complete set patterns, which are designed to test and showcase the athletic ability of a working ranch horse.

remount cavalry term for a "fresh" horse.

saddle   a supportive structure for a rider, fastened to an animal's back by a *girth*.

Saddler   general term for "gaited" breeds which naturally perform man-made gaits such as the *rack* or fox-trot.

shank   side piece of a curb *bit* attached to the mouthpiece.

shy   sudden evasive action a horse takes, usually sideways, due to being scared by something real or imaginary.

sideboard   dining-room furniture having compartments and shelves for holding articles of table service linens and silverware.

snaffle   common type of bit used for riding horses; acts by direct *rein* pressure. Composed of a mouthpiece with a ring on either side.

sorrel   horse hair color, another term for *chestnut*; may indicate a more reddish shade.

spavins   potentially disabling condition of a horse's *hock* due to bone growth or fluid accumulation in the joint.

splint   ailment of the *splint bone*; new splints are characterized by swelling and lameness; once healed these become hard, bony areas without pain.

splint bones   two long, narrow bones that descend down either side of the *cannon bone*, tapering from the knee.

spot   a horse's point of takeoff when jumping an obstacle.

spurs   device attached to a heel of rider's footwear to assist in signaling a horse to move forward. Spurs range in severity from short, rounded nubs to longer or sharper spikes and pointed wheels.

stable   a building in which horses are kept. Usually divided into separate *stalls* for individual animals.

stag   male deer; especially a mature animal with developed antlers.

stall   individual enclosure to house horses. Typical size for an adult horse is an area 12′ square.

stallion   male horse aged 4 years or over.

star   forehead patch of white hair, placed between or slightly above a horse's eyes.

stifle   joint in horse's hind leg below the croup; analogous to knee.

stone bruise   contusion to the hoof, usually by a blow to the sole on rocky ground.

Stroller   (1950-1986) British pony who took his young rider, Marion Coakes, to the top of international show jumping competition. Winning 61 international competitions over his long career, the 14.1 hands high Stroller is the only pony to have competed at the Olympics in Show Jumping. Won the Silver Medal in the 1968 Games in

Mexico City before the infamous Team competition that followed, in which the pony fell but bravely finished the course to keep British medal hopes alive, only to be eliminated for time faults.

sulky light 2-wheeled single-driver vehicle used in harness racing.

tack saddlery or horse equipment such as a *harness, saddle* and pad, *bridle, reins,* or *halter.*

Thoroughbred athletic, hot-blooded breed of horse descended from three stallions given to Britain in the 17th-18th century of Arabian, Barb, and Turkoman breeding.

throatlatch area beneath a horse's jaw where the head meets the top of the windpipe. The strap of a bridle that loops under this area is also called a throatlatch.

Transylvania University the oldest university in Kentucky, formed while Thomas Jefferson was governor of Virginia.

Triple combination obstacle in equestrian competition that has three obstacles or elements placed in a row, so that the horse will take no more than two strides between. If the obstacle must be re-taken, the whole combination must be jumped. (see *Double combination*)

trot stable, two-beat gait in which the horse moves its legs in unison in diagonal pairs. Faster than a walk but slower than a canter, the trot averages 8 mph but has a wide variation of potential speed.

trotter horse used in harness racing; horse that races at the trot instead of the gallop.

ungulate general term for a hoofed mammal.

verdad Spanish word for truth.

vetting veterinary examination of a horse's health and soundness.

vice a bad habit learned by a horse, including *bucking*, head tossing and rearing.

walk slowest natural gait of a horse, a four-beat gait averaging about four mph.

wasp-waisted condition in which a horse's waist below the flank is "tucked up" and thin with insufficient abdominal development.

webbing elastic band stretching across a racetrack, used to start races before automatic gates came into use after the 1920's.

whinny long, high-pitched sound made by a horse.

withers the highest part of the horse's back, usually seen as a slightly raised area above the shoulders.

yearling a horse between one and two years old.

BIBLIOGRAPHY

Books that informed the historical eras of 'Into the Dark'

American West & Civil War (1860's)

Fiction classics

McMurtry, Larry. <u>Lonesome Dove</u>. N.p.: Pocket Books, 1988.

Michener, James A. <u>Centennial: A Novel</u>. N.p.: Random House Trade Paperbacks, 2007 (1974).

Michener, James A. <u>Chesapeake: A Novel</u>. Random House Trade Paperbacks, 2003 (1978).

Mitchell, Margaret. <u>Gone With The Wind</u>. 60th anniversary ed. N.p.: Scribner, 1996 (1936).

Shaara, Michael. <u>The Killer Angels</u>. N.p.: Ballantine Books, 1987 (1974).

Taylor, Robert Lewis. <u>Journey to Matecumbe</u>. Texas: Mcgraw-Hill, 1961.

Twain, Mark. <u>A Connecticut Yankee in King Arthur's Court</u>. New York: Oxford University Press, 1996 (1889)

Nonfiction and Memoirs

Ambrose, Stephen. <u>Undaunted Courage: Meriwether Lewis, Thomas Jefferson, and the Opening of the American West</u>. N.p.: Simon & Schuster, 1997.

Beal, Merrill. <u>I Will Fight No More Forever</u>. University of Washington Press, 2003 (1984).

Brown, Dee Alexander. <u>Bury My Heart at Wounded Knee: An Indian History of the American West</u>. N.p.: Vintage Books USA, 1987.

Budiansky, Stephen. <u>The Bloody Shirt: Terror after Appomattox</u>. First edition. Viking Adult, 2008.

Catton, Bruce. <u>A Stillness at Appomattox (Army of the Potomac, Vol. 3)</u>. N.p.: Anchor, 1953.

Mattes, Merrill J. <u>The Great Platte River Road: The Covered Wagon Mainline via Fort Kearny to Fort Laramie</u>. revised ed.. N.p.: University of Nebraska Press, 1987.

BIBLIOGRAPHY *continued*

Turn of Century America – Prohibition (1890-1920)

Tuchman, Barbara W. The Proud Tower: A Portrait of the World Before the War, 1890-1914. Pbk. New York: Ballantine Books, 1996 (1966).

Allen, Frederick Lewis. Only Yesterday: An Informal History of the 1920's. N.p.: Perennial Library, 1931.

Farley, Walter. Man O'War. N.p.: Random House, 1983.

Cooper, Page, and Roger L. Treat. Man O'War. N.p.: Julian Messner, Inc., 1950.

World War II

Shirer, William L. Berlin Diary: The Journal of a Foreign Correspondent, 1934-1941. N.p.: The Johns Hopkins University Press, 2002 (1941).

Show Jumping / Equestrian

Williams, Dorian. Dorian Williams' World of Show Jumping. N.p.: Purnell, 1971.

Steinkraus, William. Reflections on Riding and Jumping: Winning Techniques for Serious Riders. Rev sub ed. Trafalgar Square Books, 1997.

ACKNOWLEDGEMENTS

Many dedicated artists and friends have contributed to *The Legend of the Great Horse* trilogy, and without their assistance this work would not have been possible.

I was fortunate to have the skill and dedication of JENNIFER AHLBORN, the original editor who brought the books into readable form. Special thanks go to talented young writer ASHLEY WELCH, who helped bring the story home.

Several artists contributed their unique vision to the trilogy. JOE MILSTEAD created the early inspiration for the coin artwork. The cover images are original paintings by the talented equestrian artist MARTI ADRIAN. *TheGreatHorse.com* web design by CAROLYNNE SMITH of Pixelgraphix shows the artist's vision. Special thanks and recognition is owed to my friend ALLEN GRIFFITH and his cover work for Book II: *The Golden Spark*.

I am grateful for the personal support I received from family and friends. In particular I would like to extend my heartfelt gratitude to the community of readers who took the journey with Meagan. Bev, Angéla, Peter, Cayce, Darla, Ed, Sabrina, Rea … each are special supporters who gave encouragement and motivation.

Thank you to all who have joined in the Great adventure!

—◆—

The Legend of the Great Horse *trilogy*

Book I: Eclipsed by Shadow
Book II: The Golden Spark
Book III: Into the Dark

—◆—

The author resides in Boston, Massachusetts, where he first discovered a passion for history. His experiences with (great) horses gave him a love and respect for the animal.

It is Mr. Royce's dream that American culture will rediscover its equestrian heritage. He also wishes Latin would again be taught in grade school. These hopes qualify him to write fiction in our time.

Please visit <u>TheGreatHorse.com</u> for additional information about the series and author.